You're invited to...

Return to Tyler

Where scandals and secrets
are unleashed in a small town
and love is found around every corner....

Walk through the town square
where towering oaks shade young children
playing together.

Come into Marge's Diner, where everyone
meets for coffee and company.

Visit the Quilting Circle at Worthington
House for the latest romantic gossip.

Spend the night at the Breakfast Inn Bed....

And discover the secret identity of the
mysterious new girl in town.

Return to Tyler and stay awhile.
You'll be glad you did!

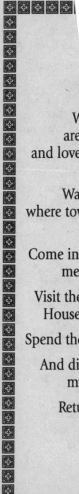

Dear Reader,

Welcome to Harlequin American Romance...where each month we offer four wonderful new books bursting with love!

Linda Randall Wisdom kicks off the month with *Bride of Dreams*, the latest installment in the RETURN TO TYLER series, in which a handsome Native American lawman is undeniably drawn to the pretty and mysterious new waitress in town. Watch for the Tyler series to continue next month in Harlequin Historicals. Next, a lovely schoolteacher is in for a big surprise when she wakes up in a hospital with no memory of her past—or how she'd gotten pregnant. Meet the last of the three identical sisters in Muriel Jensen's WHO'S THE DADDY? series in *Father Found*.

Bestselling author Judy Christenberry's *Rent a Millionaire Groom* launches Harlequin American Romance's new series, 2001 WAYS TO WED, about three best friends searching for Mr. Right who turn to a book guaranteed to help them make it to the altar. IDENTITY SWAP, Charlotte Douglas's new cross-line series, debuts with *Montana Mail-Order Wife*. In this exciting story, two women involved in a train accident switch identities and find much more than they bargained for. Follow the series next month in Harlequin Intrigue.

Enjoy this month's offerings, and make sure to return each and every month to Harlequin American Romance!

Wishing you happy reading,

Melissa Jeglinski
Associate Senior Editor
Harlequin American Romance

BRIDE OF DREAMS
Linda Randall Wisdom

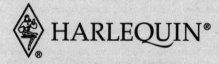

TORONTO • NEW YORK • LONDON
AMSTERDAM • PARIS • SYDNEY • HAMBURG
STOCKHOLM • ATHENS • TOKYO • MILAN • MADRID
PRAGUE • WARSAW • BUDAPEST • AUCKLAND

Special thanks and acknowledgment are given
to Linda Randall Wisdom for her contribution
to the RETURN TO TYLER series.

A very heartfelt thank-you to the group
at the Murrieta, California, post office
who take such good care of my manuscripts
and make sure they get to where they're supposed to go.
Antonio, Barbara, Frank, Mark, Melinda
and Rita are my postal angels.

ISBN 0-373-16865-9

BRIDE OF DREAMS

Visit us at www.eHarlequin.com

Printed in U.S.A.

ABOUT THE AUTHOR

Linda Randall Wisdom is a California author who loves movies, books and animals of all kinds. She also has a great sense of humor, which is reflected in her books.

Books by Linda Randall Wisdom

HARLEQUIN AMERICAN ROMANCE

Who's Who in Tyler

Cooper Night Hawk—His dreams are haunted by a woman some say will be his bride.

Caroline Benning—Falling in love wasn't in her game plan when she came to Tyler.

Laughing Bear—His Sauk wisdom and the Spirit guides have served him well.

Brady Spencer—He wants the truth about Caroline... no matter what.

Delia Mayhew—A town librarian can tell a lot about people by the books they read.

Anna and Johnny Kelsey—There's no hanky-panky going on in their boardinghouse!

Brick and Karen Bauer—This cop couple will bring peace back to Tyler, even if they have to handcuff Cooper and Caroline together.

Henry Farris—He has a roving eye for Caroline—even if he is ninety!

Lieutenant Steve Fletcher—His beat is the local lovers' lane.

Tyler Quilting Circle—Whose wedding quilt are these matchmaking women working on now?

Prologue

"I wasn't ready for you to go just yet, Dad. I wanted you here so you could hold your grandchildren. Remember what you said you wanted to do? You were going to spend all your mornings on the golf course and avoid all those widows trolling for a new husband. The ones you claimed talk endlessly about taking cruises, and want a partner to go with them. Hopefully, you."

Caroline Bennedict folded the last piece of clothing and carefully placed it in a box. Her movements were economical as she sealed the box with packing tape and marked it for one of the charities.

"I'm only twenty-two years old, Dad. I still need you." She began clearing off his chest of drawers. She knew if anyone heard her talking out loud to her father, who'd died the month before, they'd think she was losing it. They had no idea that talking to him as if he was still there made the pain more tolerable. Plus she believed, in a sense, he still was with her.

Now she was involved in a task she hadn't looked forward to but knew needed to be done—packing her father's personal items. Tears pricked her eyelids as she emptied each drawer, then moved on to the closet.

Caroline frowned when she discovered a large box set

back in the far corner of the top shelf. She stood on a chair and carefully maneuvered it forward so she could get a good grip on it. She carried it over to the bed. When she opened the box, the faint scent of Chanel wafted upward. Her dad always said Chanel reminded him of Mom. Caroline's mother had died having Caroline, so she'd never had a chance to know her, and had to rely on stories from her father. Now she didn't even have that.

The box held a quilt. She stared at the lively pattern of blue, white and green and gathered up the heavy fabric, allowing it to spill over her lap. She carefully smoothed it across her legs.

"Where did this come from?" she whispered to herself, picking up one corner and examining the tiny stitches.

Even her inexperienced eye could tell the quilt was handmade, put together with a great deal of care and love. She knew right away it wasn't designed for her father's navy-and-burgundy bedroom. As she turned the quilt over, additional colors in one of the corners caught her eye.

She pulled it toward her so she could examine it more closely. Her brows knitted in a confused frown as her fingernail traced the names embroidered in one corner of the quilt.

Violet and Elias Spencer
Seth, Brady, Quinn

Violet Spencer? The same Violet Caroline knew of as Violet Bennedict? The woman who'd died seconds after Caroline's birth?

"Mom?" she whispered. "Who are these men? And what do they have to do with you?"

Chapter One

He couldn't see her face, but he knew she was beautiful. The mist wrapped around her in the way a lover would protect her from outside forces. Even though her face was shrouded by the mist, he instinctively knew she was looking at him. Her slim figure was garbed in a cotton gown that clung to her form.

The mist swirled around her as she lifted her hand and reached out to him. She didn't speak a word, but somehow he knew she was beckoning to him. Asking that he take her hand.

He didn't move from his spot. Somehow he knew that taking her hand and allowing her to lead him into the mist would mean changes to himself and to his life. Changes he wasn't ready to make. Instead, he stepped back. Once. Twice.

He still couldn't fully see her face, but he knew she was disappointed.

Oddly enough, so was he.

But not enough to take her hand.

Cooper Night Hawk awoke a good two hours before his alarm was ready to blast him out of bed. Sleep was something he treasured because he knew there was always a chance it would be interrupted.

Tyler might not be the crime capital of the world, but mischief still happened. And some nights he was the one selected to settle it.

He left his bed and headed outside. He filled his lungs with the chilly, clean air in hopes it would clear his head. Cooper settled in one of the chairs by the back door. The wood creaked softly under him as he leaned his head back and looked up at the sky. He liked the idea of counting stars instead of counting sheep.

"You worked so many nights that your body cannot understand why it has to sleep now."

Cooper cocked a dark eyebrow. "Look who's talking, old man. You need your rest more than I do." His voice was filled with gruff affection toward his visitor.

The silver-haired man shook his head, his braids swinging gently. "The time will come soon enough when all I will do is sleep. Until the time comes, I will enjoy what the night has to offer." Cooper's grandfather, Laughing Bear, walked slowly over to the chair next to Cooper's and carefully lowered himself into the seat.

"You'll still be around telling all the old stories when I'm in my grave," Cooper argued good-naturedly. "What are you doing up this time of night?"

"The stars are only good when everyone else is asleep," Laughing Bear informed him in a low, even voice.

Cooper stretched his legs out in front of him, bare feet crossed at the ankle. "How come you're not sitting by your own house looking at the stars?"

"I do not see them as well up there. That is why I come down here to sit on your porch. The view is nicer down here," he said calmly. "The Spirits like it better down here, too."

Cooper shook his head. He knew enough not to voice

his disbelief about the Spirits who allegedly accompanied his grandfather wherever he went. Any time he even hinted his doubt of invisible beings, his grandfather would give him that long silent look that spoke volumes. The elderly man never told him how disappointed he was in his grandson's refusal to accept the legends he grew up with. The sorrow in his eyes was telling enough.

"She is here," the man said.

Cooper stifled the sigh rising in his throat. Damn him! He wasn't going to say another word.

No way. No how. This time he wasn't going to ask. In all the years he and his grandfather had done this form of one-upmanship, the older man always won. Just for once, Cooper wanted to win.

He continued sitting back with his laced fingers resting on his bare abdomen, enjoying the chilly air on his skin. He didn't have to turn his head to know his grandfather wasn't looking at him. That was part of the battle of wills that grandfather and grandson had waged over the years.

"She will take a heart while she is here," Laughing Bear said, breaking the silence once again.

Cooper bit the inside of his cheek. Anything to keep from asking.

He would have been better off talking to one of his grandfather's spirit friends.

"I can't imagine she'd want yours. It must be pretty leathery by now," Cooper said.

Laughing Bear slowly turned to face his grandson. "The heart she takes will be a younger one. A strong heart and more succulent."

Cooper cocked an eyebrow. "Succulent? Are you reading romance books again, old man?"

Laughing Bear showed no displeasure with Cooper's irreverent manner of speech. They understood each other only too well. In the beginning, the grandfather had taken care of his orphaned grandson, dealing with his pain and anger at the death of his parents. Now the grandson took care of his grandfather, making sure he saw his doctor on a regular basis and had enough firewood during the winter. With Laughing Bear's small cabin only a hundred yards away, he was close enough for Cooper to feel as if he could look after him and far enough away so that Laughing Bear could have his privacy and feel a measure of independence. It was a comfortable arrangement for both men.

Every day Cooper saw the stiffness increasing in his grandfather's body, his eyes dimming with age and his steps growing slower. Cooper didn't want to think about the day the older man would no longer be here.

"Mrs. Riley brought me one of her peach pies today," Laughing Bear said.

Not at all what Cooper expected to hear. The faint smile on the older man's lips told him he knew that.

"Funny. I thought her specialty was blackberry pies."

"Her blackberry pies are very good, too, but she knows I like her peach pies best."

Cooper tightened his lips. No sir. Not one word. A declaration that flew right out the window at the prospect of needling his grandfather.

"I heard Mrs. Riley used to put one of those sexual potency drugs in her pies for her husband up until he died," Cooper said, in the same casual tone his grandfather used. "Some say she's looking for another husband. I bet the man who shows the most appreciation for her 'pies' gets her in the bargain."

"Mrs. Riley is a nice woman, but she continues to mourn for her husband. She had never allowed his spirit to rest." Laughing Bear tilted his head back, looking upward. "Another man cannot share a life with her until she decides it is time to let him go."

Cooper chuckled. "My grandfather, the philosopher."

"No, a man wanting to stay free." The older man slowly rose to his feet. "And now a man who is ready to seek his bed." He shuffled off a few paces before he stopped and turned around. "She will capture your heart, Grandson. It will do you no good to fight the Spirits' wishes."

"Are you sure you haven't been reading vampire stories?" Cooper asked.

Laughing Bear stared at him with dark eyes that may have dimmed over the years but had lost none of their power.

"I wonder what *your* grandson will say to you when you tell him about the Spirits and their wishes." Having said his piece, he turned around and slowly walked up the well-worn pathway to his cabin.

"Deputy Night Hawk, are you listening to me?"

"Yes, ma'am," he said obediently, pen racing across his pad. "You want whoever did this to be charged with vandalism and anything else we can think of."

As owner of Gates Department store in Tyler, Nora Gates Forrester was used to people deferring to her. That Cooper wasn't giving her the attention she felt due her left her irritated.

"I'm beginning to think it's deliberate," she said angrily. "I've even heard that people claim it was Margaret Ingalls. The woman is dead!"

"Yes, ma'am," he said obediently.

Cooper wished he hadn't answered the phone this morning. He wasn't even due to go on duty yet. Then

Hedda, one of their dispatchers, had called and asked if he'd stop by Mrs. Forrester's house on his way into work.

"Mrs. Forrester..." He paused, well aware that whatever he said wouldn't be welcome. It hadn't been appreciated the last four times he'd been out here. He stepped carefully through the verbal minefield. "So far we haven't been able to come up with any tangible clues as to who is destroying your things."

The scent of Shalimar invaded his nostrils as she leaned closer. "When personal property is deliberately vandalized, you call the police. That is what I have done, and I expect results."

Cooper mentally vowed to never answer the phone first thing in the morning. At least not before he had his breakfast.

He looked around the neatly kept yard. He knew a neighbor's teenage son mowed the lawns every other week, and Mrs. Forrester tended her flowers with the same care a mother gave to her child. As he looked around, his gaze swept across the clothesline that occupied a corner of the yard. Underneath, pieces of brightly colored silk and lace dotted the green lawn—victims of the heinous crime.

He took a deep breath. "There have been some complaints about a goat wandering around in this neighborhood. You've got that hole in the back part of your fence and maybe the goat got inside the yard. They're known for eating anything."

Mrs. Forrester flashed him a look that implied she thought his idea of an underwear-eating goat ranked right up there with idiocy.

"I cannot imagine a goat would wander in here to steal and destroy my clothing," she insisted.

"I don't know. My grandmother had a goat who liked to eat dish towels."

Mrs. Forrester glared at him. "Just find out who did this."

"Yes, ma'am." He put away his pad and allowed her to escort him through the house and outside. He climbed into the Blazer and fingered the radio. "Dispatch, this is Cooper," he announced. "Finished at the Forrester house and rolling out."

"Is Nora's complaint of vandalism the same as always?" Hedda, the dispatcher, asked.

"Got it in one."

"I heard that Margaret Ingalls might have done it. What are you going to do if it does turn out to be Margaret?"

"What do you think? Call Ghostbusters." He signed off before his laughter joined hers.

He'd driven barely halfway along the street before he was flagged down. He stopped and rolled down his window.

"'Mornin', Mrs. Gray," he greeted the woman who'd been his fourth-grade teacher and still kept nine-year-olds in line at the grade school.

"Good morning, Cooper. Tell me, does Nora think Margaret Ingalls is destroying her underwear?" she asked.

"I think she's starting to think that, ma'am. Do you have anything new that might help the case?" *Such as seeing a ghostly Margaret Ingalls slipping into the Forrester yard.*

"Nora's a sensible woman except when it comes to this," she said bluntly. "If she truly wants to settle this, she should see about holding a séance. If someone can conjure Margaret up, Nora could then tell Margaret to her ghostly face to steal someone else's underwear."

Cooper coughed into his curved palm.

Mrs. Gray narrowed her eyes and gave him a look that still froze him down to his toes. "That tactic didn't work back then, Cooper Night Hawk, and it doesn't now."

"Yes, ma'am," he said soberly.

Her usually stern features relaxed in a smile. She rested her hand on the windowsill. "Did I ever tell you you grew up just fine?"

"Last week." His dark eyes twinkled.

She slapped the windowsill with her hand. "Just so you remember. Of course, I knew once you and Freddie Martin stopped hanging around together, you'd do all right." She stepped back, her own way of saying the conversation was over. "I understand Freddie is up for parole in two years."

Cooper nodded goodbye and drove on.

He knew becoming a sheriff's deputy in Tyler, Wisconsin, meant he would be dealing with people he'd known all his life. In a small town it was a given.

There were pluses and minuses in his job. Here, he knew everyone and they knew him. There'd been a time when all he thought about was getting out of Tyler for good. But that was when he was young and stupid. Now he knew this was where he belonged.

Life was predictable here but never boring. He knew many people wouldn't like predictable, but there were many times when it was pretty nice. Such as now when he was heading for Marge's Diner for his breakfast of blueberry pancakes with hash browns, sausage, orange juice and plenty of coffee.

No wonder he felt the town of Tyler gave him all the nurturing he needed.

"HEADS UP, DARLIN'."

Caroline automatically ducked as a heavily laden tray

swept over her head. Alice, the other waitress in Marge's Diner that morning, flashed her an apologetic smile.

"Sorry, sweetie. I had a head of steam going and didn't want to conk you on the noggin like the last time," she said over her shoulder as she sailed across the room.

"Thank you. Mashed potatoes weren't exactly the best conditioner for my hair," Caroline admitted, swapping the empty coffeepot for a full one.

Breakfast was a busy time in the bustling diner, and coffee was the all-important staple for the hungry diners. She'd barely finished refilling coffee cups before she had to return for another pot.

After almost ten months on the job, she was feeling more confident with her duties as one of the waitresses at Marge's Diner in Tyler. Everything here was a far cry from her life in Santa Barbara, California.

In Tyler, she didn't play tennis, laze by the pool or head for the beach with her friends. She wasn't "Caroline Bennedict" any longer. Now she was Caroline Benning—a stranger who'd driven into town, liked its looks and, since the diner was advertising for a waitress, applied for the job. Luckily, her lack of experience didn't seem to matter. Marge, the owner, warmly assured her she'd pick it up in no time.

Caroline had lost track of the number of broken dishes and incorrect orders she was responsible for—though she hadn't forgotten that time she gave Ray Hickman crab cakes instead of the fish sticks he'd ordered. She'd had no idea he was allergic to shellfish.

Caroline knew that in any other restaurant she would be history by now. Luckily, Marge was a great deal more patient with her fledgling waitress than most bosses would be. It didn't hurt that a majority of the men in town had asked that she be given a second chance. And a third.

And a fourth. Caroline was learning that small towns were very much a world unto themselves.

When Caroline had decided to seek out her mother's other family, she'd had no idea the trail would lead to Wisconsin.

She hadn't found anything in her father's papers about the Spencer family's involvement with her mother. It was pure luck there was a small note with the words *Tyler Quilting Circle, Tyler, Wisconsin* on the bottom of the box holding the quilt. Caroline hadn't stopped to think whether it was a good idea to just throw clothes in a few suitcases and take off for Tyler. She'd just done it. So far, she hadn't regretted her decision.

While she was eager to know her half brothers, she knew she couldn't just walk up to the Spencer front door and announce she was their half sister. It wasn't long after her arrival that she learned the Spencer family was well regarded in Tyler. The father and three sons were known as men not to be toyed with. They were wealthy, and she guessed they would naturally be suspicious of anyone suddenly appearing with the claim of being related.

Having grown up in a moneyed community, Caroline understood the caution they would undoubtedly display. She didn't need to watch the daytime dramas to which Alice was addicted to know she would have to get to know the Spencers first. Especially since she wasn't sure if Elias Spencer, head of the family, would accept her as his sons' half sister.

Her first thoughts were to stay in town for a while and see what she could find out about the Spencers. Then perhaps get to know them on a casual basis. She began by renting a room at the Kelsey Boarding House and looking around town for a job. In no time, she had a job where she was guaranteed to meet just about the entire population of Tyler at one time or another.

At first, she'd pretty much kept to herself. Then she'd stupidly tried to see into Elias Spencer's house and had ended up in the rose bushes, much to her embarrassment. Not something that would happen to the quiet, almost mousy Caroline Benning she'd been portraying. No wonder, since as Caroline Bennedict she'd devoured mystery novels and convinced herself she could do anything those heroines could do. After picking the thorns out of her skin, she'd decided it was time to act more like herself. She'd even dug out her own clothing, and now wore it instead of the drab, nondescript things she'd been wearing.

It wasn't long before people started to talk to her more. Marge took Caroline's sudden transformation in stride and told her she was glad to see she was settling in.

"Caroline." Marge's voice interrupted her daydreaming, and the owner flashed her eyes in the direction of the booths that were Caroline's responsibility.

Caroline felt the skin on her face turn warm. Not because of embarrassment that her boss had caught her daydreaming, but because a pair of dark brown eyes watched her with an intensity that unnerved her.

Deputy Cooper Night Hawk.

She was positive he'd looked at her and deemed her an imposter. She feared the time would come when he would reveal her lies to the town. And they would promptly run her out of town on a rail.

Until then, she would suffer while, every morning, he settled in one of her booths and ordered his usual blueberry pancakes, sausage and hash browns, coffee and orange juice.

She snagged a cup on her way over to him.

"Deputy." She greeted him with a warm smile as she set the cup on the table and filled it with hot coffee.

She was a coward, but she wasn't going to drop to her knees and beg him to understand the reasons for her lies about her name and why she was here. After all, what if she was wrong and he didn't know who she was?

Caroline vowed to stop reading mysteries. They had her believing she could get away with anything the heroines in the books could. They were getting her into a lot of trouble.

"Good morning, Caroline."

The way he said her name in his low, husky voice was enough to send shivers down her spine. Not to mention the way he looked at her, as if she was the blue plate special of the day. She managed an impersonal smile as she held her order pad in one hand and pencil in the other.

"Let me guess," she said. "The usual?"

He nodded without returning her smile. "I'd say that sounds like a plan."

"I'll be back with your juice." She whirled away and headed for the counter to drop off the order slip, although she knew Marge would have already started Cooper's breakfast.

SHE WILL STEAL YOUR HEART and give you her own.

Cooper hated the thoughts provoked by his grandfather's words that swirled inside his head. Especially when he was looking at a lovely young woman who was about as off-limits as a woman could get.

Caroline Benning was new in a town that boasted few newcomers. No one knew all that much about her other than she was twenty-two, had lost her father not long ago and had been traveling because she felt the need to get away. Cooper wondered if that need to get out of town had anything to do with a boyfriend.

His cop's eye gauged her to be about five foot eight and too thin, at around one hundred twenty pounds. He was certain the blond highlights in her light brown hair weren't real, but the dazzling green eyes were, since he didn't see any hint of contact lenses. For work, she kept her just-past-chin-length hair back in a barrette. The pink-and-white-striped, short-sleeved shirt she wore with a short denim skirt made her look younger than her twenty-two years.

She seemed a little shy, uncertain about people, but around him she actually appeared wary. He couldn't think of a reason why he'd cause that reaction in a young woman he barely knew.

Unless she had something to hide.

He didn't want to think that was the case. He liked looking at her too much.

"Hey, Cooper, heard Margaret Ingalls stole more of Nora Gates Forrester's underwear," Henry Farris called out from his usual perch at the counter. His cronies, not one of them under the age of seventy, surrounded him. Leathery fingers, gnarled by time and arthritis, wrapped themselves around coffee mugs or held on to a rich breakfast pastry. "When ya goin' to bring her in for questioning?"

"It hasn't been easy to find Margaret. I thought I'd call on Psychics R Us for help," Cooper called back.

The elderly men cackled their appreciation of his joke.

"Maybe Nora needs to put those special tags on them. You know the ones I'm talking about," Barney Metzger interjected. "Like the ones she puts on clothes in the store."

"I'll let you make that suggestion, Barney." Cooper lifted his coffee cup in a silent salute.

When Caroline set his glass of orange juice on the table, he inclined his head in a thank-you. The moment she was gone, he returned to reading the morning paper, until she returned with his food.

THE SCENT OF BLUEBERRIES and sausage, mixed with something light and floral, alerted him before she stood by his table.

"Have you ever ordered anything different for breakfast?" she asked curiously, setting the plate in front of him.

Cooper studied the stack of five pancakes, the golden surface dotted with blueberries he knew to be fresh. His mouth was watering in anticipation of that first bite.

"Not for the past sixteen years," he replied. "When you find something good, you tend to stick with it."

"Some day you ought to go wild and try them with bacon," she whispered as she refilled his coffee cup. She moved away as Marge called an order for pickup.

Cooper settled back to savor his breakfast. And visually savor Caroline. Some would say his interest in the young woman was because she was pretty. No, there was more to it than that. He just wasn't sure he was ready to further explore those thoughts.

"That's what I like to see first thing in the morning. A member of our esteemed law enforcement team sitting here stuffing his face with blueberry pancakes instead of out there fighting crime. Makes me feel downright safe."

Cooper looked up. "Up yours, Spencer. I do this to keep my energy level up, so I can catch all those bad guys you're worried about." He waved toward the empty seat across from him.

Brady Spencer slid into the seat across from Cooper. He made a face as he stared at Cooper's plate. "One day a breakfast like that will catch up with you," Brady pointed out.

"You're just jealous because I have a better metabolism than you. Comes from being more active than your average sedentary surgeon."

Brady's retort was interrupted by Caroline's appearance.

"Would you like a menu, Dr. Spencer?" she asked.

Cooper noticed that Caroline's usually bright smile appeared a bit strained. If he didn't know better, he'd swear she was nervous.

Brady looked up and flashed the smile that quickened many a woman's heart. "Just coffee, thanks, Caroline."

She quickly set a cup down in front of him and filled it. She topped off Cooper's cup before leaving.

Brady glanced at her. "Lovely woman."

"You don't want Eden to hear you say that," Cooper advised him. "She'd have your hide for sure."

Brady's smile broadened at the mention of his new wife. "Nah, she wouldn't damage anything serious. She'd just make sure I never looked at another woman again."

Cooper thought of the Spencer men and the women who'd enriched their lives. He admitted, only to himself, that he wouldn't mind finding a woman who could do that for him. He didn't hold out much hope for it.

The last woman he'd had a relationship with had told him he was too serious. She couldn't imagine him going out and cutting loose. He told her that wasn't him, and if she cared for him, she'd take him the way he was.

She took herself out of his life the next day.

"So what brings you here?" Cooper asked.

Brady shrugged. "Just wanted to talk with an old friend. Anything wrong with that?"

"Depends on what that old friend wants to talk to me about."

Brady glanced toward the counter, where Caroline was taking an order from old Henry Farris. He had to be at least ninety, but it didn't stop him from trying to look down her blouse as he ordered his usual oatmeal and a bran muffin.

God love them, nothing ever changed in this town.

"What do you think the Woman of the River looks like?" he asked suddenly.

Cooper refused to rise to the bait. He used the side of his fork to cut off a bite-size piece of pancake, and brought it to his mouth. Brady, used to his evasion tactics, patiently waited.

"Laughing Bear knows more about that story than I do," he said finally. "Why don't you ask him?" He flashed a mock-threatening stare at Brady as the other man started to reach for a sausage. Brady shrugged and backed off.

"I would think the woman in the legend could have blondish hair and green eyes. What do you think?"

"I don't think about it," Cooper lied as he took another bite. He didn't want to think about Caroline. He wanted his life to go back to the way it was. He especially wanted to consider his pancakes, which had fresh blueberries folded into the batter, the best pancakes in the world. As far as he was concerned, he rated them right up there with his first taste of coffee in the morning.

Brady leaned across the table. "I need to talk to you about something," he said in a low voice.

Cooper read the gravity in the other man's eyes. "How

serious are we talking?'' He also kept his voice low, so no one could overhear their conversation.

"Caroline came to the wedding with Marge,'' he began. Cooper nodded, silently urging his friend to continue. "Sometime during the reception, Dad went inside the house. While there, he noticed Caroline standing by his desk, looking at a family picture.'' His glance slid sideways to ensure the object of their conversation wasn't nearby.

"Since she must have been invited, I can't arrest her for trespassing.'' Cooper said. "Do you have another reason for telling me this? Did you ever stop to think she might have been admiring the Spencer boys? Although with all of you falling into the marriage trap, the odds of her landing a Spencer are now zip.''

Brady shook his head. "Not likely. This one was taken when we were boys.'' He paused and looked down at his hands, which were cupped around his coffee mug. "All I'm asking is that you see what you can dig up on this woman. Nothing heavy-duty.'' Brady looked up at Cooper. "Dad wouldn't ask you. You know how he is.''

Cooper certainly knew Elias Spencer. The older man and his three sons were like family.

And more than anyone, Cooper knew the story about Elias's wife and how she'd left him and their sons. After all, it had been last fall when Brady's brother Seth had asked Cooper to find information on their mother, Violet. The sad part was her leaving them in order to be with another man. Elias had never spoken her name again, until recently, and the Spencer brothers likewise acted as if they'd never had a mother. They had, however, discovered they had a half sibling out there somewhere. Apparently Violet had died in childbirth.

Still, Cooper balked.

"Why me? Why not ask her yourself?" he asked. "It still could have been something innocent. Lots of people like to look at family photographs."

Brady shook his head. "Dad said there was a look on her face that had nothing to do with idle curiosity." He glanced at his watch and quickly finished his coffee. "I've got to get to the hospital." He started to rise, then stopped and looked at his friend. "Will you see if you can find anything out?"

Cooper didn't tell him he'd had a few suspicions of his own about Tyler's new resident. "There's no reason for me to do it through official channels."

"Hey, she's single. You're single." Brady arched an eyebrow. "It wouldn't hurt for you to get out a little more."

"Now you sound like my grandfather," he muttered into his orange juice. "Go on. I'll do whatever I can."

Brady nodded and headed for the front of the diner. He stopped at the register and talked to Marge for a few moments before leaving.

Cooper envied people like Brady, who could talk to anyone about anything. As for him, he was never much for small talk, so the idea of finding out about Caroline Benning wasn't going to be easy. Too bad she hadn't stolen something at Elias's house. Then he'd have a good reason to haul her in for questioning, and he'd have a chance to find out everything he needed to know.

He guessed he'd have to let the good ladies of the town do some of the work for him. He was certain they'd do a hell of a more thorough job of it, too.

He'd wondered about Caroline more than usual. Part of it had to do with the fact that during the short time she'd been in Tyler, she showed more interest in the Spencer men than was normal for a newcomer.

It had Cooper asking why.

His cynical side said it could have something to do with the fact that the Spencer brothers were each successful in their own right. Along with being good-looking.

Cooper had returned to his newspaper when Caroline came by to refill his cup. He shook his head and placed his hand over the top. "No more for me, thanks. In fact, I'll just take the check."

"You're in luck, Deputy Night Hawk," she told him. "Dr. Spencer paid for your breakfast. He said it's your retainer." Mild curiosity darkened her eyes.

He tamped down the curse that threatened to erupt, and swallowed the last of his coffee. "No matter how it looks, we're not talking bribery here. The good doctor is regretting he can't eat blueberry pancakes any longer. Delicate digestion," he confided, reaching into his back pocket for his wallet.

Caroline shook her head. "Dr. Spencer left a tip also."

Cooper picked up his newspaper and folded it. "Have a good morning, Caroline."

"You too, Deputy."

His departure was slow but steady as he left the diner. People stopped him, some voicing mild complaints. It was nothing new to him, and he listened to the usual tales of dogs barking late into the night, kids riding their skateboards over lawns and little Rocky Edwards teasing Miss Smythe's nasty-tempered cat, Orlando. Cooper assured Miss Smythe he'd have a talk with Rocky.

With a full stomach and a feeling of contentment, Cooper walked past the town square as he headed for the police substation, located just beyond.

"Mrs. Forrester called," Hedda told him the minute he entered the building. She waved a pink message slip decorated with a vivid purple ink. Hedda believed the more colorful the note the easier it was to remember.

Cooper closed his eyes. "She's missing more underwear?"

"She wants to file a complaint against Mrs. Gray," Hedda explained, slipping her reading glasses on. The brightly colored frames highlighted her face, which was expertly made up.

Cooper couldn't remember ever seeing Hedda without makeup on. Her graying brown hair was pulled up and back in a bouncy ponytail tied with a colorful turquoise-and-pink scarf. She said if she had to wear a black uniform, then by God, she'd wear color anywhere else she could. No one dared ask her where else that color might be. A good idea, since they all knew if they asked she'd be only too happy to tell them.

Cooper always felt he needed sunglasses when facing her.

"Do I want to know why?"

Hedda smiled. "It seems Mrs. Gray told her she was tying up the local law office with nonsense when they could be doing something better suited to their talents. Mrs. Forrester insists there was a threat in there somewhere. I have no idea where that threat is, but I'm sure you'll find it." She beamed as she handed over the slip.

"I guess I should be grateful she's not insisting aliens are behind the so-called thefts," he muttered.

"Be careful, that just might be next."

Cooper headed for the rear of the station.

After the way his day had begun, the rest of it should turn out to be a piece of cake.

Chapter Two

Caroline liked the idea that she could walk anywhere she wanted to. Since she'd arrived in Tyler, she'd only taken her car when she wanted to explore outside of town.

She ignored her tired feet as she left the diner when her shift was over. She was grateful the Kelsey Boarding House was only two blocks away. The late afternoon sun was still warm on her face as she walked down the sidewalk.

This was what she liked best—the chance to watch the townspeople interact. She'd never thought of herself as a people watcher until she came here.

"Good afternoon, Caroline." Ed Martin greeted her with a grimace that she knew was his way of smiling. Rumor had it the video store owner had a fear that too much smiling would cause his dentures to slip out of his mouth. He stood in the doorway to his store as if he planned on dragging in customers off the sidewalk.

"Mr. Martin." She smiled back and stopped. "We didn't see you today for lunch."

"Had to unpack and set out the new releases. They arrived late today. But you'll see me tomorrow," he promised. "Can't go too many days without having Marge's meat loaf."

"You're not the only one." She walked on.

When Caroline reached the walkway leading to the boardinghouse, she noticed one of the sheriff's department vehicles cruise by. As it slowed down, she realized Cooper Night Hawk was in the driver's seat. He nodded a silent greeting toward her before driving on. She managed a jerky nod as she turned to walk up to the house.

"It's about time he noticed you as more than the one taking his breakfast order," Anna Kelsey said from the porch, where she sat in a rocking chair with a bowl of snap beans in her lap. A fat ginger-colored cat lay nearby.

Caroline felt her cheeks heat. "I thought you said you didn't believe in matchmaking." She glanced down at the cat. "Hey, Sam. Are my feet safe today?" She kept a wary eye on the cat as she dropped into the rocking chair next to Anna. She released a sigh as she kicked off her denim flats and stretched her legs out in front of her. She still kept a close eye on the cat, which was known to attack feet when the owner least expected it. "It's so nice to sit down for more than five seconds."

"Busy day?" Anna asked.

"Uh-huh. I think the entire population of Tyler, with the exception of you, came in to the diner today."

"Even Cooper Night Hawk?" she inquired in a mild voice, continuing to snap beans. Caroline studied her feet.

"Deputy Night Hawk comes in every morning for breakfast," she replied.

"The way I hear it, he always sits at one of your booths. He never did that before."

"Do you need my room so badly you'd throw me to any man who drives by and acknowledges me?" Caroline joked, trying to keep the conversation light. She was still feeling that strange sensation in the pit of her stomach when he looked at her. Nothing she'd want Anna to know about.

"Didn't you know? Matchmaking is our largest source of entertainment here in Tyler. My mother would say that you ended up here for a good reason."

"Or maybe I ended up here because I liked the looks of the town, you had a spare room and Marge needed a waitress," she said, moving the chair back so she could prop her feet up on the railing. "I really like this."

Anna shot Caroline a look of amusement. "Changing the subject?"

"No, just talking about something more interesting." She waved her hand to indicate the street in front of them. "You can sit out here all day and everyone passing by is someone you know. I lived in a city that was considered small by some standards, but it was nothing like this."

"For a city girl, you've settled into small town life like a fish takes to water." She smiled. "As if you were meant to be here all along."

"Long lost daughter returning to the fold," Caroline sang out, holding her arms out wide. She froze. "Listen to me. I sound like someone in a soap opera. Next thing you know I'll suffer a debilitating disease and lapse into a coma."

"Brady will be your doctor. He'll tell us he has no idea what caused your illness." Anna continued the fiction. "We could have Cooper ordering Brady to do whatever he can to cure you."

"I thought comas were an automatic death sentence for the actress," Caroline said, going along with the script Anna was happily writing.

"Not in our show, dear. *Tyler's Own* will be an Emmy-winning show," she insisted. "That's why we need you in a coma."

"The coma might be a good idea, since it was strongly suggested I drop out of drama class in high school," Caroline confessed.

"Honey, every woman has a bit of actress in her," the older woman soothed. "That's how we take those men and wind them around our fingers."

"So that's how it was done." Johnny Kelsey walked out of the house and kissed his wife's cheek. "Don't listen to her, Caroline. If you want to catch a man, you need a man's advice. So who are you plotting against? And does he have any idea his days are numbered?"

"No one," Caroline firmly stated, at the same time Anna offered, "Cooper Night Hawk."

Johnny raised an eyebrow. "Why don't you just throw her to the wolves, Anna? Couldn't you have started her out with someone easier?"

"You didn't see the look Cooper gave her when he drove by a few minutes ago," she replied.

"He was just being polite," Caroline explained. "Nothing more."

Anna smiled knowingly. "Yes, dear. And that's why you're blushing right now."

Caroline pushed herself out of her chair and headed for the front door. "I am not blushing," she declared haughtily as she made an escape worthy of a dramatic actress.

Husband and wife exchanged looks that said it all.

"You're really going to try to match her up with Cooper?" he asked.

"I don't think I'll have anything to say about it. You know how romance works in this town. It's all up to the quilting circle," she answered, thinking of the brightly colored quilt that had been presented to them at their wedding, and since then had adorned their bed.

Johnny shook his head in fatalistic agreement. More

than one single man cringed when they learned the Tyler Quilting Circle was beginning work on another quilt. Their success with the wedding quilts was the stuff legends were made of.

"God help them both."

CAROLINE WAS INDULGING in her favorite form of relaxation: a bubble bath.

At the moment, she was the only boarder in the house, so she didn't need to worry about anyone else needing the bathroom. She could take all the time she wanted.

She set her towel by the tub next to her CD player, stepped into the large, old-fashioned claw foot tub filled with hot water and floral-scented bubble bath, and slid down until her neck was resting against the edge of the tub, where she'd set a rolled-up towel. She turned on her CD player, slipped the headphones on and adjusted them to her ears.

Now she could truly relax. She closed her eyes, waiting for the music to flow through her body and complete the mood.

Except her body didn't calm down. And her eyes refused to remain closed. If she didn't know any different, she'd swear the music that usually soothed her now sounded downright annoying.

"Take deep calming breaths," she directed herself. "Your body can't relax if your mind won't relax."

Caroline wished her body would listen to her, but she could tell this time of relaxation wasn't soothing her as it usually did.

But how could she, when Cooper Night Hawk was firmly planted in her thoughts?

Why now? She'd been waiting on him since that first day she worked at Marge's. She'd even managed to serve him his breakfast without dropping it into his lap or scalding him with coffee.

From that first day she was aware of the intensity that surrounded him like a blanket. She didn't need to see his badge to know he was in law enforcement. He had that air about him. He was a man dedicated to protecting the people.

She sensed a dedication like his would not hesitate in protecting the Spencer men from her if he felt she posed any kind of threat to them.

There was another, more elemental reason why he unnerved her; he was the most attractive man she'd ever met.

Coal-black hair pulled back and tied with a leather thong. Eyes so dark a brown they were almost black. Copper skin stretched tightly over a face that could have been carved from granite. And a body that could inspire many a fantasy.

Caroline recalled she and friends in high school reading popular historical romances where the hero was a Native American. They'd giggled over the descriptions of men she always thought came strictly from the author's imagination. After meeting Cooper she was positive the books were nothing compared to the cold hard reality of the man.

"Caroline, dear, dinner in half an hour." Anna's voice filtered through the door.

"Thank you," she called back. Instead of waiting another twenty minutes before climbing out of the tub, she leaned forward and pulled the plug. She grabbed her towel and wrapped it around herself as she stepped out.

So much for relaxation.

"This is when I hate cars," Caroline muttered between clenched teeth as she turned the ignition key one more time. As before, the engine refused to turn over. She slapped the steering wheel with the flat of her hand as she leaned back in the seat.

It was clear she wouldn't be going any farther. She grabbed her small backpack, which doubled as her purse, and climbed out of the car. After locking the door, she walked down the road in the direction of town. With luck, someone might drive by and pick her up.

Caroline hadn't gotten far before she realized the sandals she'd put on that morning weren't meant for walking along a dusty road covered with gravel. Not to mention it was starting to get dark, and sounds she hadn't noticed before, coming from among the trees on either side of the road, seemed to grow louder.

"Lions and tigers and..." she whispered, looking left to right. She tried to pick up her pace, but the rocky road hampered her steps. "Oh, boy. Okay, no lions here. Wrong country. Tigers, no. Bears, could be. Bigfoot is in the Pacific Northwest. And I'm not."

She stopped to empty pebbles from her sandal for what felt like the twentieth time. Her balance was precarious as she stood on one foot, slipped off one shoe and brushed off the dirt. She wobbled when a truck slowed down and stopped by her.

"I heard Californians liked to walk, but I thought you'd be wearing something a bit more...sporty," Cooper said, eyeing her black tank top, which skimmed the waistline of her white-and-black-print capri pants molded to slim, tanned legs. Black thong sandals displayed feet gray from road dust. He could smell a light floral scent coming off her skin, sweeter than that of the colorful flowers growing alongside the road.

Caroline just stared at him. "You know, right now I

would love nothing more than to come up with some witty little comeback, but I'm too tired to think of one," she admitted. "My car died down the road."

He leaned over and pushed open the passenger door. "Get in. I've got a tow hook in the back, so I can tow your car to the garage if it's something that isn't a quick fix, like a loose wire or you ran out of gas."

"Unfortunately, I know from personal experience what happens when you run out of gas, and that wasn't it. I have no idea about a dead battery."

She climbed up into the cab and dropped onto the seat. She noticed the earthy aromas of horse and man mingling companionably in the small interior. Instead of his black deputy's uniform, Cooper wore a denim shirt with the cuffs rolled back to reveal dark forearms, and jeans that had seen better days. His boots were scuffed and dusty. His aviator-style sunglasses hid the eyes she sensed never displayed any emotion. An equally battered hat perched low on his forehead.

He looked as imposing as he did in uniform. Now she understood about a man with presence. Cooper Night Hawk had it in spades.

"I was beginning to think I wouldn't run into anyone," she admitted. "I heard that country roads are quiet. They're more than quiet. They're downright empty. I guess I should feel lucky my car didn't break down after dark. Who knows what I might have run into?"

"The only critters you'd find around here after dark are horny teenagers," Cooper said. He glanced at her lap. "Put your seat belt on."

She secured the harness and sat back against the door so she could face him. She slipped her sandals off and rubbed her feet. "What were you doing out here? Planning to pick off the teenagers when they show up?"

"We only come out here every so often," he replied. "That way they don't know when to expect us. We look around, see which car has the most steamed-up windows and tap on them. The area usually clears out within five minutes."

"What a spoilsport you are, Deputy." She grinned.

"That's my job."

"Right now you look more like a cowboy who's been out on the range."

He shook his head. "More like helping my grandfather with his garden. Which means he stands there and directs while I do the heavy work. He claims he's the one doing the work through my hands. Yet I always seem to be the one with the blisters and muscle aches."

"It sounds as if your grandfather knows how to delegate," Caroline pointed out. "It's considered a highly prized skill in the corporate world."

"I don't know if the corporate world could handle Grandfather and his insistence of consulting his spirit guides before making important decisions."

"I'm afraid I don't know very much about Native American culture," she confessed. "But I have heard of spirit guides. Are your spirit guides your ancestors or just someone who appears in your life?"

He drove with lazy confidence, one hand on the steering wheel, the other arm braced on the open window. A glance in her direction showed him she was genuinely interested. "Everyone has different guides. Your guides can be an ancestor or someone from your tribe. Animals are also spirit guides."

She studied him closely. "But you don't believe in them."

Cooper took his time answering. For a while she wasn't sure he was going to say anything. "My grandfather clings to the old ways. He uses herbs for healing, asks for guidance before planting, goes off to commune with his guides before making any important decisions. I believe in antibiotics, I check the almanac, and usually just flip a coin before making important decisions.''

"I have a friend who visits her psychic once a month," Caroline said. "The woman isn't always right, but Sheila never minded. She said she only sees Rena for a second opinion. Perhaps that's what your grandfather is doing. Looking for a second opinion."

Cooper quickly glanced her way. "Sounds as if you saw that psychic once in a while for those second opinions."

"I went to Rena once. She told me my life would take some surprising turns and I should just go along with the ride." Caroline thought of the turns her life had taken in the past months. " I guess she was right," she murmured.

"So that's how you ended up in Tyler? This psychic sent you here?" he asked.

She lifted her shoulder in a shrug. "She didn't exactly give me a map."

"Funny, I would have thought someone would have directed you to come this way," Cooper said casually. "It's not as if we're on all the major maps. Tyler isn't a typical destination for just anyone."

"I guess the reason I ended up here was because I decided to go off the highway and do some exploring. I drove into town and liked what I saw," she replied.

"It's not always a good idea to go off the main road. It's been known to be hazardous to a single young woman's health. More than one woman has disappeared because she wanted to see more of the countryside," he said. "Not all small communities are friendly."

"Now you sound like one of those true crime programs.

I try not to watch them. They give me nightmares.'' She leaned her head back, resting it against the partially open window. She twitched her nose in a way that reminded Cooper of a puppy sniffing the wind.

He doubted she'd appreciate being compared to a puppy. Even a cute one. He mentally kicked himself and returned to his lecture.

"They're meant to scare you," Cooper said flatly. "All it takes—"

"I'm careful, Deputy," she interrupted. "But I refuse to live my life under a cloud of fear."

He nodded. "Admittedly, our crime rate in Tyler is low, but you still have to be careful. People lock their doors now, when ten, fifteen years ago, they didn't. Still, Tyler is a small community where people look out for each other. Maybe everyone knows your business, but when the chips are down, it's nice to know there's people around who will care."

"That's quite a switch—from a warning to an advertisement on reasons to move to Tyler," she told him.

"I don't know. It seems they both cover you." He favored her with a sideways glance. "Any other surprises in store for us where you're concerned?"

She turned her head to look out the window, as if she was afraid he'd read something in her expression. "I'm not really the surprise type. I'm known as a very up-front person."

Now why did he have the feeling she was lying? She had the face of a Madonna. He didn't want to think she might have the soul of a devil. But he also felt she wasn't telling the complete truth.

"It seems a lot of the families in Tyler have lived here for many years," Caroline said.

"Some go back to the founding of the town. Others

arrived later. It's been said you're not considered a true local resident unless you can count back at least five generations," he explained. "My family can count back even further."

"So your family still lives around here?"

He shook his head. "Most live out of the area. My grandfather has a small cabin on my land. He claims it's so he can keep an eye on me."

"You're close to him, aren't you?" she guessed.

"Yeah, I am. He's an old coot but I guess I have to say he's my old coot." His voice was warm with affection. "What about you?"

"No one," she murmured. She wasn't aware of the wistful longing in her voice, nor did she see the quick look he flashed her.

Cooper steered the truck off to the side of the road and stopped behind Caroline's car. He silently held out his hand. "Keys?" he prompted when she looked at him blankly.

"Oh!" She dug into her bag and pulled out the key ring. She grasped the correct key and held it out to him. "I locked it up before I left."

He opened the door and climbed out. "I had an idea you would. Stay here. No need for you to get out."

Cooper unlocked the little sports car and lifted the hood to check the engine. After making sure the radiator was filled and she had oil, he returned to the driver's seat and tried the ignition. Just as Caroline had said, the engine refused to turn over.

He walked back to his truck and leaned on the open window.

"You've got a dead battery," he told her. "I can jump-start the engine, which should get you back to town okay. I'll follow you to make sure it doesn't die on you before you get to Carl's Garage. You'll need a new battery right away."

"This is when I hate cars," she confessed.

"That's a sweet little car you have. You need to take good care of her if you don't want to end up stranded again," he told her.

"I should have remembered that it needs more than filling up with gas and having the oil changed on a regular basis," she admitted.

In a matter of minutes, Cooper had his truck turned around to face Caroline's car. He instructed her to wait for his signal while he attached jumper cables to his truck battery, then to her car's.

"Okay, start her up," he called out.

He whistled a victory tune when the little car roared to life. He yelled for Caroline to back off on the accelerator, and quickly took off the cables.

Cooper trailed behind Caroline who kept to a fairly sedate pace as they headed toward town. He doubted she normally drove this slowly. The sporty red Miata convertible didn't look like a car that enjoyed staying at the speed limit.

"Why does someone who drives a car like that work as a waitress in a town that has little to offer anyone?" he mused as he watched her drive away. Normally, those kind of questions would raise a red flag in his mind. He'd see it as something he'd want to check out.

Temptation to run her license plate rose strongly. It was the best way to find out if she'd left any secrets in California she wouldn't want anyone to know about. Except his sense of honor was stronger than his curiosity. If the lady ran a stop sign or exceeded the speed limit, then yeah, he'd do everything by the book, along with running her plate and checking for outstanding warrants. Until then, he'd have to find other methods in his quest to find out just who Caroline Benning was.

"I COULD HAVE WALKED HOME from the garage," Caroline protested after Cooper had bundled her back into his truck and headed for the Kelsey Boarding House.

"No reason for you to when I'm driving past the house." He pulled up in front of it and stopped. He climbed out and helped Caroline out of the truck.

"Thank you," she said sincerely. "You saved me a long painful walk back to town."

"Just part of my job."

"You were off duty," she reminded him.

"Cops are never off duty," Cooper explained. He took a deep breath and seemed to look off into the distance. "The spring dance is next Saturday night. I was wondering if you'd like to go."

She blinked in surprise. "You're asking me out?"

He instantly backpedaled. "Look, if you're going with someone else…"

"No," Caroline said just as quickly. "No one else has asked me, and yes, I'd like to go with you."

Cooper nodded. "I'll pick you up at six-thirty, then," he said gruffly as he turned back to his truck.

Caroline strolled up the walkway, listening to the low rumble of Cooper's truck as he drove away.

"You wanted to keep a low profile," she told herself. "You knew it was best that you let the people get to know you while you got to know them. You have to be careful not to step over that self-imposed line. But going to the dance will give you a chance to see more people." She gave the dozing Sam a wide berth as she opened the front door. The cat opened one eye, then closed it as if Caroline offered no threat to his peace and quiet.

Anna walked out of the parlor. "What are you doing here? I thought you went for a drive." She looked surprised by her boarder's dusty appearance. "What happened to you?"

"I was, but the battery went dead," Caroline replied. "Luckily, Deputy Night Hawk drove by while I was walking toward town. He jump-started the battery, then followed me back to Carl's Garage. Carl's putting in a new battery."

"Just one of those times when cars are more trouble than they're worth." Anna nodded in understanding. "It's a good thing Cooper drove by."

Caroline headed for the stairs. "Yes, it was." She paused when she reached the first step. "Anna, does Deputy Night Hawk date a lot?"

"Cooper? He keeps his love life pretty much to himself," she chuckled. Then she noticed the expression on the younger woman's face. "Why do you ask?"

"Because he asked me to the spring dance. I have got to clean off this dust. I feel as if it's in my teeth," she confessed, running up the stairs.

"Caroline!" Anna called after her, with no response. She quickly turned around and headed for the rear of the house. "Johnny!" she called out to her husband, who was in the backyard bent over a lawn mower.

He looked up, his screwdriver in his hand. "I don't care what you say. I know I can fix this damn thing."

Anna rolled her eyes. "That's what you said about the toaster. We ended up buying a new one. This is something entirely different." She walked swiftly over to her husband and lowered her voice as she gave him the news. "Cooper just asked Caroline to the spring dance."

He raised an eyebrow in surprise. He grabbed a rag and wiped the grease from his hands. "Did she say yes?"

"Since she just told me he asked her, I'd guess she accepted. Not to mention she couldn't look at me after she told me about it."

Johnny raised his eyes heavenward. "The man doesn't have a chance."

"None of that!" She playfully swatted him. "And no teasing her about it, either."

"No worries there. But I will ask him if his intentions are honorable."

"You will not! This will be the first time that child has gone out since she arrived here. I think she's nervous about it as it is."

Johnny returned to his task. "I don't know why you're worried about Caroline. It's Cooper who's a goner."

Chapter Three

If Caroline hadn't already known that the spring dance was a major social event for the citizens of Tyler, she quickly learned. No matter where she went, it was the main topic of conversation during the week before the dance.

She was looking forward to the evening because it would give her a chance to meet more of the townspeople in a relaxed atmosphere. She remembered her father saying it was easier to get people to talk when the surroundings were congenial.

Caroline was determined to mingle as much as possible. With Cooper as her date, she knew she had the perfect opportunity to meet people she hadn't seen in the diner. She might even be able to ferret out a little more information about the elusive Deputy Night Hawk.

She'd already learned that just because he asked her to the dance didn't mean his manner toward her would change all that much when he came in to Marge's for breakfast. She wanted to assure him his face wouldn't crack into a million pieces if he smiled.

It was turning into a campaign for her to find a way to get him to smile.

Arranging blueberries in a happy face on his pancakes didn't do anything other than solicit a quizzical look.

"The least you can do is appreciate those little touches that make your breakfast special," she told him.

He picked up his fork and poured warm syrup over his pancakes. "Believe me, I do appreciate everything you do."

His orange juice served in a borrowed Flintstones glass only had him commenting that Marge must be getting low on glassware.

"What are you doing?" Alice asked one day.

"That man has a smile in him somewhere," Caroline insisted. "I intend to find it even if it kills me."

"It just might happen with the way you're going at it." The other woman shook her head. "Honey, Cooper doesn't smile. At least, he doesn't smile the way you and I do."

Caroline leaned against the counter. "Then how do you know if he's in a good mood?"

Marge chuckled from her corner, where she'd been unashamedly eavesdropping on their conversation. "That's easy, hon. When Cooper's in a good mood, he doesn't shoot anyone."

Caroline threw up her hands. "Well, that's a comfort! Everyone knows as long as he doesn't pull out his gun he's laughing on the inside?"

The two women nodded. "That's about it."

"Then the man will just have to learn it wouldn't hurt for him to smile on the outside."

Marge and Alice exchanged looks that said Caroline would have to learn something herself.

Caroline stiffened when she noticed two men walking into the diner. They chose a booth near the rear, in her station. She snagged two coffee mugs and one of the coffeepots and headed for the booth.

"Gentlemen," she said crisply, holding up the mugs. "Coffee?"

"Yes, thank you," Elias Spencer said, barely giving her a glance.

The other man, who Carolyn knew worked at the bank, took a moment to look her over thoroughly. She didn't know his name and she didn't care to. "Definitely," he said.

She mentally poured his coffee in his lap while she filled both mugs. "Do you need a little time before ordering?"

"Two eggs, over easy, hash browns crisp and my bacon crisp." Elias's tone matched how he wanted his food.

"What would you recommend, darlin'?" the other man drawled.

"Enough," Elias snapped at the man. "The girl is trying to work here. Either order or don't."

"I'll have the same thing."

Caroline nodded and walked away to put in the order.

After all this time working in the diner, this was the first time she'd waited on the illustrious Elias Spencer, since he usually sat at one of Alice's tables. Caroline had met him at Jenna and Seth's wedding and wasn't too sure she liked the man even if she knew him to be her mother's first husband. She knew her mother must have loved the stern-looking man at one time, so there had to be something special about him. But she'd also left him to marry Caroline's father.

Elias appeared so stiff she thought his spine would snap from the pressure. Not that his sons were any different. Quinn seemed to be the only one who hadn't carried on the tradition. When she looked at Elias this morning, Caroline thought the man seemed bitter. She didn't think he smiled any more than Cooper did, although he did seem to unbend a little when he was around Lydia Perry. Maybe there was hope for the man yet.

It was tempting to blow that stiff-necked manner sky-high by suddenly asking him why he'd divorced her mother. She'd love to hear that answer.

Instead, she was the picture of the perfect waitress. Elias's dining companion had given up trying to charm her. Good thing, since she would have dumped coffee in his lap for real if he'd tried anything.

Later, Caroline was clearing the table when Elias stopped back. He looked hesitant when she glanced up.

"Was there a problem, Mr. Spencer?" she asked formally.

"No, everything was fine." He dropped a couple of bills on the tabletop. "I'd just like to apologize on behalf of my colleague. There was no reason for him to act that way."

"Don't worry about it. Perils of the trade," she quipped.

He nodded. "I just wanted you to know I don't hold with that kind of behavior."

"Thank you." She smiled. "As for your colleague, tell him if he tries anything else, next time he just might find himself wearing his coffee instead of drinking it."

Elias's somber face broke into a smile. "I guess you've had to learn to handle just about anything that comes your way." He nodded and walked away.

The dishes forgotten, Caroline watched his exit. The opening was there. She could have easily slipped it in. Maybe even gotten some answers she'd been looking for.

The only thing that bothered her was the knowledge

that Elias knew things about her mother that Caroline had no hope of knowing.

After work, she walked over to the library in search of reading material. On her way out of the library, she ran into Jenna Robinson Spencer, Seth's wife, who now moved slowly due to her blossoming pregnancy.

"Jenna! Look at you! I swear, you look ready to pop," Caroline said, giving her a hug, which wasn't easy with her belly between them.

She rolled her eyes. "Let me tell you, as far as I'm concerned, right now wouldn't be soon enough." She patted her abdomen. "You know how you can buy those turkeys with those little red pop-up thingies? I'm positive I got a defective thingie because it definitely forgot to pop up to say I'm done."

"I've always heard the last month feels the longest," Caroline said with sympathy.

"Every day seems like a year," Jenna declared dramatically.

Caroline could easily tell the other woman was tired. Looking at her, she could understand why. "Still, before you know it you'll have those beautiful babies."

"Let's see if you say the same thing when it's your turn to carry around a couple of baby elephants for what seems like forever," Jenna told her.

"Considering my serious lack of a social life, I don't think that will be happening anytime soon," Caroline said.

"I'm sure I said something to that effect. Look where it got me. Well, time for me to waddle off." She grimaced. "Just tell me I don't look like one of those inflatable clowns that just pop back up when kids punch them."

"Not even close. I've heard of some restaurants that

serve a cabbage soup that pregnant women eat and they'll go into labor the same day," Caroline said helpfully.

"Tell Marge to put it on the menu and I'll be right over," Jenna said over her shoulder.

Sensing Cooper was in the vicinity, Caroline turned around and looked up the street. She found him in front of the drugstore. He was crouched down next to a little boy who was crying. A bicycle lay nearby on the sidewalk. Cooper had one hand on the boy's shoulder, and while she couldn't hear his words, she guessed he was saying something to reassure him. She watched as he pulled a handkerchief out of his back pocket and wiped the boy's eyes, then urged him to blow his nose. Cooper stood up, picked up the bicycle and set it upright. He continued talking to the boy as he guided the bike onto the edge of the street. He helped him onto the bike and kept it steady until the boy felt confident to go on his own. The little boy grinned at Cooper as he managed to make his way down the street without too much wobbling.

At that same moment, Cooper's head snapped upward and his nostrils flared as if he'd caught a scent in the wind. His head swiveled until he looked across the street. Straight at Caroline. There was no change in his expression as he nodded his head in greeting. She nodded back.

She remained frozen in time as she watched Cooper climb back into his vehicle. A moment later, the engine rumbled to life and the Blazer headed down the street. During its progress, people would look up and call out Cooper's name, punctuated with a wave of the hand.

She noted he returned each greeting, but not once did a smile crack his lips.

Caroline forced her legs to move. With each step, her resolve to see Cooper Night Hawk smile strengthened, until it was pure steel.

"YOU ARE TAKING the new woman to the dance," Laughing Bear announced from the bathroom doorway.

Cooper stood in front of the mirror adjusting his tie. He hated the things with a passion and wore them as little as possible. He swore under his breath and started to pull the tie free from his collar. Then he remembered. The ladies in town made few rules, but maintained them religiously. One of them was that their men dress up for church and for the dances.

"Have you been consulting the Spirits lately or just hearing the gossip in town?" he asked his grandfather.

He shook his head, his shoulder length gray hair shifting with each movement. "One day you will understand the Spirits' plan for you and you will regret that you doubted them."

Cooper turned away from the mirror and followed his grandfather into the large room that was a combination living room, family room and dining room all in one. His cabin was built for comfort instead of looks. In the winter, it was warm and snug, and during the summer heat waves it was cool, even outside on the wraparound porch.

"Aren't you going to the dance?" He noticed the older man's more casual attire of a plaid shirt and jeans. As he looked at his grandfather, he realized the man's hands had grown more gnarled from his arthritis and his face showed cracks and wrinkles of a life well lived. He also noticed the older man's walk wasn't as steady as it used to be.

It saddened Cooper to think the day would come when the older man wouldn't be around to remind him to honor his ancestors and tell the story of the Woman of the River and what she meant. For some time, Laughing Bear had been convinced the woman would return and come into Cooper's life, as she had come into the Sauk chief Black Hawk's.

Cooper was convinced he'd see Homer Madison's pigs fly first.

"Dances are for young people."

"That's not what Mrs. Peabody thinks. And she's got to be ninety-four, if a day," Cooper protested. "When she's feeling frisky she can put all of us to shame on the dance floor."

"Liza Peabody was a lovely young woman who had her choice of men in the town," Laughing Bear mused. "She once told me she chose Walter because he had kind eyes. She listened to her heart instead of her head. It was the best choice she could have made."

"Oh no!" Cooper threw up his hands for protection. "You already tried that a few minutes ago and I wouldn't bite."

Laughing Bear stared at his grandson for several moments. "Perhaps it would be a good thing if I go. But my truck is not running right."

His grandfather was spinning a yarn, Cooper knew, since he'd just given the cantankerous pickup a tune-up on his last day off. The older man wanted to go, all right. As long as he went with Cooper and his date. Good thing Cooper didn't think Caroline would mind.

"Go on and change," he said gruffly. "You can ride with us."

Laughing Bear appeared to hesitate. "She will not mind?"

"I have a pretty good idea Caroline won't mind at all. Go on home and change. I'll drive over there to get you."

Cooper knew his grandfather had done what many a teenager had tried and failed to do with the deputy. The elderly man had just neatly manipulated him.

"You would have made a great lawyer," he called after his grandfather.

"Yes, I would," was his serene reply.

Cooper didn't bother coming back with a retort. His grandfather was happiest when he had the last word.

"YOU LOOK LOVELY, dear," Anna told Caroline.

"It's all right?" Caroline struck a pose worthy of a haughty model in a fashion magazine. "I wasn't sure what to wear, then I discovered I had this outfit and thought it would work. It's one of my favorites."

"It's perfect," her landlady proclaimed, but looked skeptical as she stared down at Caroline's feet. "Are you sure you can dance in those shoes?"

Caroline's black, silk knit top boasted a scoop neck and cap sleeves, and skimmed the waistline to her red-and-white checked skirt with its flirtatious ruffled hemline. Her strappy, high-heeled sandals showed her legs to their best advantage. She had the top part of her hair, divided into three sections, twisting the strands around to be held in place with red pearlized butterfly clips. Her only other jewelry was a gold bangle bracelet.

Caroline had just reached the bottom step when the doorbell rang.

"I'd say that is your date," Anna said, moving toward the door. She opened it and stood back. "Cooper, now don't you look handsome."

"Anna," he greeted the woman as he stepped inside. His gaze immediately shifted to Caroline. His voice turned husky. "You look lovely."

She brightened immediately. "Thank you." She headed toward him.

"We'll see you at the dance," Anna told them.

"I hope you don't mind, but my grandfather wanted to come to the dance and he said his truck is acting up,"

Cooper said apologetically as they went down the walkway.

"I don't mind at all."

Caroline looked at the Blazer with its official seal.

"There's not enough of us to be off duty totally," he explained, opening the passenger door.

Caroline looked in, noticed the rifle and the low voiced static coming from the radio. "I don't think I've ever felt safer," she quipped, as he helped her into the seat.

"With two of us, you will feel even safer."

Caroline shifted, so she could rest her arms on the back of the seat. "You must be Cooper's grandfather. I'm Caroline Benning." She offered her hand.

"I am Laughing Bear." He took her hand between his as he smiled at her. "You are a lovely woman."

She smiled back. "Thank you. I can see where your grandson received his charm." She shifted her gaze momentarily in Cooper's direction.

"I tried to teach him well," Laughing Bear said gravely.

"Are you trying to steal my date, Grandfather?" Cooper asked as he slid behind the wheel.

"Only if she wishes to be stolen." His teeth flashed white in the dark.

"I bet all the ladies adore him," Caroline said to Cooper.

"He's a charmer, all right," he muttered.

Caroline shared a secret smile with Laughing Bear. She somehow felt that the older men approved of her.

The hall where the dance was held was brightly lit, with music floating out of the open doors. Tiny twinkling lights threaded through the trees outside the hall gave the area a fairyland atmosphere. A romantic atmosphere for those who wished some privacy. Teenagers were already disappearing among the trees.

Out of habit Cooper scanned the grounds. He didn't expect trouble. It was rare to have any problems on dance nights unless someone spent too much time in the parking lot with friends and beer. Only soft drinks were allowed in the hall for just that reason. In Cooper's opinion it was a good rule.

Caroline took his arm and hugged it against her. Her movements sent the scent of her perfume drifting his way. Tonight her fragrance was heavier, with a hint of jasmine. Something rare and exotic. Like her.

"You're off duty," she reminded him, seeing him stare toward the rear of the parking lot.

"No cop worth his salt is ever off duty," he said.

She kept his arm close to her. "Then I guess I'll just have to make sure that you're too busy dancing to worry about anyone else."

Cooper ignored the soft laughter coming at him from behind. He could tell his grandfather was already having way too much fun at his expense.

When they entered the hall, Laughing Bear moved to one side to join friends.

"It looks as if the entire town is here," Caroline said, looking around.

Her toes tapped and her hips swiveled to the beat of the Glenn Miller song the band was playing.

"Just about. All ages are welcome so no one has to baby-sit and miss out on the fun," Cooper told her. "Care to dance?"

"Of course I do. I'm not letting you off that easy," she quipped, allowing him to lead her toward the dance floor.

The moment she stepped into his arms she felt her pulse

race. She moved with him as easily as if she'd danced with him all her life.

There was no missing the darkening in his eyes or the slight hitch in his breath when she rested her hand on his shoulder. In her heels, she almost met him at eye level.

"I'm glad you asked me," she said, so softly he had to lean down to hear her.

"I'm glad you accepted."

Their steps moved in perfect sync as they moved among the other couples. They ignored the curious looks directed their way and the whispers along the side of the room.

"Seeing the way they're looking at us, I'd guess you normally don't come to the dances," she murmured.

"I don't," he admitted under his breath.

She slightly drew back. "Never?"

"My grandfather comes to them. I take duty those nights."

"You're not on duty tonight. I bet they would have let you take the evening off, so you could come other times."

"I usually prefer being on duty so anyone else who wants to come can."

The tip of her tongue appeared, to dot the curve of her upper lip. *The first time he comes to a dance is with me? No wonder people are staring at us.* "Oh."

"Who else asked you to go with them tonight?" Cooper questioned.

Caroline tipped her head back, eyes half closed in thought. Her lips moved as if she was ticking off names. In his mind, she took entirely too long before she opened her eyes.

"No one."

"I can't believe that."

"Alice said I intimidate the men. I think I just plain

scare them.'' She almost yelped with joy when she saw a corner of his mouth twitch.

"Maybe you should try the smiley face on their pancakes," he suggested.

"I wanted to build a tower with the bacon, but Marge said it wasn't a good idea." Her smile faltered.

Cooper spun her around so he could see what caught her attention. Elias Spencer had just come in with Lydia Perry, a member of the infamous Tyler Quilting Circle. Cooper didn't miss the momentary expression in Caroline's eyes that he knew was yearning. But why? What did Elias Spencer have to do with her?

It would have been so easy to ask her why seeing any of the Spencer men affected her so strongly. But he didn't want to tip his hand just yet.

"See anyone you know?" he asked instead.

She looked at him blankly for a moment before she recovered. "I'm sorry, I must have zoned out," she apologized.

He shook his head, confused. "Zoned out?"

"Mentally wandered off. I usually don't do that."

"Maybe it's the company," he said lightly.

She ducked her head just enough so she could inhale the spicy scent of his aftershave.

"Fishing for a compliment, Cooper?" Her smooth voice flowed like hot silk over his skin. Her hand moved almost caressingly across his shoulder.

"I never had a woman zone out before," he said gruffly.

She smiled brightly. "Let's just call it relaxing and having fun, shall we?"

Cooper wasn't sure it was a good idea to relax too much around Caroline.

CAROLINE LOVED TO DANCE and did so any chance she had. Tonight she learned that dancing with Cooper was a whole new experience.

She couldn't remember a partner moving with her the way he did. As if they were one.

The connotation brought images to mind that were best left alone.

Dancing was giving her the chance to glance around the room and see who was where. Luckily, the people she'd hoped to see there had arrived. The Spencer men were all present, and none of them arrived alone. Since they were good-looking men, she wasn't surprised.

Brady Spencer was the only one she'd had much chance to talk to. She hoped she would have more of a chance tonight. She already knew Cooper was good friends with all the Spencer brothers, Seth, Brady and Quinn, so it would be natural for him to spend some time with them.

"Well, folks, we're going to take a short break," the band leader, who also played the trombone, announced in a voice that carried throughout the large room. "Get your-selves something cold to drink, rest your feet and we'll be back in about fifteen minutes."

As Caroline and Cooper left the dance floor, she was aware of his hand resting warmly against the small of her back. She'd never thought of it as a sensitive area until then.

"Looks as if we're being paged," Cooper murmured, guiding Caroline to the left.

"I told myself, 'That can't be Cooper Night Hawk out there dancing,'" Brady called out. He was grinning widely when the couple reached the table. "The man wouldn't attend a dance if his life depended on it. Then Eden says, 'Look out there. It's Cooper.' I was ready to

tell her she needed glasses when I saw you myself. *Ow!*"
He rubbed his arm where his wife had punched him.

"Please excuse my husband. He sometimes needs a
mouth adjustment," Eden Frazier Spencer explained to
Caroline. Her violet eyes were warm with amusement. "I
hate to think what kind of witty sayings he comes up with
at the hospital."

"I haven't lost a sponge in a patient for some time
now," Brady insisted.

"Which is why I go out of town for medical services,"
Cooper said.

"The man can make a joke, but not once have I seen
him smile or laugh," Caroline confided in Eden.

Caroline secretly envied the other woman her stunning
violet eyes. There had been plenty of talk about Eden and
Brady's romance, with everyone insisting that the charming surgeon didn't go down easy. He hadn't wanted to
get married, but he also hadn't wanted to lose Eden.

Now he looked as if marriage agreed with him a great
deal. Caroline didn't miss the secret looks and smiles
shared by the couple. It was an intimacy she hoped to
share with a special person one day.

Cooper turned to Caroline. "How about something cold
to drink?"

"Yes, please."

"Eden, Brady, I'm sure we'll see you later."

When they reached the drinks table, Cooper looked at
her questioningly.

"Anything diet is fine with me," she replied.

Cooper purchased drinks and they walked around until
they found an empty table with two chairs. Caroline sat
down so that she could see the room from her position.

"Everyone is so friendly here," she commented. "Not
that they aren't friendly where I came from," she added

hastily. "It's just that it's different here. People are genuinely interested in hearing how you are."

"They'll also be more than willing to tell you how they are," Cooper said. "There's nothing like listening to Mrs. Morgan talk about her gallbladder surgery. In great detail, no less."

"And I bet you can count on them in any kind of emergency."

"Lightning struck a barn last summer. Started up a fire and the barn was gone in no time. Three days later enough men were over there to rebuild the barn and enough women came along to make sure we were fed," he said. "I can't imagine any secrets rolling around in Tyler for too long before they're revealed."

Caroline's smile felt frozen on her lips. "Yes, I guess it wouldn't be easy to keep them here." She toyed with her straw, rolling it around in the glass. When she looked up, she noticed several elderly women sitting together. There was nothing remarkable about them that should have caught her attention, except they all seemed to be watching her. If she wasn't mistaken, she'd swear their whispered conversation was also about her. She knew her skirt wasn't too short or her upper body too bare, so that couldn't be it.

She returned her attention to Cooper. "Do I have something on my face?" she asked in a low voice.

He looked startled by her question. "No, why?"

"Because right now I feel like a bug under a microscope. There's a table across from us where some older ladies are sitting, and they're watching us," she whispered.

Cooper shifted in his chair as if he was making himself more comfortable, but so he could also see who Caroline was talking about. He muttered a curse when he saw them. "Have you heard of the Tyler Quilting Circle?" he asked.

She nodded. "Of course. The ladies at Worthington House who get together a couple times a week to work on quilts. They recently donated one for a raffle for the children's library."

"That's the one. When you're talking about people who are genuinely interested in you, you're really talking about them. They can get information the FBI wouldn't have a prayer of finding out," he replied. He wasn't about to tell her about the legend of the Quilting Circle's quilts. He wasn't the only man who believed telling the legend could make it true. For him.

Cooper was saved when the music started up again. He'd barely led her back to the dance floor when Patrick Kelsey deftly swung her around.

"Trade ya, Cooper," he called out to the deputy.

"I think you got the raw end of the deal, Cooper," Pam Kelsey teased as Cooper put his arms around her.

"Are you kidding? I got the better deal. She kept stepping on my toes," he confided.

She smiled. "Sure, she did. That's why you shot holes through my husband when he cut in."

"Yeah, well, let him see if I'll give you back," he kidded.

Cooper was glad to see Pam out socializing. Her multiple sclerosis had taken a toll on her health, but she refused to allow it to keep her down.

After that, he felt as if someone had posted an Open Season sign on his back. Other men tried to steal Caroline from him, but he was ready for them now. His trademark glare was enough to scare them off.

For a man who didn't like dances, he was having a lot of fun.

"THIS HAS BEEN a wonderful evening." Caroline's smile dazzled him as they moved around the dance floor for the last dance.

"Yes, it has." Cooper surprised himself by speaking the truth.

He tried to remind himself taking Caroline to the dance was more a duty than a date. Helping out his friend. Seeing if he could find out anything previously unknown about Caroline. Once here, though, he couldn't resist enjoying himself.

"I'm surprised your grandfather didn't dance," she commented. "He seemed to have several of the ladies interested."

Cooper shook his head. "Grandfather only comes to socialize. The ladies like to tap into his knowledge of plants and herbs. He has a pretty extensive stock of teas, for just about every ailment." He looked around for his grandfather and spotting him, gestured that they were getting ready to leave.

"Mrs. Riley kindly offered to give me a ride home," Laughing Bear told him.

Cooper cocked an eyebrow. "Don't tell me. She's suggesting you stop by her place first for a piece of her peach pie."

The older man's expression was one of innocence. Not that Cooper believed it for a minute.

"I am an old man, Grandson. You worry about your own pie." He turned around and walked away.

Cooper stood there, unable to believe what he'd just heard.

Just be grateful he didn't bring up that damn Woman of the River, he thought, not even sure it was a good idea to think of the dream that had been haunting him for far too many nights. For all he knew, the woman could appear right now, just by him thinking about her.

"If I didn't know better, I'd think you were just told he's an adult and can do anything he pleases," Caroline said softly.

"Yeah, I guess I was." Cooper looked at her. "Since the nicest place to have a drink is a fair distance, how about stopping for something less alcoholic?"

"Make it a hot fudge sundae and you've got a deal." She playfully pulled on his arm.

"I've heard it isn't wise to get between a woman and chocolate."

"You heard right, Deputy. Greater men than you have been shot down in flames for much less."

It seemed only natural that he put his arm around her shoulders as they walked toward his vehicle.

"Then what do you say that I introduce you to the perfect hot fudge sundae?"

Caroline spun around to face him and leaned against him. She smiled as she draped her arms around his neck. His own hands dropped down to her waist, making sure she didn't move away from him.

"Why, Deputy, you charming devil, you. You know all the right wo ds to say to a girl, don't you?" she said huskily. "Wi h an intriguing proposition such as the one you just suggested, I can only say one thing—take me to that sundae."

Chapter Four

Caroline closed her eyes so she could better relish the rich treat that had been set before her. The expression on her face was that of a woman in love.

Her lips parted and the tip of her tongue appeared, silently waiting for what was coming. A spoon carried just the right amount of French vanilla ice cream and hot fudge sauce and a smidgen of whipped cream into her mouth. Her lips closed and she slowly rolled her tongue around her mouth, enjoying the rich blend of tastes. When she opened her eyes, the green orbs were glazed with desire.

Cooper couldn't remember ever feeling this uncomfortable. He felt as if he was witnessing an intimate ritual. He shifted in the seat as he felt his body growing heavier with a desire that mirrored Caroline's. Except his arousal had nothing to do with a hot fudge sundae.

"Was I right?" he asked, damning the raw need he could hear in his voice.

"Mmm, oh yes, you were." The pink tip of her tongue appeared again as she daintily licked every bit off the spoon. Cooper hadn't known he could envy a spoon. "I can't believe in the time I've been in Tyler I haven't stopped into the Dairy King. Must have been because of all those pastries I've been pigging out on at Marge's.''

"The owner personally makes the hot fudge sauce. Rumor has it that it's an old secret family recipe," he explained, his eyes trained on Caroline's face.

"No wonder it's a secret. I know I'd kill for it." She chuckled. "I guess that's something I shouldn't confess to an officer of the law."

She dipped the spoon back into the concoction and brought it to her mouth. The third spoonful she held out in front of him.

Cooper reared back as if she'd just waved a snake in front of his face.

"Oh, come on. You eat blueberry pancakes every day. This is even better. You'll like it," she challenged him. A reckless light shone in her eyes as she waited for him to accept her dare.

He warily eyed the spoon in front of his face. "This has nothing to do with my eating habits."

She held the spoon steady in front of his mouth. "Come on, Cooper, open up. It won't hurt. I promise." She lowered her voice to a husky purr.

Cooper sighed and opened his mouth just enough for the spoon to slide inside. She fed him as carefully as if he was a child. He allowed the ice cream to melt in his mouth and blend with the warm fudge.

"Good, huh?" she cooed.

"I think it's a female thing," he replied.

"Then think of it as my sharing the fantasy with you," she murmured in a voice that brought to mind hot nights and even hotter sex. She dipped the spoon into the sundae with the precision of a surgeon. A smile hovered on her lips as she again brought it to Cooper's lips. "There aren't many women who would be so generous with something this good. Maybe you need to try a second helping,'' she whispered.

''One was enough,'' he argued, thinking the exact opposite.

Damn! The woman was doing something he thought was impossible. She was seducing him with a hot fudge sundae! He felt as if this was a prelude to hot sex.

Cooper always thought seduction had to do with a star-lit night, a glass of wine, maybe a roaring fire along with a few kisses. He'd never realized this kind of temptation could be spun inside a brightly lit fast-food restaurant with golden oldies playing in the background.

He opened his mouth and waited for the cold ice cream to melt in his mouth. Her emerald eyes studied him intently as he swallowed.

''Now what do you think?''

What did he think? Right about now, he was seriously thinking about driving her back to his place. Something he never considered on a first date. Especially with a woman who, in a sense, he was investigating. Who he'd only asked to the dance in an attempt to find out more about her. Instead, she'd turned the tables on him and seemed to find a way into the deepest recesses of his being. He was beginning to think the evening had been taken out of his hands.

Damn Brady for getting him into this! Cooper had dressed up, not one of his favorite pastimes, danced, another nonfavorite pastime, mingled and, dammit, somewhere along the line even managed to enjoy himself.

He even thought about asking her out again.

''I think it would taste even better another way,'' he said huskily.

She arched an eyebrow. ''Really? How?''

''If I was tasting it on you.''

Her quick intake of breath and the way her pupils constricted were proof of his success. Now he wasn't the only one thinking of R-rated activities while they sat in a strictly G-rated atmosphere.

"You are a dangerous man, Cooper Night Hawk," she said.

"Look who's talking about dangerous. The one who was feeding me this sundae the way a sultan's concubine would offer sweetmeats," he told her. "This what you do with all your dates?"

"Chocolate is something I normally don't share," Caroline said honestly.

Damn, she'd done it again! Every time he thought he might get the better of her she turned the tables on him.

He wondered what would happen next. And if he'd have the strength to survive it.

"THANK YOU FOR A LOVELY evening." On the porch of the Kelsey Boarding House, Caroline unlocked the front door and turned to Cooper. "I really enjoyed myself."

"I'm glad." His dark gaze caught her the way a flame caught a moth. "Maybe we can do it again sometime."

"I'd like that." She smiled. "Only if I don't have to dance with Jake Monahan. My feet were black-and-blue after one turn with him."

"Yeah, he caught me a little off guard," Cooper said, chagrinned that in the few minutes he'd been gone, Jake, with his two left feet, had swept Caroline away.

Caroline reached out and lightly touched the back of his hand with her fingertips. "Would you like to come in for a cup of coffee?"

He hesitated. "I don't think it would be a good idea. Good night, Caroline."

She remained on the porch and watched him walk to

his vehicle, then drive away. She'd been so sure he was going to kiss her. And she wanted him to. She just didn't have enough experience in asking for it.

She wished the mystery books she read voraciously would have been able to give her some advice on what to do in situations like this. It was certainly time to check out some romance novels at the library next time.

Caroline fanned her face with her hand as she felt the heat travel up her body.

"There is no way I can be having a hot flash."

CAROLINE DIDN'T WANT to wake up. Not that there was a need to. She wasn't working until the dinner shift tonight. She could sleep all day if she wanted to.

Besides, waking up meant leaving her wonderful dream. In it she was wearing a beautiful flowing gown in a sheer pink. She felt like a princess in a fairy tale. A princess kidnapped by a dark-eyed stranger who only had to look at her to send lightning bolts through her body. A stranger who looked a lot like Cooper Night Hawk, except instead of his hair secured back with a leather thong, it was left loose and flowing like black silk about his shoulders. Not a prince, but a knight, born to protect his lady fair.

She knew if she continued sleeping, this dream could get real interesting. She didn't want to miss that.

Except her nose started twitching. The scents of orange and cinnamon enticed her. She opened one eye. And took a deeper breath. Oh yes, orange and other good things. The other eye popped open.

Caroline groaned and rolled over onto her back.

She hadn't been able to drop off to sleep easily last night because she'd been reliving the evening in her mind.

She'd wanted to commit everything that happened to her memory banks.

With each breath she took, the zesty fragrance of orange filled her lungs calling to her.

Caroline gave up and crawled out of bed. She stopped long enough to wash her face and brush her teeth before hurrying downstairs. She didn't worry about anyone seeing her in her cotton pajama bottoms and tank top. Since Jenna's marriage to Seth Spencer, and her departure from the Kelsey Boarding House, Caroline had been the only boarder.

"You're already designing the next one?" Anna could be heard to say, when Caroline entered the kitchen. "You didn't waste any time, did you? I still can't believe how all of you seem to know these things before the people in question do."

"Oh yes." Caroline headed for the table, where a covered basket of orange muffins lured her. In short order, she'd filled a coffee mug, grabbed a plate from the cabinet and snatched two muffins from the basket. She wasted no time in breaking open one of the hot muffins and slathering it with butter.

Anna smiled at Caroline and mouthed "good morning," then returned to her conversation. "And you all agreed about this, Mother?" she asked, keeping her eyes on Caroline. "One day all of you will be wrong. Then what will you do? Your winning streak has to end sometime." She chuckled. "All right. I'll let you know." She hung up the phone and turned to Caroline. "You need some eggs with those muffins."

Caroline started to answer, realized her mouth was full, and quickly chewed and swallowed. "I'm fine with these," she protested.

"Eggs," the older woman said firmly, picking up a

frying pan and gathering a couple of eggs out of the refrigerator.

"There's the belle of the ball!" Johnny announced, walking in through the back door. He reached for the muffin basket, but Caroline was quicker. She wrapped her arms around it and pulled it toward her.

"What's the magic word?" she said in a singsong voice.

"Please, milady, may I have an enchanted muffin?" He gave an elegant bow.

She struck a haughty pose. "You may." She selected one and handed it to him. "Just be aware that if you are not pure of heart, one bite of the muffin will turn you into a toad."

"That could be difficult since he's been a toad for some time now," Anna joked.

Johnny bit into the muffin. He snagged Anna around the waist and pulled her toward him. "Ribbit," he croaked.

"Green is definitely your color." She laughed as she pushed him away.

"You and Cooper looked very cozy last night," Johnny teased, sitting down across from Caroline. "Is there anything we should know about? Should I get out my shotgun and ask him his intentions?"

"Johnny," Anna warned.

"Don't think about calling a preacher just yet," Caroline advised. She quickly demolished another muffin and looked up to mouth "thank you" when Anna set a plate of fluffy scrambled eggs in front of her. "It was a first date, nothing more. Besides, I don't know how long I'll be in town."

The couple exchanged a glance that spoke volumes, but

Caroline couldn't quite follow. She wasn't sure she even wanted to.

Johnny took pity on Caroline and turned to his wife. "How's Martha feeling after last night? She was sure out there kicking up her heels."

"Mother said she woke up feeling better than she has in some time." Anna paused dramatically. "She said the Circle started designing a new quilt this morning."

Johnny released a low whistle. "Already? In another era, those ladies would have been called witches."

Caroline looked from one to the other. "What's so wrong with them designing a new quilt? I've heard how popular their quilts are." *Especially with your mother,* a voice said in her head.

"Not popular to everyone," Johnny muttered. "Hey!" He rubbed the back of his head where Anna had thumped him.

"People are always interested in seeing what the new design will be," Anna explained after shooting a warning glare in her husband's direction. He held his hands up in silent surrender. "Each quilt is unique. Many recipients consider them heirlooms to be passed down to the next generation."

Caroline got up to refill her coffee cup. She topped off Anna's cup at the same time. "I like the idea of having family heirlooms passing down to children and grandchildren," she said.

"Didn't your parents have anything that had been passed down to them?"

Caroline looked wary for a moment before she was able to mask her expression. "A few things," she said evasively. "Maybe my ancestors didn't have a lot of what they considered important."

She assumed her quilt was one of the Tyler Quilting

Circle's designs. Not that she could take it over there and ask the ladies outright. One day, when she felt the time was right, she would ask, and hoped she would get the answer she was seeking.

"What do you plan to do today, since you don't have to go in to work until late this afternoon?" Anna asked.

"Wander around town. Do some window shopping. If you need anything while I'm out, I'll be more than glad to pick it up for you," she offered.

"I can't think of anything. I did all my grocery shopping yesterday."

Caroline eyed the last muffin, then looked up at Johnny, who was also eyeing it.

"Rock, paper, scissors," she proposed.

"I always lose," he protested even as he clenched his fist. And promptly lost his paper to her scissors.

"Next time, flip a coin," Anna advised.

Caroline grinned as she picked up the muffin. She took pity on the man and gave him half.

"Ha! I wouldn't have bothered to share with him," Anna said.

"There's a method to my madness. If he ever wins, he'll feel obligated to share with me," Caroline explained, as she got up and carried her dishes to the counter. She remained downstairs, helping Anna with the dishes. She airily dismissed the older woman's protests that there was no need for her to stay and help.

Afterward, Caroline showered and dressed. As was her habit since arriving in Tyler, the last thing she did before leaving her room was run her fingers over the corner of the quilt bearing the Spencer family names. Then she put it away in her closet where it couldn't be seen.

Instead of heading for the shops, Caroline decided to do what she'd been putting off since she first arrived in

Tyler—do some research at the Alberta Ingalls Memorial Library. While the two-story Greek revival building was a testament to the town's history, the interior was completely modernized. This wasn't the first time Caroline had been in the building; she'd checked out many a book there. She just hadn't found the courage to utilize the facilities to investigate more personal matters.

"Don't tell me you're already back for more reading material," Delia Mayhew exlaimed when Caroline walked inside. "After last night, I would think the phone at Anna and Johnny's would be ringing off the hook with men asking you out."

"The phone's been for Anna this morning. And that's fine with me. I came in because I thought I'd spend some time digging through your old newspapers," she said. "I thought it was the best way to learn more about the town."

"You're in luck. We have copies of the *Tyler Citizen* on microfiche," she told her, leaving the desk and gesturing for Caroline to follow her. "Unfortunately, at this point they only go back to World War II. We're hoping to have the rest of them done in the next couple of years."

"That's good enough for me. I just thought I'd go back, oh…" she quickly calculated how far back she might have to go in hopes of finding out anything about her mother and the Spencer family, "…twenty-five years or so. That should give me plenty to do."

Delia quickly set Caroline up, then told her to call if she needed anything else.

Caroline ignored everything but the main and social pages. The *Tyler Citizen* wasn't as extensive as the paper she read in Santa Barbara. It didn't take her long to find a mention of Elias Spencer and his wife, Violet—a short article about them and their three sons arriving in Tyler.

"Oh, Mom," she whispered, tracing Violet's name on the screen with her fingertips.

From then on, she slowed down her search so she wouldn't miss anything. One of the first things she found was a notice that Violet Spencer had filed for divorce, and then another mentioning she'd left town. Caroline found sports articles with the Spencer boys' names mentioned. Apparently they all were quite the athletes.

Wanting a chance to study them more carefully at her leisure, she made copies of everything she found. She folded the papers into a small packet and stuffed them in her purse.

"Did you find everything you needed?" Delia asked, as Caroline stopped at the front desk on her way out.

"I made some copies of the more interesting articles so I could study them further," she explained, paying for the copies. "Tyler has a lot of interesting history."

"Yes, it does. I wish more of our own residents had the same interest in our beginnings as you do." Delia smiled. "See you later."

Caroline had gone to the library in hopes of finding a way to approach Elias, maybe even pinning down a few answers. She'd just ended up with more questions.

An unsettled feeling gripped her as she left the building and walked down the street. At the moment, she had no idea where she was going.

Farther up and across the street, Cooper stood outside the post office talking to the postmistress, Annabelle Scanlon. As he later walked toward his vehicle, he happened to glance up and notice Caroline. He only had to see the expression on her face to know she hadn't been in there perusing the latest reading material. He hazarded a guess that whatever she'd done in the library had left her upset.

Which had him wondering just what the hell she'd been doing in there.

"If you want to know, there's only one way to find out," he muttered, moving away from his truck and walking across the street. He heard the soft hum of the air conditioner as he stepped inside the building.

"Hello, Cooper," Delia greeted him, looking surprised when he approached the front desk. "Anything I can help you with?"

He looked around at the shelves, then past to the atrium. "I don't think I've been in here since high school," he admitted, resting his arms on the counter. "It hasn't changed all that much since then, either."

"You'd see a lot of changes if you bothered coming in more than every fifteen years," she teased him. "Why, I see your grandfather about once a month, when he comes in."

That surprised him. "*My* grandfather?"

She smiled. "Obviously you had no idea Laughing Bear enjoys reading horror novels."

Cooper was stunned by her revelation. "My grandfather reads horror novels?"

Delia nodded. "He once told me that some of the stories he'd read had to have come from your tribe's legends."

Cooper shook his head to clear it. "That sounds like something Laughing Bear would say. And here he claims he has no secrets. Next thing I know you're going to tell me that Caroline Benning was in here to pick up some of those men's adventure novels." He knew if he gave Delia an opening she'd take it and run with it.

And she did. "Not even close. She comes in every ten days or so and picks up mystery novels. Today was different for her."

"Oh?" He looked at the librarian expectantly, prompting her to keep talking.

She nodded. "Yes, Caroline asked about looking up the town's history. I told her that her best bet would be to look through our old newspapers, since they're on microfiche," she volunteered.

He agreed. "You're right, that is a good way to find out about the town. I didn't realize the *Citizen* was on microfiche."

"Oh yes. We're very up-to-date here," she said proudly. "Caroline must have spent a good three hours going through them. She even made copies of the articles she wanted to study more. I wish some of our own people had the interest she does."

"Maybe I should take a look at the setup. Bring myself up-to-date," he said.

"It's back here." She led him toward the rear, where two microfiche machines were set up. She explained how the system worked and left Cooper alone.

He skimmed the files Caroline had looked through. She'd gone through the last twenty-five years. He scanned a few of the papers, and the only thing he figured she could have been looking for was any mention of the Spencer family.

"What were you hoping to find here, Caroline?" he murmured to himself. "You didn't look all that happy when you left, so you must not have been successful."

When he left the library, he felt as frustrated as he had when he went in.

"THIS IS THE QUIETEST it's been in some time. It would almost make you think aliens came down and abducted everyone," Marge said to Caroline.

Caroline had retrieved all the salt and pepper shakers

off the tables and set them up in a row on the counter. She occupied herself refilling them.

"If that's what happened, they missed the two fun people. Boy, are they going to be sorry they didn't take us, too." She finished the last set of shakers, and put them all on a tray and began replacing them on the tables. She stopped long enough at the only table occupied at the moment to see if the customers required anything else.

As she walked back to the counter, she noticed Marge's lips tightening. It was easy to guess the reason when she saw three men walk in and snare a table near the window. Their voices were loud, the words off-color as they pretended to tussle over the menus. Caroline picked up the coffeepot and three cups and walked over.

"Well, look what we have here." One man gave a low, appreciative whistle as he watched her approach them. "When did you start here, honey?"

"Does anyone want coffee?" She ignored his question as she tried not to breathe. She wondered when any of them had last bathed.

"I'll take anything you've got to offer, sweetheart," another man said as he leered at her.

"Let me know when you're ready to order." She walked away.

"I'll take care of them, Caroline," Marge told her when she returned to the counter. "They behave up to a point because they know I won't tolerate any horseplay. Trouble is, they look as if they're going to be up to no good tonight."

"I'll be fine." Caroline smiled at her boss, even though her stomach was rolling uncomfortably. "They're just guys who haven't grown up yet. They think they're being funny. When they realize I won't rise to their bait, they'll knock it off."

"Unfortunately, they come in every so often. Their idea of humor is crude, and they've been told if they can't behave they won't be allowed in here again. Then they'll behave for a while. Tonight doesn't look like one of those nights. If they act up too much, I'm calling the station," she said firmly.

Caroline was taking their food order when Cooper walked in. She managed a brief smile of greeting as he settled in one of the nearby booths. She gave Marge the order, then went over to Cooper.

"Good evening, Deputy," she said in a low voice, holding her order pad ready. "What can I get for you?"

His gaze shifted toward the men two tables over. His mouth firmed as he listened to their overloud voices. "They giving you any trouble?"

"No more than I can handle," she replied.

Cooper didn't look convinced by her words. He glanced at the menu. "How about some of Marge's meat loaf and mashed potatoes?"

"She'll tell you you have to eat the green beans, too," Caroline warned.

"Every bite." He kept his eyes on the three men, who were now laughing loudly. "If any of them give you trouble, give me a sign," he murmured.

Caroline's gaze shifted toward the other table. "I can take care of myself."

"Yeah, but guys like that aren't something any woman should have to put up with."

She smiled, hoping to lighten the moment even though she quickly realized Cooper wasn't about to relax as long as the men were in the diner. "You just want to act like the big bad cop, don't you?"

His face didn't alter its expression. "I can arrange that."

''My hero,'' she whispered, before moving away.

Caroline was aware of Cooper's watchful gaze as she delivered the food to the unruly table, as she now dubbed it. She'd thought that Cooper's presence alone would tone down the men's behavior, but she'd thought wrong.

''Think you can take a quick break?'' Cooper asked after she'd set his plate in front of him and refilled his coffee cup.

She glanced around. At the time, only two other tables were occupied. Marge caught her eye, guessed the nature of Cooper's request, and nodded.

''How long will you be working the dinner shift?'' he asked.

''For the rest of the week. It's a nice change, and I don't have to get up at the crack of dawn.'' She wrinkled her nose. ''I'm not exactly a morning person,'' she confided.

He was surprised by her admission. ''You sure seemed perky whenever I came in for breakfast.''

''By the time you come in, I've had enough coffee in me that I almost think I am perky,'' she admitted. ''Catch any bad guys today?''

''Pulled Fred Chaney over for speeding. Found Marvin's hog walking along the road,'' he replied. ''Had a talk with some ten-year-olds about their spending time in the drugstore reading high-fashion magazines. Their main interest was in the underwear advertisements,'' he explained.

''Wow, it's a hotbed of crime out there, isn't it?'' she said with mock intensity.

''That's why I carry the big gun,'' Cooper said with a straight face.

''Hey, sweetcheeks, can we get some more coffee over here?'' one of the men hollered.

Cooper's face darkened. He started to rise out of his seat.

"It's okay," Caroline said hastily, standing up.

Cooper sat back, but she knew he kept a close eye on her as she retrieved a coffeepot and walked over to the table.

"Is there anything else you'd like?" she asked in a cool, professional voice.

One of the men grinned. She held back a cringe when she noticed he had two front teeth missing and the rest were tobacco stained.

"What time do you get off, honey?" he asked, reaching out.

Caroline didn't see the straying hand in time, so she was startled when she felt his hand run up her bare thigh. She jumped backward, earning a snort of laughter from the men. She was so furious at the blatant touch she didn't notice Cooper leaving his seat.

"You creep!" She slapped the man on the head with her order pad at the same time she kicked him in the shins. "You're lucky I don't pour this coffee in your lap!"

The other two men guffawed.

His face reddened as he realized she'd embarrassed him before his friends. "Why you—!" he snarled, starting to get up.

"Gentlemen." Cooper fixed each of them with his dark gaze. "I don't think you want any dessert, do you?"

"She assaulted me!" The man pointed at Caroline, who glared back at him. "I want to press charges."

"That's your right, but I don't know if it's necessarily a good idea. You see, her father is a judge here," Cooper said, straight-faced. "And he's a mean SOB who dotes on his only daughter. You press charges, she'll say she was defending herself because you copped a feel. I can tell you the judge won't like hearing that. In a lot of places what you did is called sexual harassment. Who knows what the judge will call it. Or who he'll decide in favor of, being he can be a might prejudiced where his baby girl is concerned.''

The man's expression told Cooper he was torn between doing whatever he could to embarrass Caroline or facing the wrath of a judge who could do more than just embarrass him.

He pulled his wallet out of his jeans back pocket and took out a couple of bills, tossing them on the table.

''C'mon,'' he muttered to his friends, who left fast on his heels.

Cooper raised his voice. ''Sir, you forgot to tip your waitress.''

The man turned around, muttered a few choice words as he stalked back and dropped another couple of bills on the table.

''My father, the judge, thanks you,'' Caroline said, picking up the money. She returned his glare with a deadly one of her own.

''You can find another place next time,'' Marge called after them. ''You're not allowed in here anymore. You try coming back and I'll call the cops.'' She walked over to Caroline and Cooper. ''Thanks, Cooper.'' She stopped by his booth and picked up his plate. ''I imagine this needs reheating by now.'' She looked at Caroline. ''You might as well finish your break.'' She looked meaningfully at Cooper as she walked away. ''He'll need a big slice of peach pie when he's finished with his dinner.''

''That's something I won't turn down.''

Caroline gathered up the dirty dishes from the other table and carried them to the kitchen. She picked up Cooper's reheated meal and carried it back to him.

"You've got a mean kick there," he told her.

"I just wish I had something heavier than my pad for his thick head." She looked at the mangled sheets on her order pad. "Like a sledgehammer."

"Probably just as well you didn't. I would have had to take you in for assault with a deadly weapon." He dug into his food. "You must have met guys like that before. I'd've thought it was an occupational hazard for a waitress."

"I guess I've been lucky so far." She smiled.

"No offense, but you don't seem like a career waitress."

She frowned as if thinking about it. "I can't imagine waiting on tables when I'm fifty, but then you never can tell." And it certainly wasn't her ambition as a child. "Tell me, what does a kid do while growing up in Tyler?"

"Hike, fish, play football or baseball. Chase girls," he added promptly. "What does a kid do while growing up in California?"

"Surf, go to the beach, play tennis, although I was a terrible player, and we won't even talk about what I do with a golf club."

"Sounds like the lifestyle of the privileged," he said casually.

"Comfortable," she corrected. "Where I grew up, golf was the game of choice. I saw it as a major yawn. The only time I went out on a sailboat I got so seasick I was in bed for three days. And tennis, well, let's just say I couldn't have hit the ball if the racket was six feet wide."

"Not too athletically inclined, are we?" he murmured.

"There are sports out there where I'm not expected to hit a ball," she protested.

"So what did you do that didn't involve hitting a ball?"

"Oh no, you'll just make fun of me." She picked up the plates and carried them back to the kitchen. She returned with a shallow bowl holding a large slice of peach pie topped with a scoop of vanilla ice cream.

"I promise I won't make fun of you. I'm a cop. I have to keep my promises," he assured her.

Caroline took a deep breath. "Water ballet."

Cooper looked confused. "Excuse me?"

"Water ballet. It's also called synchronized swimming," she explained. "I started doing it in high school. We would never have made the Olympics, but we enjoyed it."

"That's what Esther Williams did." Marge spoke up, not the least bit embarrassed she'd been eavesdropping on their conversation. "A lovely lady. She seemed to dance in the water."

"That I understand," Cooper said. "You do any ballet on land?"

"I took classes until I was fourteen and discovered boys were more fun," Caroline confided.

That explained her unconscious grace when she moved. He could easily imagine her moving through the water like a mermaid. Come to think of it, didn't mermaids wear practically nothing?

"I'd say you caught up just fine," Cooper said once he dug his mind out of a deep blue ocean and a near-naked Caroline swimming in it. His fantasy had nothing to do with the Disney cartoon, either.

He knew what the problem was. He was used to interrogating prisoners where you got as much information as you could in as short a time as possible. Caroline wasn't a prisoner and he couldn't insist she answer his questions. If he wanted to find out just exactly why she'd come to Tyler he was going to have to take it slow and easy.

Maybe he should just come right out and ask her why she was so interested in the Spencer family. And if she was so interested, why she hadn't approached them. Which brought a burning question to mind. Why hadn't she done something to get closer to them? Or at least get in with their women and go at it that way? After seeing her in action tonight, he knew antagonizing her wouldn't be a good idea. If he was lucky, she'd only freeze him out.

No, he'd prefer to bask in her warmth.

Chapter Five

"I don't think this is such a good idea." Caroline frowned at the large monster standing in front of her.

"There's nothing to worry about. She's as gentle as a lamb," Cooper assured her.

She didn't look all that reassured. "There has to be another way." She stepped back.

"Not for where we're going," he said patiently. "You'll be fine. I promise."

"But she's so tall." She looked at the horse, whose head was above her own. The chestnut with a white blaze on her face had sweet brown eyes, but Caroline still didn't trust her. "And she has big teeth."

He tugged on her hand. "You'll find her easier to ride than a carousel horse," he told her.

"I don't think so. Carousel horses don't run away with you or buck you off." She still wasn't convinced.

When Cooper had asked her if she'd like to go for a horseback ride, she'd immediately accepted because she wanted to spend time with him. She hadn't thought far enough about the logistics of the matter—that she'd be expected to climb onto an animal and, well, ride it.

He didn't miss the uncertainty on her face. "You said you know how to ride."

"I do know how. And I have ridden," she said faintly.

Cooper grew suspicious by her tone of voice. "When exactly was the last time you were on a horse?"

Caroline looked upward. "I think I was fourteen."

He laid his hand against the chestnut's withers, stroking the silky coat. The horse turned her head, nuzzling his arm.

"Riding Mame is like sitting in a comfortable rocking chair," he explained. "That's why I borrowed her for you. But if you'd rather not—"

She took a deep breath. "No, I'll do it. Just give me a leg up."

He bent down and laced his hands into a stirrup. Caroline placed her foot in it and allowed herself to be boosted up into the saddle. Cooper handed her the reins and moved around her horse. He mounted a black gelding, settling in the saddle with the ease of a man who spent time there.

"Don't worry, Mame will follow Jack," he assured her.

"Mame and Jack. Whatever happened to horse names?" she asked, as she grabbed hold of the saddle horn for balance. Just as Cooper had promised, her mount ambled up the trail behind him. Caroline tightly gripped the horse's sides with her knees, as she feared she'd slide right off the saddle.

Cooper half turned in the saddle. "Horse names? What do you consider horse names?"

"Oh, you know the kind of names I'm talking about. Trigger. Silver. Blaze," she said, forcing herself to relax in the saddle. The motion wasn't like a rocking chair as he'd promised, but it wasn't uncomfortable, either. "Names that tell a person you're talking about a horse."

"Jack's full name is Jackknife because he used to have a nasty habit of doing a jackknife motion whenever anyone tried to climb into the saddle. Mame was named after the movie. That's right," he approved, noticing her starting to relax. "Just go with the motion. Mame will do all the work and you can sit back."

Once she felt secure, she swiveled her head from side to side. "It really is pretty out here," she exclaimed.

"And a lot easier to see than from a car window when you're speeding down the road."

"Is this what you do on your days off? Go horseback riding?" She relaxed her white-knuckled grip on the saddle horn a fraction.

"Sometimes. It's a good way to clear the mind."

She laughed out loud when she saw a squirrel race up a tree. Its angry chatter told her it didn't appreciate the intrusion.

They spoke little as they climbed the trail that wound its way upward. When they reached the top, Cooper reined in his horse and dismounted. He walked over to Caroline and helped her down. She grabbed hold of his arms when her legs started to give out from under her.

"You okay?" he asked, keeping a firm hold on her arms.

"Oh sure," she muttered, wincing as painful pins and needles traveled up her legs and into her thighs. "I may never walk again, but I'm fine." She winced as she took a tentative step forward. "Now I remember why I haven't ridden a horse since I was fourteen." She made her way to a nearby boulder and dropped down onto it. She winced as she realized her butt was as sore as her legs. She pulled her T-shirt away from her sweaty midriff. She wrinkled her nose. "I smell like a horse."

"Another horse wouldn't mind," he told her.

"Maybe not, but I don't think it would ever be a bestselling fragrance for humans.'' She wiped her forehead with the back of her hand. ''Eau de Equine No. 8.''

Cooper pulled two insulated bottles of water out of a saddlebag and walked over to the boulder, sitting down next to her.

''You just need to get out more,'' he told her, handing her one of the bottles.

She opened the top and drank thirstily. As she reclosed it, she looked down the hill, seeing a thin ribbon of water below. ''I didn't know there was a river nearby.''

''It's an important river for my people,'' he explained. ''They believe that many years ago, a woman came from that river to keep peace in the land. The Sauk chief Black Hawk found her and they fell in love. My grandfather seems to think that one day she'll return and make us whole again.'' He was uncomfortably reminded of his dream and the woman who now haunted him at least once a week. A dream woman who was starting to remind him more and more of Caroline.

''What a nice legend. Especially when you look around and feel as if you've gone back in time,'' she said dreamily. ''You can't see any hint of modern civilization. It's as if it's a hundred and fifty years ago. Maybe there was a bank robber's hideout nearby.'' Her face betrayed her excitement as her imagination took flight.

''Sorry, no robber's hideouts. No famous gunfights were fought in the area. Although rumor has it that some of the booze runners from Canada during the Prohibition era drove through here on their way to Chicago. Will that do?'' he asked.

Caroline exhaled a deep sigh. ''I guess it has to, but I was hoping for something more exciting.''

Cooper looked off into the distance. ''If you want to find out about the town's history, you should try the library,'' he said a shade too casually. ''They've got a pretty extensive section devoted to the history of the town. I heard they even have old copies of the local newspaper.'' He felt her body stiffen.

''I go in every so often and check out books, but I never thought of looking at the town's history. I'll have to check it out the next time I'm in there,'' she murmured as she toyed with her water bottle.

Cooper studied her profile. He would have thought she could have come up with a better story than that. Regardless, she'd lied. At least avoided the truth. What exactly was she trying to hide?

By rights he shouldn't be thinking about kissing her. He was crazy to even consider it. But there was something about her that invited his touch.

He rested his fingertips against the delicate curve of her jaw as he turned her head toward him. Her skin was warm and silky as he lifted her face to his. A soft intake of breath was her only response when his mouth lowered to hers. He should have known her lips would be as warm and silky as her skin. And just as intoxicating.

She twisted her body more so she could curve her arms around his neck while his arms slid around her waist and pulled her onto his lap. His tongue probed and gained entrance into the parted softness of her mouth.

Caroline pulled back and looked at him through glazed eyes.

''Gee, Cooper, if I'd known you could kiss this good I would have given you my entire hot fudge sundae that night.''

''IF I DIDN'T KNOW any better, I'd say you'd had a personality transplant,'' Lieutenant Steve Fletcher said stopping by Cooper's desk.

Cooper looked up from the paperwork he had put off so long he now had no choice but to stay there until he finished it. The last report had to do with another theft and destruction of Nora Gates Forrester's underwear. The woman wasn't pleased with the inability of Tyler's law enforcement officers to catch the culprit. He was seriously thinking about making it his duty to track down that goat and turn him into goat steaks.

"Meaning?"

"Meaning you're actually lightening up," Steve told him. "There's been a betting pool on who would be the lucky woman to turn you into a human being. I lost fifty bucks because I thought for sure it would be Megan Kilmore."

"Megan Kilmore only went out with me to make Jerry Donner jealous," Cooper told him.

"She wanted Jerry? Man, I didn't think she had that bad a taste in men." Steve shook his head. "She should have chosen me."

"Yeah, and you would have been the one with five kids," Cooper pointed out.

Steve whistled a low tune as he realized he was better off. "Good point." He ambled away. "Since you're loaded down with paperwork, I guess I'll stop by Marge's for dinner and keep your girlfriend company." He tipped his hat toward Cooper as he headed for the door.

"Maybe she'll spill the plate on you," he muttered, returning to his paperwork with a swiftness he hadn't shown before.

With Caroline working the dinner shift and Cooper working days, he didn't see her in the mornings. He'd stopped by the restaurant most nights after he got off duty because it was his only chance to see her. Each time, he'd delicately probe for more information about her background, but found little.

He knew the gossipy tongues had started wagging the night he took Caroline to the spring dance. Since then the gossips had been working overtime. If they knew he'd kissed her, he had a good idea they'd waste no time in planning the wedding.

She wasn't the only woman he'd ever kissed. But she was the only woman who set his world on fire with just the touch of her lips. He hadn't expected her to be so dangerous to his senses.

He had been ready to kiss her again the day they went for a horseback ride, but the sound of voices coming up the trail had put a damper on anything more happening. Within the space of seconds, he'd watched Caroline's expression turn neutral and her body angle away from his. By the time a group of teenagers on horseback arrived, they looked like two acquaintances who just happened to meet up.

Within twenty-four hours word of Cooper and Caroline's horseback ride on Tyler Hill had raced through town like wildfire.

Compounding it was Brady Spencer leaving a message on Cooper's answering machine asking if Cooper wasn't going above and beyond the call of duty. Brady's advice was to be careful.

That was a reminder Cooper didn't need. He was seeing Caroline and not learning a damned thing. He could have called Brady back and told him just that. The trouble was, he didn't want to stop seeing her.

After he finished his paperwork late that afternoon, he climbed in his vehicle and forced himself to drive home instead of stopping at Marge's Diner. He punished his taste buds by heating up a can of chili instead of enjoying Marge's pot roast and letting his eyes feast Caroline.

By the time he crawled into bed, he was calling himself every kind of fool.

"THE WEATHER IS GETTING warmer. And I still have plenty of firewood," Laughing Bear told his grandson. "I do not think I will need any more wood until fall."

"Maybe you think you don't need more, but the nights are still cold. And you know your bones will want the heat," Cooper said, as he lifted the heavy ax.

The exercise had warmed him up quickly, so he tossed his shirt to one side. He'd tied a bandanna around his forehead to keep the sweat from dripping into his eyes. His muscles rippled under his skin as he lifted the ax and brought it down, splitting the log into kindling. He had no doubt he'd feel the effect of his exertions tonight, but for now, it was just the kind of exercise he needed.

"You should be in town spending time with Caroline instead of out here chopping wood," the elderly man said. "Is that not why you try to work the same hours she does whenever you can? So the two of you can see each other?"

Cooper almost lost his grip on the ax, which would have probably taken off a few toes in the process. He muttered a curse that used to guarantee a mouth full of soap when he was a kid.

"You like her, don't you?" Laughing Bear slowly settled himself on a nearby log. He braced his hands on his knees. "I cannot think of any man who would not like her. She is pretty, smart and healthy. A good combination for a wife."

"I didn't know you were looking for one," Cooper said, setting the ax to one side. If his grandfather was going to make any more surprise comments he wanted to make sure nothing valuable was in the way. He pulled off his gloves and tucked them into his back pocket. "I bet there's a few ladies who'd snap you right up."

"I am not looking for a wife, but that does not mean I do not notice these things. And I am not the only one. Caroline is new to the town. There is a lot of talk about her. Especially that she has not gone out with anyone until you took her to the spring dance. I think she has secrets, Grandson," he concluded. "Secrets you feel a need to learn."

"You should have been a cop, old man," he muttered, not liking that Laughing Bear had figured out as much as Cooper already had. Not that he ever doubted his grandfather's intelligence.

Laughing Bear shook his head, his silvery braids swinging gently with the motion. "I have always had other things to do."

"Such as trying to set up a love life for me."

"I do not interfere in one's fate." The elderly man looked a little too smug for Cooper's peace of mind.

"How did Grandmother put up with you all those years?" he asked.

"She loved me," he said simply.

Cooper thought of the woman who'd died when he was in his early teens. There had never been a question that his grandparents shared something very special. He might have been a child, but he could see the strong love the couple shared. It wasn't until he grew into an adult that he realized a part of his grandfather had died with his wife. Cooper could only hope he would be lucky enough to have a fraction of what his grandfather had.

"Caroline isn't planning on staying in Tyler permanently, Grandfather," he said quietly. "She only stopped here because she felt the need for a change after her father's death. The day will come when she's decided she's had enough of small town life and she'll return to her old life in California."

Laughing Bear studied him with eyes that might have been dimmed with age but still saw more than most.

"People only leave if they feel there is not enough to hold them in the place where they are."

Cooper muttered a low curse. "Are you sure you weren't Confucius in another life? You should be writing fortunes for fortune cookies."

Laughing Bear looked as serene as the legendary philosopher of China.

"Chinese food gives me gas."

"THERE'S THE WOMAN who's managed to snag the attention of one Sergeant Cooper Night Hawk. Now the question is what will she do next?"

Caroline turned around, to find Jenna pushing a double stroller. Her face brightened with her smile.

"Jenna!" She leaned over and hugged the woman. She stepped back and viewed the stroller's occupants. "I know it isn't possible, but the twins seem to have grown a foot since they were born. They're what? Almost four weeks now?"

"Four weeks, three days, and if you give me a minute, I'll figure out how many hours, minutes and seconds. Considering all they do is eat, I wouldn't be surprised if they've grown several feet," she replied, laughing. "Seth disagrees. He feels the end result of all those feedings is just more diaper changes. At least I got rid of those pesky basketballs." She patted her much flatter belly. "With luck and a lot more stomach crunches, I'll be able to get back into my favorite leather pants in no time."

"You are such a focused person. You seem to accomplish everything you set out to do. You're very lucky," Caroline told her with a touch of envy, looking down at the twin babies, who were peacefully sleeping. She'd heard Susan and Dominick were named after the matchmaking couple who got Jenna and Seth together.

Jenna's face lit up. "I think so, too," she acknowledged. "Don't tell Seth, because it will just swell his head, but he has a lot to do with it."

Caroline remembered only too well what had gone on during Jenna and Seth's stormy courtship since Jenna had lived in the Kelsey Boarding House before she married. And now she was a part of the family Caroline wanted so badly to be with.

"I guess being a Spencer puts you in a special category. What with them being practically Tyler icons," she said.

"If you're going to talk about being in a special category, let's talk about you and Cooper Night Hawk," Jenna replied. "I wouldn't be surprised if there was a betting pool going on as to when the two of you will get married."

Caroline flushed. "You have got to be kidding. I can't believe some people have so little to do that they started a betting pool about me."

Jenna shook her head. "Are *you* kidding? I remember once hearing there was a pool as to who you'd go out with first," she said. "From what I remember, I don't think Cooper even made that list. I couldn't understand why, either, because I would have bet on him."

Caroline felt her cheeks grow warm with embarrassment. "That is so crazy. Who had the best odds?" she couldn't help asking.

"Greg Lowell."

"Greg Lowell?" She made a face. "People actually

thought I would go out with him? No offense to Greg, but I swear every time he's come in to the diner, he's smelled like a wet dog. And I'm not talking about a fresh-from-the-bath wet dog, either.''

"There is that rumor that all six of his hunting dogs sleep with him.''

"If that's the case, it's no wonder he has trouble getting a date.''

The two women burst into shared laughter.

"Cooper keeps his private life so private that his dating anyone here in town is tantamount to a miracle,'' Jenna said. She looked around to make sure she couldn't be overheard. "So what's it like dating the tall, dark and handsome deputy?''

"Interesting.''

"Oh no, you are not getting away with a nonanswer like that. I want all the delicious details,'' she insisted.

"He's about as perfect as you can get. He actually listens to what you're saying, and you know how rare that is in a man. When he asks you about what you've been doing, he's sincerely interested.''

Jenna nodded. "I'd say he's a definite keeper. You better hang on to him.''

"Don't even think about ordering wedding invitations,'' Caroline warned. "I'm not going to be here forever.'' She didn't like the little critters taking swan dives inside her stomach when she uttered the last word.

Jenna's smile was unsettling. "You can't fight it, Caroline. Don't even try. Take it from one who knows.''

"We're just dating, nothing more,'' she argued.

Jenna nodded and hugged her. "I said pretty much the same thing and look what happened to me. I'd better get home before Dominick and Susan realize it's almost time for a feeding. It was good to see you, Caroline. It's been too long. I'll stop by Marge's for a pastry fix soon.''

Caroline hugged her back. ''You do that.''

As she watched Jenna push the stroller down the sidewalk, an empty feeling centered in her body. She thought about what Jenna had gone through with Seth.

Her friend had been so unhappy with Seth's leaving her in New York. Then when he found out she was having his child and they reconciled... Well, suffice to say now she looked as if she'd never spent one second agonizing over the man.

Caroline tamped down the feeling and turned toward the video store, her original destination.

That morning she'd offered to pick up the videos she and the Kelseys would be watching that evening. Anna said anything was fine with her, and Johnny said anything was fine with him, too, as long as Michelle Pfeiffer was in it. Anna told her if that was the case she'd take Harrison Ford, thank you very much. Caroline cruised the shelves and settled on something she felt they all would like. She enjoyed the evenings she spent with the Kelseys having ''movie night.'' They'd watch one or two videos and consume a large bowl of buttered popcorn. The last couple of weeks she'd been tempted to ask Cooper if he'd like to join them, but she held back. She didn't fully understand the feelings he generated inside her, but she knew they were growing stronger each day.

More than once she thought of confessing to him her true reason for coming to Tyler. But each time she held off. That he was a good friend of the Spencers was a good reason not to say anything. At least, not until she knew exactly what she was going to do.

So far, all she had to show for her efforts was a handful of newspaper articles about the brothers as they grew up.

Articles detailing Seth Spencer's appointment as president of the Tyler Savings & Loan. Brady leaving town for college and medical school, then another article when he returned to work at Tyler General Hospital as a surgeon. Quinn's graduation from law school and his also returning to set up his practice in Amanda Baron Trask's law office.

Caroline had waited on each of them numerous times at the diner and overheard gossip about Elias Spencer and his sons. She wished she could initiate a conversation, bring up the subject of Elias's former wife, Violet. Except she couldn't think of any logical reason how she might even know of the woman.

She thought of the hours she'd spent digging through her father's papers, finding nothing that told her about her mother before her marriage to her dad. Caroline was upset she could find nothing about her mother's former marriage and especially information about her other children. It seemed as if Violet had wiped them out of her life, so that they didn't exist for her.

In Caroline's eyes that omission was the same as a lie. She didn't want to think her parents had lied to her. But since they had, she wanted to know why.

"Funny thing, I never thought of you as the type interested in the latest manure spreader," a male voice murmured in her ear.

Her heart skipped a few beats at the husky sound of Cooper's voice. A blink of the eyes and a screeching return to the present showed her she was standing in front of Murphy's Hardware Store.

"You don't think Johnny would like one for his birthday?" she asked, injecting a teasing lightness in her voice.

"I don't think he'd want one guaranteed to cover fifty acres in no time. You might think about a much smaller model."

Caroline never told Cooper that she thought he looked sexy in his black uniform, which intensified his dark good looks. His sunglasses were aviator style, with reflective lenses so she couldn't see his eyes.

She had a pretty good idea what *he* saw. Since the day was warm, she'd chosen to wear her lilac cotton shorts with a sleeveless, white eyelet top that bared her midriff. Her backless sandals were nothing more than narrow bands of lilac leather across her toes and the top of her feet. When she'd left the boardinghouse earlier, she'd felt pretty darn cute. Something told her that Cooper saw her the same way.

It frightened and excited her at the same time. Cooper Night Hawk was more man than she had ever known before. Right now she was thinking she was more than enough woman for him.

Cooper looked beyond her shoulder. "I was wondering if you were free tonight," he said slowly.

"Anna, Johnny and I are doing our movie night," she explained. "We do videos, popcorn and sometimes brownies. You're welcome to come over and join us."

"What time?" He surprised her with his question.

"Seven."

Cooper nodded. He started to turn away, then looked back. "We're not talking about chick flicks, are we?" he asked warily.

"Can you imagine Johnny even willing to watch a chick flick?" she asked. "If Anna and I want one, he sneaks out to that poker game that supposedly doesn't exist."

While Cooper didn't smile, his features lightened. "See you tonight." He walked back to his vehicle.

Not wanting to stand there and drool while she watched

him drive away, Caroline forced herself to walk down the sidewalk.

"It's amazing he didn't run in the other direction. He'll think you're showing him what family life can be like," she muttered, quickening her steps.

"HE THOUGHT NOTHING of saying yes?" Anna asked after Caroline told her there'd be one more for their moviethon.

"Cooper did seem relieved when I said we wouldn't be watching any chick flicks," she said. She peered into the large mixing bowl and inhaled the rich chocolate scent. "No one makes brownies like you."

Anna looked pleased with the compliment. "Thick, fudgy and filled with all sorts of goodies. Dangerous to our figures, but I can't make myself stop making them."

"Dangerous doesn't scare me. I'd rather run a few extra miles in the morning than give up your brownies."

"Play your cards right and Johnny and I will decide to make it an early night," the older woman teased.

Caroline laughed as she ran upstairs. She had a feeling this would be one movie night she'd remember for a long time.

"THIS IS NOT FAIR! You rented a chick movie!" Johnny protested from his easy chair as the opening credits ran.

"It's a comedy," Caroline pointed out. She handed Johnny his can of beer and walked over to the easy chair Cooper was sitting in and gave him a glass of Coke. "Anna said you've never seen it and we know you'll like it. Besides, I got an action film for your bloodthirsty nature."

"*When Harry Met Sally* is a classic." Anna set a plate of warm brownies and a bowl of popcorn on the coffee table.

"I heard about that scene in a restaurant," Johnny muttered. He spared Cooper a quick look. "You know what I'm talking about?"

"Like you, I've heard, not seen." Cooper looked up at Caroline. The message in his eyes was unmistakable.

She wasn't going to tell him she'd stopped off at the video store and deliberately picked that film. She merely scooped popcorn into a bowl and handed it to Cooper.

"No brownie?" he asked.

She smiled, picked up a fudgy square and plopped it on top of his popcorn. Unable to leave it alone, she tore off a corner and popped it into her mouth.

"This is so good," she cooed, stealing another corner and holding it in front of his lips. He glanced toward Anna and Johnny, who kept their gazes glued to the television screen. He parted his lips and Caroline slipped the piece of brownie inside his mouth.

"Seems you're always sharing your chocolate with me," he murmured.

She picked up a few pieces of popcorn and tossed them into her mouth. "Luckily, Anna makes a big batch of brownies."

"Jeez, this is the kind of movie that embarrasses a guy," Johnny muttered.

"Maybe I should have picked up *Thelma and Louise* instead. A chick flick with major action," Caroline teased.

"I won't even tell you what movies she's brought in the past," Johnny told Cooper. "She doesn't understand what a good movie is."

Caroline leaned back in her chair, stretching her long legs along the chair arm.

Cooper's eyes naturally followed the delicate lines of her body, garbed in an off-the-shoulder, rose print top and a solid rose, ankle-length skirt that split up to her thigh.

He couldn't help but notice the gold ankle bracelet with a tiny heart hanging from the chain. More ammunition for his imagination. As if he needed any.

The subtle scent of her cologne teased his nostrils as she leaned closer to him, her arm stretched across the back of the chair.

There was no way he was going to be able to concentrate on the movie. At least, he thought so until the infamous scene came on the screen. Anna whooped with delighted laughter while Johnny groaned closing his eyes and covering his ears with his hands.

It might have been Meg Ryan proving to Billy Crystal that a woman could easily fake an orgasm, but in his mind's eye Cooper was looking at Caroline's face and hearing her cries in a real orgasm. He shifted uneasily in the chair, praying no one could see his lap.

It was one long movie.

As the video rewound, Anna and Caroline made a second bowl of popcorn and brought in more drinks.

"She's a great kid," Johnny said to Cooper.

Cooper read the line as "I'll get out my shotgun if you hurt her."

"She's definitely not like anyone I've met before," he admitted, listening to the soft tones of Caroline's voice and laughter.

"She's one of a kind," the older man agreed. "And even though she appears to be in control of her life, she's still vulnerable. She hasn't said a lot about her family, but there's no mistaking she and her father were close. She's still grieving over his death." His eyes bored straight into Cooper. "And she's far away from her home and everything familiar to her."

"Makes you wonder why a woman would suddenly pull up stakes and end up in a town practically two thousand miles away, where she has no family or friends,'' Cooper said casually. ''You'd think she'd want to be where everything is familiar to her.''

''Not necessarily,'' he countered. ''Caroline's a pretty independent young lady. She needed a change, and lucky for us, she chose Tyler.''

Cooper narrowed his eyes. ''Johnny, is the Quilting Circle working on a new quilt?''

''There's the church bazaar coming up,'' he said. ''You know they always make a quilt for that.''

''And your mother-in-law is part of the Circle, so you'd know what they're doing. Who their next victims are.''

Johnny was saved a reply by the reappearance of Caroline and Anna.

As promised, the second showing was an action film that Johnny loudly applauded and declared was more his idea of a good movie.

Cooper was intensely aware of Caroline perching herself on the arm of his chair. There was nothing she did to draw attention to herself other than merely be there. He felt her arm brush against his when she stole popcorn from his bowl. He inhaled her cologne when she shifted her body into a more comfortable position.

''Now that is what I call a movie,'' Johnny declared when the end credits rolled.

''Yes, dear, and now it's time for bed.'' Anna stood up and gestured for him to follow her. She shushed Caroline when the younger woman insisted she'd clean up.

''There's nothing that can't wait until morning,'' Anna said. ''Good night, Cooper.''

''Just because you're tired doesn't mean I am.'' Johnny's protest could be heard as his wife pulled him up the stairs.

"But you are tired, dear," she told him. "You'll realize it just as soon as you're in bed."

Caroline stood up and stretched her arms over her head. "Too tame an evening for you?" she asked Cooper.

He grabbed hold of her hand and pulled her down next to him. "*Tame* isn't a word I'd use." He slanted his mouth over hers.

Caroline tasted of salt and chocolate. He couldn't imagine anything more delicious than her intoxicating flavor. She moaned his name when he redirected his mouth to the curve of her jaw.

"I didn't think it would be a good idea to do this while Anna and Johnny were down here," he murmured. "Johnny would have gotten down his shotgun in record time."

"He would have changed his mind once Anna told him he'd have to clean up the mess," she said, pressing the palm of her hand against the hard planes of his chest. "My head is spinning."

"So is mine," he whispered, rounding his hand along the curve of her hip as he drew her closer against him. "That's what you do to me."

Caroline melted against him as his mouth returned to hers. Her tongue met his, daring him to dance with her. Encouraged with her following his lead, he deepened the kiss even more. All too soon, it threatened to flare out of control. Cooper drew back. Caroline's eyes showed confusion as she looked up at him.

"It would be just like Johnny to suddenly wander in here looking for his glasses," he murmured.

She frowned. "He doesn't wear glasses. He's quick to remind people of that fact, too."

"But it makes for a good excuse if he wants to make

sure I'm not compromising your virtue," Cooper pointed out.

Caroline's lips started to twitch. "We could give him an eyeful."

He gently placed her to one side and stood up. "Not when he's got a rifle always loaded with either buckshot or rock salt. Nothing smarts more than one of those in your butt."

"Are we speaking from experience?" She adjusted her top.

Cooper swallowed before he could answer. "Unfortunately."

Caroline smiled as she took his arm, walking with him to the door. "That's one story I can't wait to hear."

"I'm taking the Fifth."

"You'll eventually give in and tell me all," she said confidently. "I'm really glad you came tonight."

It might have been the kind of statement a polite hostess would make, but the look in her eyes and the womanly smile on her lips said she wasn't thinking all that politely.

It was definitely time for him to get going. But not without another kiss that was guaranteed to keep him awake for the rest of the night.

"Next time you won't get off so easy," he warned, after he released her.

"Is that a promise, Deputy?"

"Count on it." He opened the door and escaped before he returned for more.

Even breathing in the fresh cool air of night didn't settle him down enough. Right now, a good long swim in ice-cold water seemed like a good idea.

Chapter Six

"Caroline..." A low voice invaded the hazy mist of her mind. It was meant to entice her to rise to the surface of wakefulness.

Except she didn't want to wake up. Waking up meant leaving her dream, and it was too wonderful to abandon.

She didn't want to leave the beautiful grassy meadow that was lush and green under her feet. She felt the warm sun on her face. She was wearing a beautiful dress that floated around her ankles. As for Cooper, well, he had on a pair of faded jeans and nothing else. His embrace was warm and his hair was like coarse living silk between her fingers. And his mouth... It was doing wonderful, incredible, maybe even illegal things to her.

No woman in her right mind would want to abandon this dream!

But her sense of smell was a rude intruder. Instead of the spring scent of flowers she smelled the rich aroma of coffee and the homey fragrance of yeast and cinnamon. If she didn't know any better, she'd swear they were right under her nose.

"Caroline..." The male voice beguiled her, the husky tone silently urging her to open her eyes no matter how badly she wanted to keep them closed.

It was easy to give in when the voice sounded just like Cooper Night Hawk's.

She cautiously opened one eye. She was fully prepared to close it again if there was no one there.

Cooper crouched by her bed, one hand holding a mug of coffee and the other holding one of Anna's richly frosted cinnamon rolls. Caroline whimpered. For a moment she wasn't sure which looked better: Cooper or the coffee and cinnamon roll.

She voted for the coffee. She took the mug out of his hand and sat up so she could drink the hot liquid.

"What are you doing here?" she whispered.

"Waking you up."

She looked past his shoulder at the window. "It's still dark outside." Then she turned her head to squint at the clock. "It's four-thirty in the morning." She handed him back the coffee cup and slid back down under the covers, pulling them over her head.

Cooper pulled them back. "Come on. You've got ten minutes to be up and dressed for riding."

"Riding?" She screwed up her face in a grimace. "I don't think so. I'm still recovering from the last time."

"You'll recover just fine on horseback. You haven't lived until you've seen a Tyler sunrise." Undaunted, he pulled her out of bed. He placed the coffee mug back in her hand, patted her on the behind and gently pushed her into the hall in the direction of the bathroom. "Be downstairs in ten minutes," he ordered. "And if you try sneaking back into bed, the next time I'll come up with a glass of ice water."

Caroline's eyes were at half-mast as she stumbled toward the bathroom. "Leave the cinnamon roll," she commanded before she closed the door.

Caroline had no idea how Cooper managed to charm

her back onto a horse. She was relieved to see he'd brought her Mame. At least she didn't have to worry about a strange horse suddenly running away with her.

"Would you care to tell me what is so special about riding somewhere to see a sunrise?" she demanded in a less than friendly voice. She hadn't imbibed enough coffee yet to feel completely human.

"For someone who works the breakfast shift, you sure are cranky first thing in the morning."

Caroline muttered that she'd show Cooper cranky. Luckily, he ignored it.

By the time they reached the top of the hill, the sky had turned a pale gray. Cooper helped Caroline off her mount and led her over to a rocky outcropping. He returned to his horse and pulled off the saddlebags.

Caroline cooed with delight when he unscrewed the thermos and she caught the aroma of coffee. He poured the hot liquid into two plastic cups and handed one to her. She blew on the surface and sipped cautiously. Her enthusiasm increased when he handed her a still-warm cinnamon roll wrapped in a napkin.

"I guess I'll have to let you live, after all," she said after she'd practically inhaled the cinnamon roll and was leisurely nibbling on a second.

"I am still amazed that you don't try to live on a few lettuce leaves," Cooper said, watching her enjoy her breakfast. "Now I know why Anna gave me so many," he muttered, refilling his coffee cup. As he looked past Caroline, his eyes lit up. He grasped her shoulders and turned her around, pulling her back to rest against his chest. "Tell me this wasn't worth it."

Caroline's sticky treat was forgotten as she stared at the slivers of grayish light widening and brightening into pastel pinks, blues and purples. She watched in awe as the sky seemed to burst into colors.

"I have never seen anything so incredible," she whispered, as if speaking in a louder voice would destroy the mood. "It's as if someone splashed fairy dust across the sky." She turned to him with eyes glowing like two brilliant emeralds.

"See what you miss by sleeping in?" he teased gently, resting his chin on her shoulder as he wrapped his arms around her.

She turned her head and pressed her lips against his chin. When she leaned back, she noticed the sky wasn't the only thing lightening up.

Cooper's lips were slightly turned up at the corner. Not a full-blown smile, but it was close enough to the real thing to please her. She turned around and cupped his face with her hands. The coppery skin was smooth and warm under her touch. She found herself wanting to touch him more each time she was with him.

"Thank you for giving me something so beautiful," she murmured before she kissed him again.

Cooper caught her about the waist and increased the pressure, sending Caroline to dizzying heights.

She closed her eyes, but she could still see the colors of the sky behind her closed eyelids. Cooper's mouth sent her flying toward the sky. All Caroline could do was hang on for the ride. She scrambled to pull his T-shirt out of his jeans, so she could feel the heat of his bare skin. At the same time, he was pulling her T-shirt out of her jeans and unhooking her bra in one easy motion. She drew in a sharp breath when she felt the chilly early morning air against her bare breasts.

"Did I ever tell you how beautiful you are?" Cooper asked in a raw voice that sent fire streaking through her veins. His hand cupping her breast rapidly warmed her skin.

"Yes, but don't let that stop you from saying it again," she gasped when his lips replaced his hand.

"You're beautiful, you're beautiful, you're beautiful," he chanted as he explored the round contour.

Caroline's head was spinning. She could swear she heard little cherubs flying around them, their tiny wings fluttering in the air. She turned her head to rest her cheek against his chest. She opened her eyes, expecting to see a rosy-cheeked cherub flying in front of her face. Instead, she saw a squirrel standing on a rock, chattering away in a scolding tone.

"Cooper," she whispered, "we have company."

He didn't seem to be worried. "Anyone we know?"

"Not unless you have friends with grayish-brown fur and a tail."

Cooper drew back and looked where she pointed. "I guess we woke him up." Just as easily, his lips began exploring her ear, while his fingers deftly rolled her nipple.

Caroline couldn't keep her eyes off the squirrel, which was still chattering his displeasure at being disturbed.

"Cooper," she said in a low voice, "he's still watching us."

"Maybe he's looking for some pointers." He was engrossed in the sensitive skin just behind her ear.

She reluctantly released the cozy warmth of his chest and sat back. "I can't," she confessed. "I don't care if it is a squirrel. It's still an audience."

Cooper glared at the offensive squirrel that was ruining his morning. "I could shoot him."

"It's a good thing I know you're kidding." She fumbled with her bra clasp, finally managing to fasten it. She pulled her T-shirt back down and tucked it into her jeans. She sneaked a peek as Cooper did the same, and felt satisfaction seeing that his hands were as unsteady as hers were. He handed her her coffee mug and cinnamon roll, which he'd put to one side.

Caroline drew her legs up so she could sit cross-legged. She tore off a bit of her roll and tossed it to the squirrel. She swore he chattered thank-you as he scooped up his treat and scampered off.

"There were times when I was up at dawn because I hadn't gone to bed yet. I was too tired and ready for bed to bother looking at the sunrise," she said. "At the beach we saw more spectacular sunsets than sunrises."

"Then you've missed a lot of beauty." Cooper poured more coffee into his mug and sipped. "There's nothing more special than getting up first thing in the morning and watching the day begin."

She combed her hair back with her fingers, tucking the loose strands behind her ears. "Did you come up here and wait for the sunrise when you were a kid?" she asked.

"Hell, no," he chuckled. "It was sheer misery to just drag myself out of bed for school."

"But you do it now."

Cooper nodded. "It's peaceful up here."

"And peace is important to you."

He thought for a moment. "Yes, it is."

"So you were a hell-raiser as a boy and peacekeeper as an adult."

The barest hint of a smile touched his lips at the double meaning to her words. "I guess I am."

They sat there in companionable silence for some time until Cooper glanced at his watch. "Time for me to go play cop," he said reluctantly.

Caroline helped gather up the trash and stuff it in the

saddlebags. She groaned as Cooper gave her a boost into the saddle.

"At this rate, I'm going to end up bowlegged," she grumbled as Mame followed Cooper and Jack down the trail.

COOPER FELT AS UNSETTLED as hell. He couldn't remember the last time he'd had a decent night's sleep in the past couple of weeks. He'd asked to be switched over to the night shift, figuring if he couldn't sleep, he could at least do something useful.

Useful, right. Break up steamy necking sessions that were going hot and heavy along the side roads. Toss Clay Matthews's butt into jail after he got drunk and ran stark naked through Worthington House. Rumor had it the elderly men sighed and recalled their wild and crazy days, and a few of the women wanted to know if Clay was single.

Every time Cooper turned around his thoughts were about Caroline.

Kissing her had only whetted an already hefty appetite. It didn't help that his nights on duty were generally quiet, which gave him plenty of time to think about her.

Anymore, he wasn't sure which was worse—his grandfather's knowing looks or the woman still haunting his dreams. He felt as if Caroline and the Woman of the River had somehow merged into one being. And it scared the hell out of him.

He couldn't afford to fall for her. She'd showed up in Tyler one day and she'd probably leave another day, when she decided she'd had enough of small town life. Or, more likely, once she discovered whatever she wanted to know about the Spencers. People just didn't wander into Tyler and decide to stay.

He could have started pushing more under the guise of casual conversation. And he should have. Except he didn't want to scare her off. Plus he wasn't sure he wanted to know. He didn't want to think she planned any harm for Elias or his sons. It was easier to think she was there to check them out because someone had left old Elias a couple million dollars.

Not a great story, but one Cooper could live with until he discovered the truth.

"Are you doing okay?" Karen Bauer asked one morning when he'd come into the station to pick up some papers to take over to Belton.

"I'm fine," he said gruffly.

She didn't look as if she believed him, but luckily for him, she left it alone.

"What the hell happened to you, Night Hawk?" Brick Bauer demanded the moment Cooper walked into the Belton station. "You look as if someone wrung you out to dry."

"Must be tough to look as ugly as you and then try to convince others they're the ones who don't look so good," Cooper grumbled.

Brick grinned. "So it's true. Ha!" He roared with laughter as he clapped Cooper on the back. "My wife is right, guys. Another one bites the dust!" he announced to the other officers in the station.

Their applause was punctuated with foot stomping and ear-piercing whistles.

Cooper glared at them all and planned to give Brick's wife Karen a piece of his mind when he returned to Tyler.

"Can I have your black book?" one of the deputies called out.

"Who's had time enough to date to even compile a black book?" he barked back. "As if you'd know what to do with one if you had it.'' He slapped the envelope he'd come to deliver against Brick's chest. ''You guys need to spend less time with your hunting dogs and find yourselves some women. You still act as if you're in kindergarten.'' He stalked out of the station with the sound of male laughter ringing in his ears.

He knew if he thought about it long enough he'd come up with a suitable revenge for Brick and company. If he planned it right, he could guarantee the men would never know what hit them.

ONE THING CAROLINE WAS good at was research. Her interest in digging for facts had kept her grade level up in college, and helped on this personal mission.

Now she was researching something entirely different. As before, she knew that what she needed could be found at the library. She took a free afternoon to spend time there.

''I have to say this is a change from your usual reading material.'' Delia studied the titles of the books Caroline brought to the front desk.

''That's why I chose them,'' she said. ''I needed a change.'' She silently prayed her face wasn't a bright red.

Delia put cards in each book. She smiled as she handed the stack back to Caroline. ''Good luck.''

''Oh, I'll get them all read before they're due,'' Caroline assured her, as she tucked the books into a canvas tote she'd brought with her. She walked swiftly toward the door.

''I meant good luck with Cooper Night Hawk,'' the librarian called after her.

It was pure luck Caroline didn't drop the bag. She managed a garbled reply before she fled. She was positive her face now flamed a brilliant shade of scarlet.

As she walked up Oak Street toward the town square she was positive everyone knew the contents of her tote bag. Her smile was brief and wary each time she ran into someone she knew. Considering Tyler wasn't all that large a town and she'd pretty much met everyone, she convinced herself she passed every resident that afternoon.

Funny, it never bothered her when she was lugging a stack of murder mysteries back to the boardinghouse. All it took was for her to switch over to romance novels. She convinced herself that everyone in town now knew she was using the books to figure out the best way to properly seduce Cooper Night Hawk.

"DON'T TELL ME. The meat loaf with gravy, mashed potatoes, green beans, coffee and berry cobbler, warmed up, with vanilla ice cream." Caroline wrote as she spoke.

Cooper looked up at her. "That's way too predictable. Let's leave off the vanilla ice cream this time," he suggested.

"That's what I like about you, Deputy. You're such a wild man." She spun around and headed for the kitchen.

Cooper settled for the lovely sight of her graceful walk and the gentle sway of her hips. He wasn't sure he liked the other men watching her. But he wasn't the type to make a scene and kick some serious butt. He reminded himself that he was the one taking her home when her shift was over. He'd deliberately waited to have a late dinner so he could time his meal to finish about the same time she finished her work.

He watched her serve coffee to old Henry Farris and stay a moment to chat with him. Cooper figured she was listening to the same stories and jokes for the hundredth time, but the attention she gave him made it seem as if this was the first. The saucy smile she flashed the man would have him thinking he was a young stud again.

She's not going to be here forever. She's here for a reason, and once she's accomplished what she's come for she'll be out of here. A lady like that can't necessarily be trusted.

He ignored the warning inside his head. Just like he'd ignored it other times.

"Mr. Farris is a sweetie, but he's also a major lech," Caroline complained good-naturedly as she placed a plate filled with food in front of Cooper. She slid into the seat across from him and set down the glass of iced tea she'd brought for herself.

"He still trying to look down your blouse?"

She shook her head. "He's graduated to a little pinch on the behind."

"I didn't hear any screams and accusations of sexual harassment." Cooper dug into his meal. Lunch had been a long time ago and his stomach hadn't appreciated having to wait for dinner.

"The man is what, close to ninety? If I screamed I'd probably scare him into a heart attack."

"His father lived to be one hundred and four, his grandfather made it to one hundred and six. I don't think you need to worry on that score." He broke open the roll and slathered butter on the flaky surface.

"There's always an exception to the rule, and I don't want to be the one to test the theory." Caroline stretched her legs out and playfully kicked Cooper's shin. "What about your family? How many hundred-year-olds in your family tree?"

"I never checked all the branches. My grandfather has no idea how old he is. He doesn't have a birth certificate," he explained. "The closest we've been able to figure is about eighty-four or -five."

She sipped her tea. "The strong sense of family has always fascinated me," she said. "Families who are so closely knit that they do everything together, as if they couldn't imagine what it would be like if they didn't have each other."

"Didn't you have that kind of family?" he asked, relieved he was able to question her for once without it sounding as if he was interrogating her.

She looked off into the distance. The wistful look that crossed her face had a sorrow there that seemed to come from her very soul.

"No," she said softly. "No, I didn't."

"No brothers or sisters?" he pressed.

"There was just me," she murmured. She managed a wan smile.

He pretended an interest in his food he didn't feel, because he wanted to keep this as casual as possible. "Only child like me," he commented, hoping to open up some kind of discussion.

Caroline shrugged. "I'd like to have more than one child," she stated.

"I always figured I'd end up with a beautiful daughter I'd have to lock up until she was at least forty," Cooper said.

She was surprised by his statement. "You'd keep your daughter locked up until she was forty?"

"That and I'd have a loaded shotgun by the front door. Back in high school I remember taking out a girl whose father liked to sit at the kitchen table and clean his gun whenever her dates picked her up."

"That would ruin my social life in no time," Caroline chuckled. "My dad usually just asked them if they knew where the cemetery was. They usually said yes whether they did or not. They had no idea where he was going with that question.''

''What happened if they said yes?'' Cooper was intrigued by her story. He was also surprised, since she'd said very little about her family before now.

She grinned. ''That was the best part of all. Because then he'd put his arm around their shoulders and say he was glad to know it because if they harmed one hair on my head they'd end up owning some land out there.''

''That's one I'll have to remember,'' Cooper stated. He forked up the last bite of meat loaf.

''I'll get your cobbler.'' She slid out of the booth.

''Caroline.'' He grabbed hold of her hand.

She stopped, her head cocked to one side as she waited to see what else he had to say.

''I'd like to change my order back to ice cream on the cobbler.''

''I was going to make it up that way anyway,'' she said in a mock whisper.

A moment later, she exchanged the dinner plate for a shallow dish holding warm cobbler and ice cream melting on top. Cooper could feel his taste buds working overtime.

''Hey, Cooper!''

He looked up to see Brady and Eden and Seth and Jenna walk into the diner. As he nodded in their direction he spared a quick glance toward Caroline. If he hadn't been looking directly at her, he would have had trouble believing a person could change so quickly.

Within seconds her expression suddenly smoothed over and a polite, impersonal mask covered her face. The warm and laughing woman he'd been talking to moments before disappeared, as if she'd deliberately shut down a vital part of herself. He watched and noted each change. He doubted anyone else would have noticed what she'd done, but to him, the differences were glaring.

Her walk almost seemed reluctant as she approached their table. Her smile wasn't as open and honest as it had been with him. Unlike her usual chatty self, she made as little small talk as necessary as she took their order.

Outwardly, she was the perfect waitress, but she was nothing more than a hollow shell. Because he was watching her so closely, he didn't miss the furtive looks she directed toward Brady and Seth. Or the strange expression on her face that he swore looked wistful. He also didn't miss Brady watching her with speculation in his eyes.

He heard Marge call out and ask who was taking care of Susan and Dominick, and Seth's explanation that Elias and Lydia were baby-sitting.

Cooper hid his smile as he noticed Seth placing his cell phone on the table. Obviously, he didn't want to remain too far out of touch. He'd heard Seth had turned into the model father who did more than his fair share of taking care of the babies. Obviously, it was true.

Then he noticed Caroline's furtive glance in their direction.

What is so damn important about them?

She'd been caught in the rose bushes outside Elias's house. She'd been seen studying family photos during the wedding reception. She'd made copies of newspaper articles about the Spencers.

What else had she done since she'd arrived in Tyler? If Elias hadn't seen her in his office, would anyone have been aware of what she was doing? Of course, the question was still why.

Caroline's smile looked a little strained when she stopped at his table long enough to refill his cup. ''I need to stay until they're finished," she told him. "There's no need for you to stick around waiting for me."

"I'm not going anywhere."

His quiet assurance warmed her smile. She nodded and stepped back before returning to the Spencer table.

Cooper drank his coffee and watched Caroline move around the diner. A couple of times she looked in his direction and smiled.

He didn't miss that Brady noticed the exchange and shot him a questioning look. Cooper pretended not to see it and forked up another bite of cobbler. When Caroline stopped by with the coffeepot, he nudged his cup in her direction.

"If I had this much coffee I'd be spinning in circles all night," she told him.

"Cops and coffee go together."

"And here I thought it was doughnuts and cops that made up the dynamic duo." She flashed him an impish grin before she moved away.

After the two couples finished and were getting ready to leave, Brady walked over to Cooper. "You and Caroline seem to be pretty cozy," he murmured.

"She's single. I'm single. Just a natural progression," Cooper said blandly.

"You learn anything about her that can tell me why she's been pulling some of those stunts?"

Cooper's gaze was flat as he looked up at a man he thought of as a friend but wasn't sure he liked too much right now. Brady was reminding him of his request. It was bad enough it had tormented him since the morning Brady sat down across from him. Not to mention that Cooper had broken down and informally contacted the Santa Barbara Police Department to run a check on Caroline. Nothing urgent, no top priority. He hadn't heard from them—and now he hoped he never did.

"Caroline uses blueberries to make smiley faces on my pancakes. She tries to tell jokes, but she always forgets the punchline."

"That's what you've learned in all this time?"

Brady quickly glanced in Caroline's direction, then turned back to Cooper.

"If there's anything I think you should know, I'll tell you," Cooper stated in a voice that strongly suggested Brady back off.

Brady cocked an eyebrow. "So that's how it is," he said. "Be careful."

He walked away and joined his wife, sliding an arm around Eden's waist. Her head immediately found a niche against his shoulder, as if it belonged there. When Brady looked down at her, his eyes were dark with love.

Cooper felt as if he'd stumbled upon an intimate moment.

He was relieved when Caroline was ready to go.

"Don't you worry about anything here. You just go on." Marge shooed them out the door while Caroline protested she could help finish the cleanup. "I don't have a good-looking man waiting to walk me home." She winked at them.

As they walked down the sidewalk, Caroline noticed other businesses getting ready to close up.

"It's as if some unknown entity rings a bell and everyone starts to roll up their share of the sidewalk," she commented.

"Except for the Dairy King and a few places outside of town where a body can get a beer or something stronger," Cooper said.

She nodded. "I've noticed those places. Not my idea of fun."

"Good thing or we'd be breaking up a lot of fights once the men got a look at you."

Caroline grabbed hold of Cooper's hand. She playfully bumped her hip against his.

"There're some places where that would be considered assaulting an officer of the law," he told her, bumping her back.

"Oh sure, like anyone would believe l'il ole me could assault big bad you!" She laughed. "Go for it." She bounced away from him and held out her wrists. "Take me in, Deputy."

"There's an offer I wouldn't refuse, Cooper!" someone shouted.

Cooper muttered a few exasperated comments about crazy women, and braceleted one wrist with his fingers instead. He pulled her alongside him as he walked rapidly along the sidewalk.

"Have you always been like this?" he asked.

"Like what?"

He shook his head. "Are you sure you weren't the one drinking all the coffee?"

"I had a couple caffeine-free Diet Cokes. No, this is just my effervescent personality. Hadn't you guessed by now?" She wiggled her fingers in a wave as she passed by storefronts. More than one person waved back or offered a helpful comment to Cooper on how to properly treat the lady he was with.

Cooper ignored them all and concentrated on getting them to the Kelsey Boarding House where, if he was lucky, he could cheerfully wring Caroline's neck without any witnesses.

He was a man who'd always valued the truth. All right,

it made him more than a little tight-assed at times, but that didn't bother him. He wanted to know a person was telling him the truth. And, dammit, there were times he knew Carolyn was speaking more fiction than fact.

He knew that within the next hour, word would be all over town that Cooper Night Hawk had practically dragged Caroline Benning through the town. If he was lucky, that's all that would be said. If not, it would just depend on who said what first.

When they reached the boardinghouse, Cooper continued walking around the side of the house toward the back. He didn't release Caroline until they reached the back steps.

"You are more trouble than you are worth," he said between clenched teeth.

Instead of appearing angry with his caveman attitude, she looked amused. She hopped up onto the first step so she was at eye level with him. She looped her arms around his neck.

"Trouble is my middle name," she murmured, just before she leaned forward to kiss him.

The lip gloss she'd applied before leaving the diner tasted like berries. Instead of smelling like the food she'd handled that afternoon and evening, she smelled sweet, with a touch of vanilla.

He wrapped his arms around her and took over until she was hanging limply in his arms.

"Exactly who are you?" he murmured.

She reared back. For a brief second something flashed across her face, but it was too fleeting for him to decipher it.

"Now I see how you do it," she whispered.

What was she trying to do now? "Do what?"

She gave him the smile that hit him all the way to his soul.

"Charm a lady." She dropped her arms from his neck and stepped back. "Sweet dreams, Cooper." She opened the door and disappeared into the kitchen.

Cooper stood there trying to get his heart rate back to a normal beat. As he walked back to his Blazer, he couldn't help but wonder what would happen next. And if he could survive the outcome.

Chapter Seven

"Really smart, Caroline. Why didn't you just extract the man's tonsils while you were down there," she scolded herself as she tossed her clothes onto the chair and picked up her pajamas.

"You acted like a maniac out there on the street." She kept up her self-reprimand as she washed her face and brushed her teeth. "What were you thinking?" She shook her toothbrush at her reflection in the mirror. "Who knows what he thought of you," she mumbled, smoothing moisturizer over her face.

He probably thought he had this hot-blooded woman on his hands. Of course, you were thinking you'd just died and gone to heaven. If the man kisses that good, can you imagine what he'd be like in bed?

The image of a naked Cooper popped into her mind. She grabbed the edge of the sink and tried to catch her breath.

Experience told her she could hold her own in kissing. When it came to anything more in the romance department she was playing strictly in the rookie league.

Caroline was a virgin. Not for lack of men in her life, but because she didn't believe in having sex just for the sake of it. And because she hadn't met a man she would want to share that experience with. Her lack of experience in that area never bothered her. It wasn't as if she was in any hurry to shed her virginity the same way she might shed a sweater. She'd know when the time was right.

Everything inside her was announcing in an extremely loud voice that the time had arrived.

She wondered what it would take to convince Cooper the time was right for the two of them.

She returned to her room and curled up on her bed with her mother's quilt draped around her. The book she'd planned to begin that night lay unopened on her lap as she thought over the past year.

It had all begun with her father's death and the discovery of the quilt. She'd set out for Tyler because she needed to find out about Elias Spencer and his three sons. She'd hoped finding them might tell her more about her mother.

What had her father told her whenever she asked him about her mother? That she'd looked forward to the birth of their child. That she'd loved Caroline from the time she knew she was pregnant.

But there were so many other things Caroline didn't know. She wished she hadn't stopped asking him about her. That she'd been more insistent. It had been too easy to back off when she felt she upset her father with her questions.

Would he have given the quilt away if he'd known he would die soon? Would he have made sure Caroline never knew about the quilt and, in essence, the Spencer men? Or had he been waiting for what he might have thought was the appropriate time to give it to her?

More questions. No answers.

She put the book to one side and leaned over to open her nightstand drawer. She pulled out a notebook she'd been keeping since she came to Tyler. She'd found it helpful to write down all the questions she had, in hopes she would eventually have the answers she was looking for. She'd clipped the articles to the back cover. So far the notebook was filled with more questions than answers. She'd also jotted down a list of names of people she thought might have known her mother. Anna Kelsey was one of the names near the top of the list.

It hadn't been easy for Caroline not to say anything these past few months, but she knew she needed the people here to feel comfortable with her. Along the way, she'd dropped tidbits about her interest in history. That she was curious about Tyler's past. She'd heard stories about the town's beginning more than one hundred and fifty years ago, founded by Gunther Ingalls and Jackie Kelsey.

It was further back in time than she cared to research, but when some of her elderly customers told her the stories—with a great deal of embellishment, she suspected— she didn't have the heart to stop them. Besides, she did enjoy hearing them.

After she finished writing down anything that came to mind about the Spencers, she realized she still didn't know any more about her mother than she'd known when she arrived in Tyler.

She was also feeling pretty guilty. She was very attracted to Cooper. Not telling him the truth about herself bothered her. And not just because he was a sheriff's deputy, either. She sensed that even if he didn't wear a badge, he would still carry that strong sense of honor, which was ingrained in him. What would he feel about her once he learned she wasn't who she claimed to be?

He was a careful man who didn't take unnecessary

chances. He loved and revered his grandfather. She knew he was well respected in town and very well liked.

She also knew he kissed like the devil and tempted her more than any man had ever tempted her before.

When she thought about it she realized she'd never dated a man like Cooper. Anyone before him fell into the young man category—guys who had no idea what they wanted to be when they grew up. She wouldn't be surprised if Cooper had known what he wanted to do with his life since he was age five.

Caroline worried she was moving swiftly past attraction to seriously falling for the man. Not a good idea. The practical part of her nature told her there was still the chance the Spencers would not want anything to do with her when she revealed her true name.

And she had no idea how Cooper would take the news. She couldn't bear it if he hated her because of her deception.

With the notebook safely tucked away in the drawer, she picked the book back up and opened it.

After a few pages, Caroline began to squirm uncomfortably. When she'd chosen the volume she hadn't realized it was actually a book of erotica for women. That would teach her to just grab a book because it had a sexy cover. What she was reading turned out to be a great deal more graphic than anything she'd read before. And written so effectively she was feeling much too warm even with the cool breeze coming in through the open window.

She skimmed the rest of the chapter, then stopped when something caught her attention. She read several pages, then backtracked and read them again. Keeping her finger in the book to hold her place, she closed her eyes and tried to imagine the position she'd just read about. She prided herself on having a good imagination, but this was turning out to be more than she ever expected to think about. Her eyes popped open.

"There is no way that can be physically possible."

"WHY DON'T YOU TAKE HER out to dinner at Timberlake Lodge?" Brick asked Cooper the next time he was in Belton.

Cooper made a show of checking the calendar hanging on the wall. "Yep, thought so."

"Thought what?"

"Thought it couldn't be anywhere near Valentine's Day, yet you're wearing one of those cute little diapers and carrying a bow and arrows," Cooper said blandly.

Brick didn't look offended at being compared to Cupid. "I have to give Karen a hell of a lot more credit for putting up with you.

"Maybe I could tell your wife that you're thinking about taking *her* to Timberlake Lodge for dinner." Cooper's dark eyes gleamed.

"If I didn't know any better, I'd swear you're telling me that the subject of Caroline Benning is off-limits," the captain drawled.

"You're a smart man."

"It still wouldn't hurt you to take her out to dinner someplace, rather than her serving you dinner most of the time."

"Caroline's working the breakfast shift again," Cooper told him.

"Even better. She won't have to ask for a night off. Aunt Anna says the two of you seem to spend a lot of time in the backyard and you've even joined them a few times for their movie nights," Brick said. "All those chaperons must really cramp a guy's style."

Now Cooper was feeling downright suspicious. He was

tempted to give the government-issue desk a good kick, but if it was anything like the ones at the Tyler substation there was a chance it would collapse.

"Did Karen put you up to this?"

The slight shift of the other man's eyes told him all he needed to know.

"Dammit, Brick, can't you do something so your wife will stop poking her nose in other people's business?"

"She's a cop. It's her job to poke her nose in other people's business."

"Her job doesn't cover my business." His mouth thinned.

"Fine, I'll let you tell her you said that. Mainly because I have this irritating habit. I like to live." Brick grinned.

Cooper knew the couple was too well suited to each other for Brick to worry about his wife's reaction if he told her to knock it off. And how many couples got to share, in a sense, the same job—Karen heading the Tyler substation and Brick heading the Belton one?

"I was over there not long ago," Brick said. "Met Karen at the diner for lunch. Your little waitress waited on us. She's cute."

"I wouldn't call her a little waitress to her face," Cooper advised. "She might decide to take a swing at you, and I'd have to look the other way."

He was about ready to take a swing at the man himself.

But as he drove back to Tyler, he did have to admit Brick had a good idea about a romantic evening with Caroline.

So far, most of his time with her was spent either when he was eating at the diner or walking back to the boardinghouse. They usually sat out in the backyard, because he felt as if the entire town was watching anytime they occupied the chairs on the front porch. He wasn't about to tell Brick that lately their schedules hadn't been in sync while he filled in for deputies who'd been taking their vacation time. Who knew what the man would suggest.

But Brick had planted a seed. Cooper had a couple days off coming to him. And he knew Marge wouldn't mind if Caroline had an evening off. The woman was a romantic, even if she didn't want to admit it.

Cooper was grateful no one ever asked him what he thought of Caroline. How could he explain that being with her was like riding a roller coaster? He never knew what would happen next. She kept him on his toes and he was actually liking it. Even her single-minded determination to make him smile. He didn't know how to tell her that he didn't smile much because he didn't think it fit him. He was a no-nonsense kind of guy and no-nonsense guys didn't smile a lot. Not that his explanation would have deterred her. From what he could see of her, it would only have spurred her on.

It got so he had no idea what to expect next where she was concerned.

And that was what made him nervous.

"He's taking you to dinner at Timberlake Lodge?" Anna's voice rose to a delighted shriek. "It's beautiful there. I know you'll enjoy it."

Caroline cringed. "We don't need to tell the entire town, do we?" she muttered.

Anna immediately pushed her into the kitchen. Caroline then realized the older woman wasn't alone. Seated around the large butcher-block table was Anna's mother, Martha Bauer, her daughter-in-law, Pam Kelsey, and several other members of the Tyler Quilting Circle.

"Hello, dear," Martha greeted her warmly. "So Cooper is taking you out for a nice dinner. Seems only right, what with the two of you going out for so long.''

Caroline felt glued to the spot by the sharp blue eyes watching her. She was positive this woman missed nothing. She remembered her seventh-grade teacher having that same intensity. No one was ever able to put anything over on her.

"Cooper is a nice boy, but so serious." Tillie Phelps spoke up.

"Then Caroline is good for him," Anna said. "This girl laughs all the time."

"There are times when it isn't a good idea to laugh," Emma Finklebaum insisted with a sly smile.

Caroline was starting to feel a full-fledged panic. Luckily, Pam recognized what was going on and took pity on her. "Since I need to pick Jeremy up at day care in an hour, I hope we can finalize the plans for the church bazaar before I have to leave," she said quickly.

"We aren't going to do another white elephant sale, are we?" Emma asked. "We haven't been able to unload that horrible lamp Frederick Martin donated five years ago."

Anna filled a glass with iced tea, added lemon and cut a piece of the coconut cake she'd made for the meeting. She pressed both on Caroline, who wasted no time in escaping up the back stairs.

The women paused in their conversation until they heard a door close upstairs.

"She's an excellent balance for Cooper," Tillie said. "And so pretty. She doesn't seem like the flighty type, either. Not that Cooper would put up with a flighty woman. Remember that airline hostess he once dated?"

"They call them flight attendants now," Anna explained.

Tillie waved her hand in dismissal. "At my age, I don't

need to worry about being politically correct,'' she argued. ''She should settle in here nicely.''

Martha looked thoughtful. ''For Cooper's sake, I hope so,'' she murmured.

Anna turned to her mother. ''Mother, what do you mean?''

She shook her head. ''I have a pretty good idea, but I'm not ready to say anything just yet.'' She patted her daughter's hand. ''It's nothing to worry about.''

Anna looked toward the stairs as if the answer would suddenly materialize.

Caroline was grateful to have escaped when she did. She knew the ladies of the Quilting Circle were laws unto themselves, but she hadn't encountered that power until today.

She hadn't planned on blurting out Cooper's invitation the way she had, but it had been such a surprise that she'd wanted to share it with Anna. She hadn't stopped to think that, when she ran into the kitchen with her news, Anna might not be alone.

What bothered Caroline the most was the thoughtful expression on Martha Bauer's face as she'd studied her. She found the woman's visual examination unsettling.

Then it suddenly hit her. Martha had been with the Tyler Quilting Circle for many years. If the quilt had been crafted by the group, there was a good chance Martha had known her mother.

The urge to pick up the quilt, carry it downstairs was so strong that Caroline headed for the closet with just that intent. The moment her fingers touched the fabric, she hesitated.

A calmer voice suggested she wait until there weren't as many people present. There was no guarantee what she might hear, and there was no reason for an audience. She felt her sigh all the way up from her toes.

"They weren't kidding when they said life wasn't fair."

"MY, THAT IS A LOVELY dress," Anna said faintly, looking at Caroline as she stood before the mirror in her bedroom, using her fingers to scrunch up the tousled curls she'd fashioned with her curling iron.

"Not too short or too skimpy?" Caroline asked.

"Well…" Anna hesitated as if afraid she would insult her boarder, "Perhaps…"

Caroline smoothed the lace skirt down over her hips. "You should have heard my dad when I came home with this dress. He insisted the store cheated me, that there had to be more to it."

Caroline was glad that, when she'd done her packing, she'd thought to throw in an outfit suitable for a more formal evening out. The sleeveless lace dress over a black underslip clung lovingly to her body and ended well above her knees. Sheer black stockings and black high heeled, strappy sandals completed the sexy outfit.

"And he probably worried about you every time you went out wearing that dress," Anna said.

"Actually, he worried more about my dates than what I was wearing. He was afraid I'd give them a heart attack," she explained. "My dad could have a twisted sense of humor at times."

Anna shook her head. "He probably needed one. We parents always worry about our children. It's one of the bylaws of parenthood. I must say you look lovely, dear. Cooper will be speechless when he sees you."

As Anna started to turn, a splash of color on the bed caught her eye. She got up and picked up a corner of the quilt. Caroline froze. "This is lovely, dear. You should show it to the Quilting Circle. They love examining the competition, so to speak." She chuckled. "Sometime I should tell you about the beginning of quilting in Tyler. It started out courtesy of a mutual ancestor of both the Kelsey and the Forrester families. Her name was Tiffany Pierce Kelsey. A very formidable young lady."

"I'd like to hear about it."

Anna's attention was diverted when she heard the doorbell.

"I would say that is Cooper," she said. She walked to the open doorway and peered out. "Johnny, would you please get the door!" she called. "That way you can make an entrance," she said to Caroline before she left the room. "I better get down there before Johnny decides to act the father figure and scare the poor man."

Caroline picked up the black silk crocheted bag and dropped in her lipstick and perfume. She took one last look in the mirror. She was pleased with the results.

"The man won't have a chance," she murmured, heading along the hallway to the stairs.

She walked down the stairs in a slow measured pace guaranteed to snag a man's attention.

She was a third of the way down when Cooper looked up. The stunned look on his face went beyond the reaction she'd received the night of the spring dance.

She was feeling a little stunned herself.

Cooper in a charcoal suit and white shirt was a feast for her eyes. He'd tied his dark hair back, which only emphasized his sharp cheekbones. She resisted the urge to fiddle with his maroon-and-gray tie. Not that it needed straightening; she just would have used it as an excuse to touch him.

"You look beautiful," Cooper managed to exclaim, once he'd found his speech.

Johnny's expression was one she'd seen on her father's face more than once. "Shouldn't there be more to that dress?" he asked his wife.

"She's an adult, dear." She patted his shoulder.

Cooper couldn't keep his eyes off Caroline as they walked out to his truck. "With you looking like that I feel as if I should have rented a limousine," he said, as he helped her into the vehicle.

"You washed the truck and cleaned out the interior. That's more than a lot of men would do," she assured him when he climbed in behind the wheel.

"Only the best for you, babe," he said, straight-faced.

Caroline scrunched up her nose. "Please do something for me. Don't ever call me babe. It just doesn't sound right coming from you." She narrowed her gaze. "Aha, I get it. You don't smile, but you make jokes."

"It's a hobby." He switched on the engine and pulled away from the curb.

"So what exactly is Timberlake Lodge?" she asked. "It sounds like one of those private men's clubs you hear about. The husband leaving the house at night saying, 'Bye, hon, I'm going down to the lodge.'"

"You're not even close. I guess you'd have to say it's the place where we head when we want to go exclusive," he replied. "It used to be a hunting lodge, a summer house in early nineteen-hundreds. It's still used for conferences. There was an astrology conference held there not all that long ago."

"I bet that was one time 'what's your sign?' wasn't a come-on," Caroline quipped.

Cooper's response was a quirk of the eyebrow. "If that was intended to get me to smile, you are way off."

"Sorry, bud, I'm working big time to get a full-fledged laugh out of you." She crossed her legs, which caused her dress to hike up even farther. She didn't bother trying to smooth it back down.

Cooper's eyes followed the extended line of leg, then quickly shifted back to watch the road.

Caroline felt pretty smug.

The evening was already going as she hoped it would. And they hadn't even arrived at the lodge yet.

"Don't tell me. That's Timber Lake," she said when the headlights flashed out over a body of water.

"Good guess." He turned up a road marked by two brick columns.

"This must be incredible during the day." She looked out the window up at trees that lined the road.

When they reached the entrance, a valet ran over to take the truck and park it. Cooper kept his hand against Caroline's back as they crossed the veranda to the front door.

"I made reservations and thought we could come early for a drink," he said.

"This is beautiful," she commented, looking around at the antique furniture.

Cooper identified himself to the hostess and explained they would wait in the bar for their table.

"Was that chandelier made of deer antlers?" Caroline asked in a whisper.

"They have that sort of thing in hunting lodges."

They chose a table near the piano. Caroline asked for an amaretto and soda while Cooper ordered a glass of wine.

"I thought you didn't drink," she said, surprised.

"An occasional glass of wine, but that's pretty much it."

Caroline looked around the room, fascinated with the blend of old and new.

"You can imagine all those hunters coming in here, drinking their whiskeys and trading stories about the buck that got away," she said, settling back in the chair, which was upholstered in a deep burgundy velvet. She leaned forward. "Do you think they had women up here during their hunting parties?" she asked in a mock whisper. "And I'm not talking about their wives, either."

"Probably. We men tend to do things like that."

Cooper was wondering if he'd ever be able to breathe again.

From the first moment he'd seen Caroline coming down the stairs, he felt as if he'd been poleaxed.

The cute little number she'd worn to the spring dance gave him a lot of pleasant memories, but tonight's outfit went way past the limits of his sanity.

The black, stretch-lace dress was provocative even with the underslip. It also didn't leave a lot to the imagination, what with those tiny lace straps that left the rounded mounds of her breasts in view. Her tousled curls invited his hands to burrow there—something he was planning on doing later that evening. Along with seeing just what made her skin sparkle the way it did and smell like sin.

For now, he'd settle on savoring the lovely sight before him and relishing the fantasy that she was all his.

How his grandfather would love to hear that. He was already a little too smug after hearing Cooper was taking Caroline out to dinner. And where. He might have told his grandson to have a pleasant evening, but Cooper knew there was a pretty long message behind his words.

Laughing Bear was convinced Caroline was the Woman of the River.

Cooper knew better.

Caroline wasn't part of the legend because she had an entirely different purpose for being in Tyler than to heal a man.

For many a year, Cooper had protected his heart from injury, and he wasn't about to risk it with a woman whom he suspected of lying.

When their drinks arrived, he sipped his wine and enjoyed Caroline's fascination with the room.

"I can't help it," she confessed. "It's so easy to imagine the hunting parties, which could have been orgies for all we know. The family up here for the summer for G-rated entertainment. Picnicking by the lake, rowing a boat out on the water. Things like that."

"Don't tell me. You were a history major in school."

"And there's not much you can do with a history degree, either," she replied.

The hostess came in to tell them their table was ready.

During the elegant and delicious meal, Cooper watched Caroline and realized she belonged in formal surroundings such as this. Even though this wasn't the first time he'd been here, he still felt a twinge of intimidation. Hell, he felt more comfortable kicking back in Marge's Diner than he did in a restaurant that required a jacket and a tie that was strangling him.

A long time later, he smiled his thanks as the waiter brought them their coffee.

"I bet they wouldn't have been so quick to hire me here," Caroline confessed. "And if they had hired me, I wouldn't have lasted too long. I would have been more nervous if I was carrying the fine china they use here."

"What would you be doing if you were back in California?" Cooper asked.

She thought for a moment. "I'd be realizing that it's time to see what I can do with my history degree."

"That sounds like a challenge in itself," he acknowledged. "You said your father passed away a couple months before you arrived here."

A shadow crossed over her face. She shook her head. "I don't like to talk about it," she said tightly.

"My grandfather would say the heart heals faster if you open it to the pain."

She took so long to reply that he wasn't sure if she was going to.

"Dad was getting ready to head out to the golf course," she said softly. "He had an eight o'clock tee off with his best friend. They played golf at least three times a week. He'd asked me if I wanted to meet him for lunch at the club. I told him I'd be there to cheer him on at the eighteenth hole and he walked out to the car. Later that morning, I received a phone call. He'd collapsed on the eighth hole, with a heart attack. He was gone before he hit the ground." She blinked rapidly. "You know the odd part? He'd just had a complete checkup the week before, and been told he was in perfect health. His doctor was as stunned as the rest of us. He said it was just one of those things that can happen without any warning."

Cooper reached across the table and took her hand. "And you said your mother died when you were born."

Her smile trembled on her lips as she nodded.

"He never remarried?"

Caroline shook her head. She looked off in the distance as she thought about the past. "He dated, and some women turned into long-term relationships, but he once told me that Mom was the only love of his life and he didn't think he could be that lucky a second time. He didn't feel it was right to remarry just to give me a mother, because there was no guarantee a woman who would be a good wife for him would be a good mother for me."

When a tear appeared in her eye, Cooper pulled his handkerchief out of his pocket and passed it to her. She smiled and murmured a thank-you. She dabbed at the corner of her eyes.

"I'm sorry, I didn't mean to ruin the evening." She folded the handkerchief and tucked it in her purse.

"You didn't. You never really talked all that much about your family, and after what you'd gone through, maybe you've needed to," Cooper told her. "It sounds as if you and your father were very close. It couldn't have been easy for a single father, especially with a daughter. I'd say he did a pretty good job."

"Dad said at first he was so scared about being a father he read a lot of parenting books. Then he threw them out. He figured we'd both be better off if we just winged it. Since I didn't end up with any complexes, he felt he must have done all right."

"He sounds like my grandfather. Laughing Bear believes as long as you follow your heart, you can't go wrong."

"I like your grandfather." She smiled. "I bet you'll be just like him when you reach his age."

"I don't know. I might end up ornerier. I'm sure Laughing Bear thinks so."

"What happened to your parents?" she asked.

He knew that same shadow crossed his face. "Car accident. They were coming back from a movie and a drunk driver sideswiped them. Their truck spun out of control and wrapped itself around a telephone pole. They never had a chance. My grandmother mourned the loss of her only son for months. I once heard her say the only reason she could continue on with her life was because she was afraid what bad habits Laughing Bear would teach me if she wasn't around to make sure I grew up right. Laughing Bear used to be a hell-raiser in his day.''

"I guess we both were lucky with the adults we were left with,'' she admitted. "But—'' she leaned forward and whispered in a conspiratorial tone ''—you did turn out like your grandfather, didn't you? I know you couldn't have been an angel all these years. What was the worst thing you ever did in school?''

He recognized that she was trying to lighten the moment before they both grew too maudlin. "Are we talking grade or high?''

Her eyebrow rose in an arch. "You decide. How far back did those hell-raiser tendencies begin?''

He thought back. "I can't remember too much before third grade. That was a cherry bomb set off in the boys' bathroom. How about you?''

"I started earlier. Second grade. Nothing destructive. Just traumatic for my teacher, who wasn't married and never intended to be. I took a box of my dad's condoms for show and tell.'' She rotated her hand at the wrist, the fingers pointing at him indicating it was now his turn.

There was nothing Cooper enjoyed more than a challenge.

"Ever try pouring two gallons of vodka into the water dispenser in the teachers' lounge?'' he asked. "Funny thing is there wasn't one detention notice or tardy slip handed out that day.''

"Shame on you,'' she scolded.

Cooper nodded. "How did you end up to be such a troublemaker?''

"It's easy when you have friends who didn't like playing with dolls.'' She sipped her coffee. "Don't even try the same excuse because I won't buy it.''

He shook his head in admiration. "Are you sure you're only twenty-two?"

"I didn't think you'd believe me if I told you I was sixty," she teased. "I've always looked young for my age."

"You're right. I'd have trouble with that." He picked up his credit card, which the waiter had returned with the bill. "Can you walk in those shoes? I thought we could go down by the lake."

Her face lit up. "I'd love it."

Cooper put his arm around her waist and she slipped hers around his as they started down the path. Torches along the way gave them plenty of light.

Caroline breathed in deeply. "This is beautiful. It's so serene out here that you feel all your worries fade away."

"I'm sorry if my questions depressed you," Cooper said, bending his head to inhale her fragrance, which he decided was headier than any brandy.

How had he existed before he met her?

She turned her head so she could look up at him. "Actually, I think it helped. You were right. I haven't talked about it much. At home, the memories were too strong. I felt lost and I felt the need to find myself again."

"Do you still feel the need to find yourself?"

Caroline stopped and turned around. She framed his face with her hands. Her fingertips gently caressed his cheeks.

"You know what?" she said in a whisper that feathered its way across his mouth. "It's amazing that I had to come all the way out here to find myself." She leaned forward to kiss him. He met her more than halfway.

The electricity arced between them as their mouths merged in a heated kiss that had been eagerly anticipated by both of them all evening.

Cooper pulled her fully into his arms and immediately deepened the kiss by plunging his tongue inside her mouth. Her hands remained cupping his face. Unable to stay still, her fingers blindly traced the harsh contours. He fulfilled an earlier fantasy by tunneling his hands through her hair, watching the silken curls wrap themselves around his fingers. She tilted her head back as she looked up at him. Her eyes shone with desire and her lips were still moist from his kiss.

"Cooper," she murmured, "before someone comes out and dumps a bucket of cold water on us, don't you think it might be a good idea if we went back to your place?"

Chapter Eight

I'm crazy to do this. Certifiable.

Cooper may have been crazy but he wasn't stupid. The lady made a request and he had been taught from birth to always honor a lady's request.

He pulled away from the enticing feel of her body and walked with her back up the path to the front of the lodge.

The torches along the way shot bands of light across her face, revealing the hectic color in her cheeks. For a moment, he thought he saw trepidation in her eyes and almost stopped to ask her if this was what she truly wanted. As if she knew the question forming in his mind, she looked up and smiled. The smile was more an answer than words could ever be.

They may have only waited minutes for his truck, but Cooper felt as if it was hours. Caroline stood so close to him he felt as if she was a part of him. He glared at the valet, who shot her a blatant male look of admiration. The young man swiftly backed off, allowing Cooper to assist Caroline into his vehicle.

Once the truck was rolling down the road, Caroline slid across the seat until her thigh touched Cooper's. Her hand rested lightly on his thigh, but the heat went through the material of his pants to his skin. She looked as calm as if they were out for an evening drive, while he felt as if he would snap like a rubber band wound too tightly.

He knew it would take twenty minutes to return to Tyler and more than that to reach his cabin. His foot slightly increased its pressure on the accelerator, then eased off. The last thing he needed was to be pulled over for speeding. Word would reach all substations in no time and he'd never live it down. He kept one eye on the speedometer, making sure to never exceed the speed limit.

He was aware of Caroline softly humming along with the song playing on the radio. Aware of the sensual fragrance of her perfume in the truck. Aware of the feel of her hand on his leg and the way her fingers occasionally stroked the fabric, searing him down to the bone.

If they were lucky, he wouldn't drive off the road or do something stupid before they reached his cabin. He would thank every one of his ancestor spirits if his grandfather was watching the damn stars from his own porch tonight.

Cooper felt uneasy when he parked in front of his place. What could be called cozy by some would probably be called primitive by others. He climbed out of his truck and walked around to help Caroline down.

"This is wonderful," she exclaimed, looking around. "You have so much privacy here with the trees. How far away is your nearest neighbor? Ten miles?"

"More like a hundred yards or so," he confessed. "My grandfather has his cabin up that way." He gestured in the general direction.

"Ah." She nodded in understanding. "Bachelor hideaway." She took hold of his hand, wrapping her own hands around it.

Cooper opened the door and ushered her inside. A lamp burned in a corner of the living room.

Would she notice that his tan corduroy couch had seen better days and the easy chair faced the big screen TV for the baseball games?

She wandered around the room, trailing her fingers along the back of the couch, and paused by the coffee table covered with magazines. By the time she finished her circuit of the room, he felt she knew every corner that housed a spiderweb and how many inches of dust coated the furniture. He was grateful that he hadn't left any dirty dishes in the sink.

"I'm impressed. No deer head mounted over the fireplace," she murmured. "No girly magazines and empty beer cans stacked on the coffee table. No underwear draped over the lamps and furniture. I like your cabin, Cooper Night Hawk." She wrapped her hand around the back of his neck and brought his face down to hers. She nipped at his lower lip, then gently tugged on it. "When do I get to see the rest of it?" she whispered, sliding her arms around his waist.

"It's nothing fancy," he warned her.

"Cooper."

He swung her up in his arms and carried her into the bedroom, on the way in using his elbow to nudge the light switch that would illuminate the lamp by the bed. He set her down there.

She kept her gaze fixed on his face as she took off his suit coat, folded it and laid it over the back of the chair. She nimbly loosened his tie and dropped it on top of the coat. His shirt soon followed.

"Oh my," she breathed, unable to keep herself from running her hands over the smooth contours of his chest. When she gave in to temptation and leaned forward to tease a dark, copper-colored nipple with her tongue, he felt the shock down to his toes. She smiled as she felt the ripple of desire move through his body.

"Now it's your turn." He reached around her for the zipper. He pushed the black lace and underslip down to her waist, then down to pool around her feet. He thought he'd lose his sanity when he saw her wearing only a black strapless bra, black silk thong underwear and sheer black thigh-high stockings. "You don't make it easy on a guy, do you?"

Caroline's smile was purely female and as old as time. "I'm glad you like it," she purred, reaching for his belt and unfastening it, sliding the leather through the loops. When she reached for the waistband of his slacks, she started to falter.

Cooper brushed her hands away and finished the job. After that, all he cared about was touching Caroline and kissing her for the rest of his life. Starting now.

The soft cotton sheets caught them as they tumbled onto the bed. Caroline's bra soon ended up on the floor, and Cooper's boxers followed.

"No one should be so beautiful," he muttered, cupping her breast in his hand. "How did I get so lucky to be with you?"

"I'm the lucky one." She gasped his name as his mouth covered her nipple. She arched up when his teeth lightly grazed the sensitive skin. Pleased with her unrestrained response, he repeated the action.

Cooper discovered her skin was living silk and her mouth a temptation he was helpless to resist.

For someone so bold before, she seemed almost shy as her hands moved lower. But her smile wasn't. When she lifted her head to look at him, her eyes blazed with emerald fires.

"I want you, Cooper Night Hawk, as I have never wanted anyone before," she whispered.

He pulled open the nightstand drawer and withdrew a foil packet. Caroline took it out of his hands and with agonizing slowness covered his erection.

Cooper rolled until Caroline was lying against the pillows and he loomed over her. He nudged her knees apart and moved between them. While he wanted nothing more than to bury himself in her, he still wanted to take his time. He began dropping kisses along her collarbone and down across the curve of her breasts. She twisted and turned beneath him, begging for more. As he moved down to the dark blond thatch of hair, he felt her shocked surprise the moment his mouth covered her sensitive area. She reared up as if she was about to protest, but a flutter of his tongue against her shot that idea right out of her mind.

"Cooper!" she almost screamed.

"Just wait…" He alternately soothed and inflamed her, finding the glistening nub of sensitivity and laving it with the rough surface of his tongue.

Not until then did he move back up, kissing her rib cage along the way. As he lowered himself into her welcoming softness he felt her surround him like a taut velvet glove. Had anyone ever felt so perfect? It was only as he gently thrust forward that he realized there was something unexpected to impede his progress. Stunned by what he knew had to be there, he reflexively started to draw back.

"Cooper," she moaned, grabbing hold of him and arching up at the same time. Her eyes widened to saucer size when he was fully buried inside her.

He took several deep breaths, waiting until he felt her fully relax under him. He felt as if every muscle in his body was strung tight, but he still made shallow thrusts.

When he felt her contract around him, he felt himself falling into the abyss of pure sensation that threatened to set them both aflame.

"Thank you," she whispered in his ear.

CAROLINE HAD NEVER FELT so good. She couldn't stop smiling. But then, looking at Cooper had her smiling all the time. Feeling a bit shy about her nudity, she reached for his shirt and pulled it on. She carefully rolled the sleeves up to her elbows and buttoned enough buttons to feel covered. She ran her fingers through her hair in hopes it didn't look too much like a rat's nest, grimacing as her fingers encountered a couple of snarls.

She felt a bit sorry that Cooper didn't recover as quickly as she did. In fact, he lay against the pillows looking dazed. Her fingers itched to comb the dark, silky strands that stood out against the white pillowcase. She would have given in to temptation if it wasn't for the faint look of accusation on his face. She didn't want to think that expression was for her.

"So, was it good for you?" She fell back on the time honored cliché in hopes she could lighten the darkness crossing his face.

"Why didn't you tell me?" His quietly voiced question had a bit of a sting to it.

She knew this was a time to keep a little distance. She sat up with her fingers laced in her lap.

"If you think about it, it's not exactly a normal topic of conversation between two people," she replied. "I'm not going to date a person and say 'Oh, by the way, I'm a virgin.'"

"Some men would like nothing more than to know a woman's a virgin."

"And others don't."

"Because it's a big responsibility." His voice hardened. "Dammit, Caroline, I would have been more careful. Gone slower. Given you more time."

"More time for what? And as for going slower, I would have started screaming and—"

"You did scream," he murmured.

She shot him a look that strongly suggested he remain quiet. "All right, maybe I haven't had any prior experience in this field, but I'd say you did everything more than right. I couldn't breathe. I felt as if every nerve ending in my body was on fire. I saw God!" Her voice rose with every word until her declaration ended in a soft shriek.

Cooper's mouth twitched at each corner. Pretty soon they turned up.

Caroline's mouth dropped open in shock. "Damn you, Cooper Night Hawk, do not laugh!" She started lightly hitting his chest. She could feel the faint rumble under her hands and knew the laugh was just about ready to erupt.

Before she could react, Cooper pulled her down onto his chest, wrapping his arms around her when she tried to pull away. His laughter was rough and low in her ears as he nuzzled her neck.

"Do you know how many joke books I've read?" she mourned.

"I practically jumped through hoops to get you to even smile, and now you're sitting here laughing. This is not right."

"There were times it wasn't easy not to laugh at some of your antics, but I have a reputation as a unsmiling sort of guy," he admitted. "Yes, I was upset you hadn't told me. A woman's first time is important. It needs to be special."

"It was special," she insisted, pushing herself up off his chest. "No one could have done everything just right. I will remember this for the rest of my life because of you." *And I'll remember you.* "I wanted you to be the one."

"A little hint still would have been nice," he said, starting to relent.

"Too late now." She flopped back down onto his chest and rubbed her nose against his neck, inhaling the musky scent of his skin. She felt as if it had been imprinted onto her own. A very nice feeling, indeed. Her former sense of serenity was turning into something more elemental.

The heat of Cooper's skin seared her palms and she noticed the heat flaring in his eyes. He grasped her hips and pulled her over on top of him until she sat in the cradle of his hips. When she felt his hardness against her, she couldn't resist a little wiggle in that direction. Cooper's groan told her she'd done the right thing. He ran his hand up her bare thigh. As the shirttail hiked up, he noticed several dark spots on her hip. He lifted the shirt for a better look.

"What happened here?"

She looked down. "Oh, those. I'd like to say moles, but they don't even look close." She looked embarrassed. "Actually, they were supposed to be a rubber duck."

"A rubber duck?" Now Cooper was thoroughly confused.

Caroline shifted her position, momentarily unaware of what her movements were doing to him.

"It was my eighteenth birthday. Two friends and I decided we were going to get a tattoo. I had a thing about rubber ducks and decided that's what I wanted." She wiggled when his fingers gently touched the dark spots. "One friend got a rose. Another got a butterfly and I got these spots because I discovered very quickly I was a total wuss when it came to needles. My dad just about laughed himself silly when he found out. He said he was surprised I got as far as I did, since I hate needles so much. We won't talk about what happened every time I had to have a shot." She wrinkled her nose.

Cooper chuckled. "Too bad. A rubber duck would have looked cute there." His hand did some additional wandering.

Caroline found herself responding to the skillful manipulation of his fingers.

"And here I thought there was a lengthy recovery time for men," she murmured, lowering her mouth to his.

"I think I've created a sex maniac," he said before he showed her just how incredible it was when she was allowed to be in charge.

"Don't worry," she murmured, nipping at his lower lip. "I'll be gentle."

COOPER SHOULD HAVE BEEN dead. After the past few hours, any other man would have been ready to be buried, with a big smile on his face.

For a beginner, Caroline caught on fast. She was passionate, inventive and knew just how to turn a guy inside out with a sensual combination of hands and lips.

For now, she appeared to be content to lie curled up against him. She still wore his shirt, now a mass of wrinkles. All traces of makeup were gone from her face, and he knew if she saw her hair, she'd probably shriek. But to him, she'd never looked more beautiful. The color in her cheeks was from their lovemaking, and her deep sleep was a result of the same. He should have been ready to sleep, too, but he preferred remaining awake. He didn't want to lose any of this time with her by succumbing to sleep.

She stirred and opened her eyes. "What time is it?" She rubbed the sleep out of her eyes and half sat up.

He glanced over at the glowing digital clock. "A little after three."

Caroline combed her fingers through her hair and winced when she encountered a snag. Not wanting to cause herself any more discomfort, she gave up trying to restore order to her hair. She stretched her arms over her head and seemed to reach for the ceiling.

"You men are all alike," she said lazily, dropping her arms to her sides.

"Meaning?"

"Meaning, you were looking at my breasts. And don't say you weren't," she warned, with a narrowing of her eyes.

"I was admiring how well my shirt fit you," he retorted, defending himself.

She lifted sleeves that had been folded back several times, plucked the front of the shirt away from her chest to show how much larger it was, and shrugged shoulders the shirt literally hung off of.

"Oh yes, it fits perfectly." She struck a model's pose. Her arms suddenly dropped. A trace of uncertainty shadowed her eyes. As if she realized it was there, she swiftly masked it with a smile that didn't quite ring true.

What's really going on in that mind of yours, Caroline? Cooper asked himself catching the look that passed so quickly across her face. *Why can't you tell me what you're really looking for?*

Please, God, all I ask is that she isn't playing me for a fool.

He ignored whatever doubts he felt and pulled her

down to him. The need to touch her was strong, as if his fingers on her skin could divine her secrets.

"Caroline Benning, you are quite a woman."

He had no idea her pleasure in his words was dimmed by the fact that he hadn't spoken her real name.

Caroline clung to him the way a drowning victim would cling to a life raft. In her mind, that was just what she felt like. Drowning.

She was relieved as time passed and he didn't seem to sense her scattered thoughts. Instead, he spoke of the cabin his father had built for his young wife. The plans that had been made for more rooms when their family expanded with a baby son. Instead, the parents had died and a father and mother mourned their deaths and took a young boy into their home. When Cooper grew older, he built a cabin of his own a short distance from his grandparents. It proved a good idea when his grandmother died. His grandfather could still live on his own, but Cooper had the security of knowing he was nearby.

Caroline looked at the clock again.

"I should get back to the Kelseys before breakfast," she said reluctantly. "I don't want them to think...." Her voice fell off.

"They won't think the worst of you," he assured her, as he climbed out of the bed. "Just let me get dressed."

Caroline couldn't keep her eyes off his body as he rummaged through drawers for clothing. The muscles in his buttocks flexed with his movements as he pulled on a pair of boxers, then jeans and a dark blue T-shirt.

He gathered up her clothing and handed it to her.

"I'll make some coffee." He left her alone.

Caroline was grateful for his sensitivity. She decided she'd used up her quota of bold measures for at least the next ten years. Besides, she wasn't as comfortable walking around nude in front of him as he had been with her.

"And who knows how many others have seen him that way," she muttered, balling up her stockings and tucking them inside her purse.

She made the mistake of going into the bathroom and catching a glimpse of herself in the mirror.

"You lied to him," she whispered to her reflection. "The woman he thinks you are is nothing but a lie." Sniffing, she grabbed a tissue and blew her nose. She cursed under her breath as she looked at the raccoon eyes looking back at her.

"That's the last time I use that mascara," she grumbled, using a tissue and water to scrub out the dark stains. She picked up the toothpaste tube, squeezed a line onto her forefinger and scrubbed her teeth. She fought with her hair, gave up the battle and left the room.

When she entered the main room, she found Cooper in the kitchen filling two mugs with coffee. He turned at her entrance and handed her a cup.

She sipped cautiously.

"You okay?"

His quietly spoken question brought her head upward.

"Fine. Very good." Her voice strengthened with the knowledge his question was sincere. "I'm just not familiar with all the rules."

"There are no rules." He wrapped his hand around the nape of her neck. "We do what feels right. I'd say this feels very right." He brushed a light kiss across her lips. "Now I guess we should get you back to the Kelseys'."

Caroline was aware of the quiet in town as Cooper drove down the empty streets. When they pulled into the driveway of the boardinghouse, she noticed the light that

Anna kept on in the kitchen in case anyone wanted a late night snack.

She turned to Cooper. There were so many things she wanted to say to him, starting with the truth about who she was and why she was in Tyler.

"Thank you for dinner," was all she said.

Cooper's smile flashed white in the darkness. "Thank you." His voice held a great deal of meaning she couldn't miss.

"I think *I'm* the one who created a monster." She stole a quick kiss before he got out of the truck and helped her down.

"See you at dinner," he told her, waiting until she entered the house.

Caroline waited until she heard the truck drive away. Holding her shoes in one hand she stealthily crept up the back stairs to her room.

When she crawled into bed, she draped her mother's quilt over her. As she fell sleep she relived every second spent in Cooper's arms. The only flaw in her memories was him calling her Caroline Benning.

She wondered how much longer she could keep up the charade.

And if Cooper would hate her when he learned the truth.

COOPER WOULDN'T HAVE minded another ten hours sleep, but the incessant beeping of his alarm reminded him it wasn't to be.

The homey aroma of coffee and waffles wasn't expected. He pulled on a pair of jeans and wandered out to the kitchen, where he found Laughing Bear standing in front of the stove. The elderly man should have looked ridiculous brandishing a spatula and wearing a dish towel tucked in his waistband, but his quiet dignity carried it off. Laughing Bear took one look at him and handed him a mug filled with coffee.

Since Cooper couldn't remember the last time his grandfather had showed up and cooked breakfast for him, he knew there had to be a good reason for the older man to turn up this particular morning. He had a pretty good idea why, too.

Cooper sat at the small table while his grandfather set a plate loaded with a waffle and bacon in front of him. A mug of warm syrup was next. Laughing Bear set another plate down and sat across from his grandson.

"She stole your heart."

Cooper shook his head violently. "Nobody steals my heart," he corrected.

Laughing Bear stared at him for a long time. "Then you gave it to her. Just as she gave you hers."

"Not even close."

"Remember our great Sauk chief, Black Hawk?"

"Not all that well," Cooper said dryly. "Probably because he died a good hundred years ago."

Laughing Bear ignored his sarcasm. "His grandson, Night Hawk, dreamed of the hawk. In the dream the hawk presented his own feather, which meant the chief would have to make a great sacrifice. And in the dream Night Hawk joined with Amanda, the Woman of the River."

Cooper tried not to think of the times he'd joined with Caroline the previous night.

"I haven't dreamed of the hawk, Grandfather," he said quietly. "Your stories have always been very good, but now they're meant more at bedtime for children. I'm sorry, they don't reflect real life." Even though he didn't believe in the tales, he wouldn't hurt his grandfather's feelings by scoffing at them. "Caroline may have been here for some months, but that doesn't mean she won't get tired of small town life and leave. She's not at all like Amanda. Besides, who says I'd make a good husband?" Not that he even dared think that far ahead.

Laughing Bear shook his head. "You are talking about things you have not thought about thoroughly. You also forget you can be anything you wish to be as long as you are dedicated to working hard to attain your goals. Caroline will not leave Tyler unless she is driven out. She cannot leave when it would mean she would leave her heart behind. If she has your heart, then you have hers. I think after last night, you have shared more than your hearts."

Cooper felt the heat of embarrassment infuse his cheeks. "That subject isn't up for discussion." He snagged a third waffle from the rapidly dwindling pile.

Laughing Bear wasn't insulted by the younger man's brusque statement. He wasn't even surprised by it. The small smile touching his lips warned Cooper he'd gotten just the reaction he'd expected.

"You and your Spirits have way too much time on your hands," Cooper muttered.

"Not at all. We enjoyed watching the stars last night. The night was very clear."

Cooper studied his grandfather's face. He dreaded to ask the question.

"The chair on my porch needs a new cushion, but it was still very comfortable," Laughing Bear continued.

Cooper got up and retrieved the coffeepot, bringing it back to the table.

"She's very special to me," he conceded finally.

Laughing Bear smiled. "Yes, she is. Remember that, Cooper, because I see days ahead that will be dark for the two of you. But I know everything will turn out all right."

Cooper blew out an exasperated breath. "Have you been calling that psychic hotline again?"

"Not this time."

CAROLINE WOKE UP TOO LATE for breakfast, but managed a cup of coffee and a couple of muffins. Not that she was all that hungry.

Anna's smile was knowing, but the older woman refrained from asking any questions.

Not wanting to stay indoors, Caroline filled a sports bottle with iced tea and gathered up her collection of articles about the Spencer men and a book. With everything in hand, she walked over to the square. With no one else there, she easily found a bench that gave her a good view of the interconnecting streets and the sidewalk leading to the substation a half block off the square. She knew Cooper didn't start his shift until later in the day, but she could hope.

With her sunglasses perched on her nose, the world took on a hazy gray color. She smiled and watched a couple of little boys running across the grass and a frazzled mother chasing them. Her threats of what she'd do to her erring sons when she caught them sounded dire, but Caroline knew the words were empty. Not when she was laughing as hard as her boys. Without warning, thoughts of what Cooper's sons would look like stole into her mind.

Musings of Cooper brought memories long forgotten. Erratic thoughts about friends who'd made love with a boyfriend, only to have said boyfriend never call them again, crowded her mind. She didn't fear that would happen with Cooper.

She only had to recall the ferocity in his expression when he'd entered her. The way he looked at her, as if she was the only woman in the world, told her just how he felt. And it echoed her own feelings.

The day was warm and sunny, but she felt even warmer. A good kind of warm.

She kicked off her sandals and sat cross-legged on the bench with the pouch filled with the articles next to her.

Suddenly, reading about the Spencers didn't seem all that important. She sipped her iced tea, then lifted her face to the sun while stretching her arms along the back of the bench with her fingers dangling downward.

"Is this what they mean when they say someone is worshipping the sun? Or is this purely a California activity?"

Caroline turned her head.

"Hello, Mrs. Bauer," she greeted the older woman. "I don't think it's strictly for Californians, although I guess we're blamed for it the most. It's nice over here in the mornings, isn't it?"

"Very nice," she agreed.

Caroline quickly straightened up. "Please, have a seat."

Martha sat down, placing her canvas shopping bag on the ground by her feet.

"What did you think of Timberlake Lodge?"

Caroline was afraid she was blushing. Dinner wasn't what she was thinking about when it came to last night.

"It's a fascinating building with all the history it holds," she replied. "I'm more used to California history, which has a Spanish background. Whereas the town here was settled by Swedish and Irish immigrants."

Martha nodded. "Yes, the Ingallses and the Kelseys. We're very proud of Tyler's beginnings. Has your family always lived in California?"

Caroline shook her head. "We moved there when I was a few months old."

"That's a shame, because after grief subsides a little, you discover that the familiar can offer comfort." She looked around the square, nodded a silent greeting to one couple who walked past them.

"I was never told why we moved," Caroline said.

Martha looked at her, seeming to study her closely. "You're very lovely and obviously intelligent. Why are you working for Marge when you could clearly do so much more?"

"I've learned that waitresses need a lot of smarts along with a good sense of balance if carrying a lot of plates. And it's not a good idea to spill anything on your customers," she confided. "This is challenge enough for now."

Martha glanced at her watch. "I must be getting back to Worthington House. I volunteered to go out and pick up thread we need for our latest quilt."

Caroline saw an opening. "Anna said the tradition of Tyler quilts has been around for some time. Does the Quilting Circle make quite a few a year?"

"We don't think about making a certain number a year. The quilts we make are given as gifts or donated for special causes." Martha reached down for her bag and stood up. "Perhaps sometime you'll stop by the house and see what we have."

"I'd like that," Caroline said sincerely. "Mrs. Bauer? When your group gives someone a quilt, do you do anything special to it?"

"Such as?"

"I don't know. Sew a label on it somewhere. Maybe embroider a name on it."

"We've done that, yes. I know of many quilters who

do." She patted Caroline's shoulder. "Have a nice day, dear."

Caroline watched Martha walk slowly down the path leading to the square. She only had to ask the woman one simple question—would she look at Caroline's quilt? So why did she hesitate?

She'd been here long enough that she felt comfortable around most residents of Tyler. Even if she still felt a little uneasy in the vicinity of any of the Spencers.

It was getting to the time when she would have to talk to someone about it.

Even considering his friendship with the Spencers, she knew her most obvious choice was still Cooper. She could sit him down and explain everything to him. Ask him what would be the best way to handle her problem. If anyone would know how to approach Elias Spencer, it would be Cooper.

Suddenly, the sun didn't feel as warm and inviting as it had before. Her muscles felt tight, and her enjoyment of a pleasant morning was a thing of the past.

More and more she regretted the lie she'd started to spin the first day she arrived here.

Chapter Nine

Dammit, he didn't want her here tonight! Couldn't she understand that she wasn't to visit him anymore? Obviously no one had told her she wasn't welcome.

She should have looked lonely as she stood alone in the deepening mist. Instead, she looked filled with anticipation. She turned as if sensing his presence and held out her hand, beckoning to him. The gown she wore was ethereal, the color of new mown grass. The same color as her eyes, which smiled as they watched him.

He still held back. He couldn't take her hand. Taking it was dangerous. Besides, it was a dream! She was not real!

As if she realized his anger was directed toward her, her smile dimmed. Her hand dropped to her side and she stepped back. She turned around and disappeared into the mist.

"You're not real!" he shouted. "Not real!"

"Not real!" He shot up in bed.

"Cooper?" A cool hand rested on his shoulder.

He couldn't speak. He felt each labored breath echo loudly inside his head as he fought to regulate his out-of-control respiration. He felt the sweat pouring down his chest, chilling him in the night air.

"Cooper, are you all right?" Panic tinged the voice.
Caroline.

They'd gone to the movies, but sitting in close proximity only caused problems. Cooper didn't want popcorn. He wanted Caroline. It took only one glance to see she felt the same way. He muttered that the movie would be out on video in six months or so anyway, and they'd fled the theater.

They left a trail of clothing from the door to his bed. Cooper had fallen asleep with Caroline curled up in his arms. He hadn't expected the dream to visit him tonight.

"Sorry, bad dream," he muttered.

She scooted around on the bed until she was kneeling by his side. "It must have been some nightmare to do this to you." She brushed his hair away from his face, noting the sheen of sweat on his skin. "Sweetheart, you're drenched." She picked up a corner of the sheet and dried his face.

Cooper clenched his hands as he fought to expel the last remnants of the dream from his mind.

"Cooper?" Sensing his turmoil, she framed his face with her hands and tried to soothe him with the light touch of her fingers. "What on earth did you dream that upset you so much?"

He shook his head. There was no way in hell he would discuss it with her, of all people.

"I can't remember," he lied, not wanting to even think about it for fear it would recur.

"Well, whatever it was, it really shook you up," she said, accepting his untruth. She reached for his T-shirt, dropping it over her head before she climbed off the bed. She switched on the bathroom light and disappeared inside.

Cooper fell back against his pillow, still feeling the mad racing of his blood.

He couldn't understand why the dream affected him so strongly this time. The woman in the mist had never disappeared that way before. He didn't need to close his eyes to see the sadness in her eyes when he told her he didn't believe in her.

"This should help." Caroline plopped back down on the bed. She stroked his heated skin with the damp washcloth.

He took a chance and closed his eyes as the cool cloth passed across his eyelids. Luckily, nothing appeared.

"Funny thing," she said softly, "but I never thought of you as someone who would have nightmares. Me, that's a different story. I eat pizza too late at night and I'm dreaming that the Mozzarella Man is chasing me."

He smiled. He was discovering that he was doing that a lot when he was around her. "Mozzarella Man? Remind me to never feed you pizza past 8:00 p.m."

She combed her fingers through his hair, smoothing the damp tangled, strands. "I wouldn't think anything could frighten you," she murmured. "You're always so in control. I guess I'd think that nightmares would be scared of you."

"Maybe it was too much popcorn." He removed the washcloth and opened his eyes. The look of worry shadowing her eyes was humbling. "I'm sorry I woke you up."

"Don't be," she argued. "Actually, I'm glad I was here. I wouldn't like to think you would have woken up alone." She curled up next to him with her legs tucked under her.

Cooper stared at the shadows dancing against the wall,

realizing there must be a breeze outside, ruffling the tree branches to life.

Usually he would go outside and allow nature to destroy the last of his dream. Most of the time he was alone. Sometimes Laughing Bear would appear, as if he knew of his grandson's emotional unrest and felt his presence would soothe the demons driving him.

Tonight, he settled for the comfort of Caroline's arms around him and the scent of her skin to soothe him. He was afraid to return her embrace for fear he'd hold on so tightly she'd be spooked by the intensity.

As he'd abandoned the woman in the mist.

"You've had this dream before, haven't you?"

He was floored by her insight. Had any woman read him as easily as Caroline did?

"Sometimes." He settled for a half-truth. "Maybe I've been working too hard."

"Or there's something that's bothering you a lot," she murmured. "I once read that about recurring dreams. That there's a message there."

He swallowed the laugh that crawled up his throat. If she only knew that the dream had to do with her, and that each time he saw the woman in the mist he felt a stronger urge to take her hand and see what was beyond the that swirling wall.

He'd lied about it in his heart for too long. The woman in the mist was Caroline. She might not look like her, but in his heart, he knew she was.

Even if he was the one who'd originally brought it on himself, this was a complication he didn't need in his life. Not when there were times he felt he didn't know the real Caroline Benning.

"I feel like I should do more," she murmured. "Sing

you to sleep or something. But if I started singing, we'd have wolves in the next four states howling.''

"Tone deaf?'' he asked, realizing she'd imparted one more tiny fact about herself.

"That's probably a kind way of putting it.'' She scrunched down under the covers and rested her head against his chest. By now he felt more able to hold her. "I'm safe with humming as long as I don't break out into song.''

"Okay, no sing-alongs for you.'' He realized what she was doing. Talking about normal everyday things. If they were nonsensical, that was fine, because it would get his mind off why he woke up.

Besides, it felt good. It was the middle of the night and they were able to lie there talking about anything and everything. He couldn't remember the last time he'd been able to relax that much with a woman. Come to think of it, he didn't think he'd ever allowed himself that luxury. Probably because he feared he would give away a part of himself that he dare not expose.

What was it about Caroline that had him doing so many things he hadn't even thought of before?

It wasn't until then that he realized her eyes were closed and her breathing deep.

"And sweet dreams for you,'' he whispered, keeping his arms wrapped around her. When he finally closed his own eyes, he instinctively knew the woman wouldn't return to torment his sleep.

At least, not tonight.

"TELL ME, CAROLINE, should I act the father figure and ask Cooper about his intentions?'' Johnny asked one morning during breakfast.

"Johnny..." Anna warned him in a voice that brooked no argument.

Caroline waved her off.

"I think it's sweet that you're worried about me, Johnny," she said to him. "But you can put your mind at rest. Cooper is always a perfect gentleman when we go out. Dating a cop means you're safe." She started in surprise when Anna stood behind her and casually straightened her collar. Then she remembered she'd worn the mock turtleneck to hide the love bite Cooper had left on her neck the previous night. Always considerate, she'd bestowed one on him, too. But being considerate, she'd made sure it wouldn't be easily seen.

"Johnny tends to forget our children have lives of their own and that he needs to keep his nose in his own business," Anna said, shooting a warning glare in her husband's direction. "Perhaps it's because he doesn't have enough to do. Mother called earlier and said she needed someone with muscles to help move a few pieces of furniture around. I told her you would be over there as soon as you finished breakfast." She stared at his empty plate.

Johnny groaned. He hunched down in his chair. "Not again! Remember the last time? Those ladies had me move a couch six times because they couldn't agree on where it should be. I couldn't move for a week after that afternoon."

"That's my big strong man," Anna said approvingly, pulling him up out of his chair. "You don't have to worry. They don't need a couch moved this time." She firmly pushed him out the back door and closed it after him.

"That was one smooth maneuver," Caroline exclaimed in admiration.

Anna's eyes twinkled. "He won't think so when he gets over there and finds out they want to move the furniture around in the main room.'' She walked over to a cabinet and rummaged through the contents. She pulled out a bottle and showed it to Caroline.

"Liniment? They have really nice muscle rubs out now that don't smell like, well, like that."

"But not as effective. He'll come limping home, whispering that he'll never be able to move again and I'll tell him it couldn't have been done without him. And his mind will be off your love life for a while," Anna explained.

Caroline shifted uneasily.

"I never thought of interfering in Jenna's love life, and no matter how badly I want to play mother figure I promise to remain out of yours, dear," she declared. "I think you have enough on your plate dealing with Cooper."

Caroline unconsciously touched the side of her neck. The mark was small and would fade, but she knew the memory wouldn't. It was almost as if a primitive force had overtaken them last night. At the time she'd felt as if the mark was a brand, his proclaiming she was his. She felt the only thing to do was return the favor by marking him as hers.

For a former virgin, she'd wasted no time in discovering that she enjoyed having a sex life. Especially when the man she was involved with was Cooper. She already couldn't imagine anyone else in her life.

She had no idea a smile tipped the corners of her lips upward and her eyes turned dreamy.

Anna took one look at the expression on her face and turned away. She easily read what Caroline was thinking about. She'd done it many a time in the past. Still did. She firmly believed her Johnny only got better with age.

Caroline flashed her a quick smile and ran up the stairs.

She realized she'd let some things slide lately. Being with Cooper tended to do that to her. She sorted out books that needed to be returned to the library, clothing to be dropped off at the cleaners and, with a blush, made a note to pick up her birth control pills at the drugstore. She would have a busy day until she reported for work.

"Clean linens," Anna loudly announced as she knocked on Caroline's door.

Caroline quickly opened the door and took the sheets and towels from Anna's arms. She never minded helping out, and cleaning her room never took much time for her. She set the small pile in the nearby chair.

Anna walked over to the bed and lightly touched the quilt, which was carefully draped over the footboard.

"Did you say you received this from your father, dear?" she murmured. "The pattern reminds me of some of the quilts the Circle has made. I know my mother would be interested in seeing it."

Caroline held her breath, but luckily the older woman didn't pick it up. Caroline always folded it so the embroidered corner was well hidden.

"It's a family heirloom," she explained. "My father passed it down to me."

Anna's expression grew puzzled as she carefully traced the rows of tiny stitches that linked the pattern into one whole.

She straightened up and smiled brightly. "It's nice to see some young people value what's been handed down to them. A tradition you can carry on with your children. And, of course—" her smile grew a trace sly "—the time will come when you'll have your husband's family traditions to add to your own."

"Let's just hope that my husband will have some nice traditions to add to the list." She could feel the blush travel up her cheeks as Anna continued smiling, this time knowingly. "Anna, you're doing what Johnny did," she said gently. "Just differently."

"Habits are hard to break when you've had daughters." Anna glanced down at the quilt again. "And some still see you as a bit of a mystery woman. Someone who drove into town and decided to stay. Young people are usually eager to leave Tyler, not stay."

Caroline still found it difficult to confide in anyone. She'd known that keeping the quilt out would raise questions once Anna saw it. That's why, in the beginning, she'd kept it on the shelf in the closet and only brought it out at night, keeping it around her the way she kept a teddy bear by her when she was little.

"I guess I've always been a bit of a rebel," she replied.

Anna smiled. She patted Caroline's shoulder as she walked out of the room.

Caroline paced the room as if moving would help soothe her chaotic thoughts.

Whenever she and Cooper were together, she thought of telling him the entire story. Of asking him to help her to speak to Elias Spencer. It ate her up inside that she hadn't confided in him yet. She tried to rationalize it by saying the time never seemed right. Any time they spoke of personal matters, she imparted only a little more of herself. She never said a word that would give even a hint that her real name was Caroline Bennedict.

She laced and unlaced her fingers. Agitation boiled up inside her like acid. She never liked keeping secrets. Her kind of secrets meant lies, and she never was very good at those, either. It was only during these past few months that she'd learned she could keep secrets, after all.

Secrets from a man she feared she'd fallen in love with. Secrets that, when revealed, could turn him against her.

She turned away from the window. Her thoughts were

so jumbled, she hadn't seen anything in any case. The first thing she noticed was the quilt. The bright colors taunted her. The names stitched in one corner seemed to scream accusations at her.

Caroline began to think she shouldn't have come to Tyler. She should have remained in Santa Barbara, grieved for her father and gone on with her life. She should have stayed where she had familiar surroundings and friends who would have been there for her. Why had she felt the need to travel across the country to learn about a mother she never knew?

But she hadn't thought clearly once she found the quilt. Instead, she'd torn her father's home office apart looking for anything that would tell her why he had hid from her a quilt with her mother's name on it. When she found the name Tyler, Wisconsin, she'd wasted no time in closing up the house her father had left her, tossing clothing in a few suitcases and, with the aid of road maps, starting off to find out about her mother and the other names on the quilt.

In all the time she'd spent in Tyler, what had she learned about Violet Spencer?

That she'd moved here with her husband and three sons twenty-odd years ago.

That not long after, she'd divorced her husband, left her sons behind and left Tyler to be with Caroline's father, whom she'd been having an affair with.

When Caroline added it up, it didn't come to very much.

That left her with two choices.

She could leave Tyler and go back home. Take back the life she had there. After a while, it would be as if she'd never left. Her friends would see to that. At least, that was what she told herself. But it would never be as it was.

Because she wasn't the same person she'd been a year ago.

Or she could remain here as Caroline Benning. Work at Marge's, even see what would happen with Cooper.

She felt whole when she was with him. She enjoyed seeing the rare smiles that lit up his face. Perhaps because the only time she saw them was when they were alone. He still didn't smile in public. She was content with that. As the joke about Cooper went, it was easy to know when he was in a good mood. He didn't shoot anyone.

Not to say he might not be tempted when Caroline finally found the courage to tell him all.

"JENNA AND SETH ARE having a party in a couple of weeks, to celebrate the twins' birth," Cooper told Caroline as she set a filled coffee mug in front of him at the diner. "I'm sure Jenna already invited you. But I thought I'd see if you wanted to go with me."

"*You* want to go to a party? You do understand what parties are, don't you? Lots of people in one place. The whole socializing bit—like the dance, but no dancing at this. And you want to do this? Are you sure you wouldn't rather take someone else's shift?" she teased.

He looked pained but endured her gentle goading.

"If I did, you'd just go without me."

"Don't worry, I'll save you a piece of cake." She wrote on her order pad. There was never a need to ask him what he wanted, since he was as predictable as the sun rising in the east each morning.

Funny thing, she'd never thought predictable was exciting. She was learning that Cooper gave predictable a whole new meaning.

He reached out and took her hand. His gesture surprised her, since he'd never before made any kind of public display that intimated a personal relationship.

"I'll make the sacrifice," he said in a dry tone that told her just what he thought of her teasing.

"You're so good to me," she cooed before whirling away.

Cooper watched her move among her customers, pausing to see if others needed something and refilling coffee mugs. Every time he watched her he could see why she was so popular with everyone in the diner.

No wonder Henry Farris kept trying to look down her blouse.

Her smile alone cast a bright light across each table. She had a smile he never tired of seeing. Especially when it was directed at him. It was one he could handle having directed at him for a long time.

"Damn," he said under his breath as the truth hit him like a four-by-four.

He was doing just what he'd feared was the worst thing that could happen to him right now.

God help him, he was falling in love with her.

Chapter Ten

"I don't do this," Cooper protested, facing her down with his steeliest cop stare. Not that it did any good.

"Of course you do," Caroline insisted.

"No, I don't."

"Yes, you do," she said, undeterred by the finality in his voice.

"Not really."

"Why not?"

Cooper sighed. He should have known better than to think Caroline would just accept his statement at face value and let it go at that.

He looked around. Everyone in the diner appeared to be absorbed either in the morning newspaper or in conversation with meal partners. He knew better. Every ear was trained on his and Caroline's conversation.

He'd come into Marge's for breakfast because he knew Caroline was only working the breakfast shift and then would be off for the rest of the day. He thought about seeing if she wanted to take a drive. Find someplace to stop for lunch. He'd even wander through some antique shops with her.

That was when he told her he had the rest of the day free and suggested they might go for a nice drive. He knew he'd said the right thing when her face lit up with pleasure.

Then she suggested that along with the drive they find a spot for a picnic.

Cooper considered himself the typical male who didn't enjoy shopping, but was willing to do it every so often to make his lady happy. He'd even lug all her purchases around for her.

Picnics were another matter.

The gleam in Caroline's eyes warned him she knew just what he was thinking. Her gorgeous smile was another warning. He steeled himself for the worst.

"I bet you know lots of beautiful secluded places where we can have our picnic," she said in a sly tone that silently dared him to protest the idea.

"I'll make up a nice lunch for you two," Marge offered, raising her voice enough to be heard by all.

"You're really enjoying this, aren't you?" he said to Caroline between clenched teeth.

"Oh yes," she replied. "You're not going to disappoint all these people, are you, Cooper?"

"Pretty soon you'll probably invite them along," he muttered.

"Did I tell you about a dream I once had?" she asked conversationally, as if he wasn't scowling at her.

"You dreamed about a picnic? We didn't do anything weird, did we?" he asked warily, only too familiar with the surprises she'd come up with before.

"More like just you and me in this beautiful deserted meadow. Half-naked," she whispered. "Did I tell you this was an incredibly sexy dream?"

Cooper closed his eyes, then quickly opened them again before images she'd painted became permanently adhered to his eyelids.

"There wasn't one ant there," she continued.

He cursed the heavy material of his uniform. It wasn't allowing him to breathe.

"Thanks for the offer, Marge," he called out suddenly. "We'll take a lunch with us."

The woman smirked and turned away.

"Took a girl on a picnic once," Henry Farris announced in a loud voice. He'd forgotten his hearing aid again and forgot that everyone could hear him just fine without him shouting the words. "Went wading in a pond but she fell in and got all wet. Had to take off her clothes, so they could dry out. Her pa wasn't too happy about that." He fingered the pocket in his coveralls, looking for his pipe. But when he caught Marge's warning look, he left it where it was.

"Wasn't that Sadie Morton?" one of Henry's cronies asked. "Her pa went after you with his shotgun."

"He did, but I went in the army instead," Henry replied. "Met my Etta while I was overseas. I heard Sadie tried that falling in the pond trick with every man she went with in hopes of getting a husband. She finally landed Warren Morrisen over in Belton."

Cooper could see this was going to turn into a long-term discussion. "I'll keep her away from ponds," he said, getting up from his booth and walking over to the register.

"Stop by on your way out of town and I'll have a basket ready for you," Marge told him.

"I can see Caroline's not the only one enjoying this," he muttered, handing over the money for his breakfast.

"Why? Because she's turned our grumpy deputy into someone who almost smiles?" she teased.

He shook his head. He looked over and saw Caroline

juggling an armful of plates. "Would you do me a favor and tell her I'll pick her up in an hour?"

"No problem." Marge handed him his change. "It's not so painful, is it?"

"What?" he asked, distracted as he jammed his money in his pocket.

"Falling in love," she whispered with a sly smile.

Cooper muttered a curse. "Playing Cupid isn't your style, Marge," he growled, then escaped the diner before anything else was said.

He drove back to his cabin in record time, throwing off his uniform and taking a quick shower before dressing in jeans and a black T-shirt. He'd just picked up his wallet when he heard a vehicle outside. He walked over to a window to see who his visitor was. The last person he expected to see was Brady Spencer. The man wore wrinkled scrubs and looked tired.

"I didn't think doctors made house calls anymore," Cooper joked, stepping out onto the porch. Suddenly, the worst came to mind. "It's not my grandfather, is it?"

"My being here has nothing to do with Laughing Bear," Brady assured him. "I was just on my way home when I decided to stop by."

"I live in the opposite direction," he pointed out in a hard voice.

"I stopped in Marge's Diner for some breakfast and everyone's talking about Caroline talking you into a picnic." Brady looked off into the distance. "Cooper, I'm sorry. I made a mistake in asking you to check into Caroline. What I asked you wasn't right. I'm afraid she might be leading you on. Are you going out with her to see what you can find out? Or is there more going on?" He studied his friend's face, but Cooper was an expert at hiding his thoughts. "Come on, Cooper, is she that good in bed that you're blind to what could be going on?"

"Don't even go there, Brady." His low voice fairly vibrated with violent undertones.

The other man stared long and hard at Cooper. He didn't expect to find any clues, but something, maybe having been there at one time, told him what he needed to know.

"Damn."

Cooper didn't say a word.

"Damn," Brady repeated. "Is this a good idea?"

"Did I ask you if it was a good idea for you to get involved with Eden?" Cooper asked. "Did I tell you she deserved better than a doctor who went through women the way a person suffering from a cold goes through tissues?"

"There's something there," Brady maintained. "Deep down, I feel it."

"If there is, when the time is right, she'll say so. Until then, butt out," Cooper said in a hard voice.

Brady held up his hands in surrender. "I got it." His expression softened. "I just don't want you to get hurt."

Cooper cocked an eyebrow. "I've got a thick skin, Brady. I'll be fine." He pointedly glanced at his watch. "Now if you don't mind?"

Brady nodded and headed back to his car. "I just didn't want to think I might have made a mistake on your behalf."

"If Caroline breaks the law, I'll arrest her. Until then, she's allowed to walk around town," he said. "Remember, Brady. All she did was look at some family pictures."

Brady opened his car door and started to get inside. He halted and looked over the door. Whatever he was going to say was left unsaid. He slid behind the wheel and started up the engine.

Cooper remained on the porch until Brady drove away. By the time he drove off himself, ten minutes later, he felt a little sick to his stomach. It was all Brady Spencer's fault.

"YOU'RE NOT TOO MAD about having a picnic, are you?" Caroline asked after Cooper had picked her up. A picnic hamper was secured in the back of the truck, with everything packed in special containers to keep the food fresh. "I just thought it would be fun." She'd started to half turn in her seat with her legs drawn up under her when Cooper reminded her she needed to secure her seat belt.

From the moment he'd picked her up, she felt a one-hundred-eighty degree shift in his mood. At the diner, he'd been resigned, even a little amused, at her blatant attempt to set up a picnic. Now he appeared distracted. Almost angry. There was a faint furrow between his brows that she hadn't remembered seeing before.

She'd dressed with care, choosing a pink, cotton sleeveless dress she'd gotten on a shopping expedition the month before. She liked the way the full skirt floated around her calves, and the sweetheart neckline made her feel very feminine. She'd taken the time to curl her hair because she knew Cooper liked to wrap the curls around his fingertips. She didn't expect the picnic to end up the way her dream picnic had, but she could still hope for a quiet lazy day with a lot of cuddling.

Now she wasn't so sure.

"There's a flea market about fifty miles from here if you're interested," Cooper suggested. "I've never been there, but I hear it's a pretty good one."

"I'm sorry, Cooper, I shouldn't have pushed you into doing something you didn't want to do."

He took one look at her and quickly pulled the truck over to the side of the road.

"I'm the one who should be apologizing," he murmured. "I saw someone who put me in a bad mood, that's all. There was no reason to take it out on you. I guess I acted like a jerk about the picnic just because it was so much fun to watch you try to charm me into it." He used his fingers to tuck a stray curl behind her ear. His hand lingered to curve around the back of her head. "I promise I'll do better."

"If you don't behave, can I sic Laughing Bear on you?"

"Not in this lifetime."

Cooper pulled away and steered the truck back onto the road.

"You are not an easy man," she informed him. "You don't seem to understand the concept of just kicking back."

"You mean what we're doing today isn't kicking back?" he asked in mock shock.

"You really need to toss some of that old-fashioned work ethic and put more play into your life." Caroline dropped her arm out of the window, letting it wave to and fro in the air. "Otherwise, you're going to grow old before your time."

"Somehow, I can't see that happening," he said dryly.

An hour later, Cooper pulled into the parking lot for the flea market. He helped Caroline down from the truck. She spun in a circle, trying to see everything.

"Cool," she breathed, looking in the distance at what used to be a drive-in movie screen. "We have swap meets in some of our former drive-in movie theaters, since they're no longer used, and I guess in some areas no one wants to tear them down."

"This one is still used during the summer," he replied. He was almost jerked off his feet when she grabbed hold of his hand and dragged him toward the entrance of the market.

Cooper had no idea that suggesting the market would turn into a walking tour of every booth. When Caroline bragged she definitely shopped until she dropped, she meant it. She took her time inspecting the contents of each booth, pausing longer by ones that held something of interest to her.

She was looking at some jewelry when Cooper's cell phone rang.

"Deputy Night Hawk? This is Sergeant O'Connell of the Santa Barbara PD returning your call. You were looking for information on a Caroline Benning."

Cooper glanced furtively at Caroline. Of all times for this call to come through. "Yes, right. Look, can I ask you to hold for one second?" He hit the mute button on his phone and looked down at her. "I'm sorry, Caroline," he quickly said. "I've got to take this call." His eyes scanned the area and lit on a quiet corner behind the stalls. "I'll be over there. Just a minute, I promise."

After he left the crowd and Caroline behind, he deactivated the mute. "Yes, this is Night Hawk. Sorry to keep you waiting. What have you got for me?" He could see Caroline through the stalls, and he felt like a heel. Why was he investigating her? By now he'd forgotten his reasons, or Brady's. That was, until Sergeant O'Connell spoke again.

"Well, it's more like what I haven't got. We have no record whatsoever of a Caroline Benning here in Santa Barbara."

"What?" Cooper felt confused. "You're sure?"

The sergeant remained patient. "Absolutely. We've checked all records." As if sensing Cooper's disappointment, he said, "I'm sorry. But let us know if we can help any further."

As if on automatic pilot, Cooper hit the end button. He looked at Caroline and saw her smiling warmly as she spoke to the jewelry maker. *What's going on, Caroline?*

He kept his question to himself, knowing this wasn't the time or place to raise it. He went back to her side and ushered her away from the stall. "How about finding a place to eat that lunch Marge packed us?" he asked. "You must have worked up an appetite by now."

"I am hungry." She looked at him. "Everything okay with your call?"

He nodded. "Come on." Then he took her hand and guided her toward the exit.

Cooper found a spot halfway between the market and Tyler, a grassy knoll overlooking a large pond. He carried the basket while Caroline carried the blanket.

Unpacking the lunch took little time. Marge had gone out of her way, fixing roast beef sandwiches, baby vegetables and dip, and a variety of other finger foods. Cooper stretched out on his side, accepting the plate Caroline fixed for him.

For a few minutes they ate in companionable silence. She was obviously enjoying the beautiful day. Cooper, however, felt as if he were about to burst. He couldn't contain the questions any longer.

"Caroline, why did you lie to me about your being from Santa Barbara?"

At his blunt question, she nearly choked. "Excuse me?"

"That call I got earlier. It was from the Santa Barbara

PD. They've got no record of a Caroline Benning.'' He struggled to keep his voice down and thought perhaps he'd gone too far. Even to himself he sounded as if he were performing an interrogation.

He hoped Sergeant O'Connell was wrong. That Caroline would have a reasonable explanation. But when he looked at her, he thought he detected a blush staining her cheeks. He noticed her hand tremble as she put down the sandwich.

"Cooper, I..." She cleared her throat. "I don't know what to say..."

"How about the truth?" he said simply.

"The truth is..." She looked up at him and could see the anxiety on his face. It matched the fear she felt at the moment. How could she possibly tell him the truth? That she was really Caroline Bennedict and in Tyler to find long-lost relatives. Everything she'd done for the past several months would blow up in her face. Not to mention the fact that she'd probably lose the man she loved. The truth? Not likely. She had no choice but to lie—again.

"The truth is, Cooper, that I'm not from Santa Barbara." It was amazing how, when cornered, even an honest person could let lies roll off her tongue. Since she wouldn't tell him her real name, she had to make up another lie about a bogus hometown. "I only told people that so I couldn't be traced."

"Traced by whom?" he asked.

"By my family."

"But you told me you had no family."

Caroline lowered her gaze, her mind working furiously to come up with a story. "I have some distant relatives— no one I'm close to. But they... You see, after my father died, they started fighting me over his will. I had no choice but to get away. I needed time. I was too upset over my father's death to deal with his business, his estate...."

"I see." But his voice held no understanding, no compassion. "So just where are you from?"

"San Mateo." She lied yet again, and was instantly reminded of that line from Shakespeare, "Oh, what a tangled web we weave." Her heart ached at the thought of lying to Cooper. But what choice did she have?

"So if I ran your name through their PD, I wouldn't find a dead end? I'd find a Caroline Benning—with no arrest warrants, just an honest citizen?"

"Not even a parking ticket. Trust me." She felt sick to her stomach at her deception.

Cooper leaned over, taking hold of her chin with his fingertips. He lifted her face so he could study it, looking for even the slightest hint of untruth in her expression. He wanted to believe her. He had to believe her. If he didn't, whatever he felt for her would turn into a lie, too. He couldn't hold back his anger. He blamed Brady Spencer for talking to him that morning. For again sowing the seeds of suspicion.

"Then why didn't you tell me this sooner? Dammit, Caroline, I'm a cop. When I find out someone's lied to me, I have to question their credibility on everything else. Frustration darkened his voice. "Can you see my point?"

"Yes," she whispered. "And I'm sorry." Tears sparkled on her lashes like tiny diamonds. "Just don't hate me, Cooper."

He pulled her into his arms, cradling her head against his shoulder. If he'd seen the anguish on her face at that moment, he would have instantly known that there was much more to her story.

THE REST OF THE RIDE BACK to the Kelsey Boarding House was quiet and filled with tension. Caroline could think of nothing to say. She was suffering too much and she feared it wouldn't be the last time.

What surprised and frightened her was that at a time when she would have ordinarily broken down and told all, she had kept back the truth.

Cooper walked her to the door and kissed her gently on the mouth.

She wanted to throw herself into his arms, confess everything and plead with him to help her find a way to make everything all right.

What held her back was the realization she couldn't expect him to make things right. She'd started it. She had to finish it.

"I'll see you later," he said quietly, before he walked back to his truck.

She sadly realized it was the first time he hadn't pinned down a time when they'd see each other again.

CAROLINE FELT SHE'D BEEN going through a lot of first times lately.

She didn't see or hear from Cooper for four days—the longest four days in her life. When he did come in to Marge's for breakfast, he took his usual booth. He smiled at her and talked to her as he'd always done in the past, as if nothing had happened. She still felt as if something between them was missing.

By the end of her shift, she felt close to tears.

Caroline didn't want to go back to the boardinghouse. She finally settled on escaping to the library. She found an empty bench in the atrium and sat down. Leaning back and closing her eyes, she listened to the classical music playing softly on the radio. Caroline hoped the music and the lush greenery surrounding her would give her the comfort she needed.

"Do you think what you are seeking can be found here?"

Caroline opened her eyes and looked into Laughing Bear's deep brown eyes. They were so like his grandson's, but there was a softness that wasn't found in Cooper's. She noticed the elderly man carried several books.

He looked toward the empty end of the bench. She smiled and nodded.

"The Spirits and I like to read." He held up his booty.

Caroline took the books out of his hands and studied the titles.

"Vampires at Midnight, Feast of Blood, Terror at the Lake," she read out loud. She shuddered. "You and your Spirits have some lurid taste in reading material."

"I used to read a lot of science fiction, but I didn't like the different worlds," he explained. "Delia asked me why I don't try reading historical fiction, but I told her I lived through enough history that I do not feel the need to read any. And the Spirits tell me anything I do not know."

"Your Spirits must be better than mine then, because mine have been really quiet."

"Perhaps you are not listening."

Caroline instinctively felt she had a friend. "I meditate."

"But do you concentrate on what is inside you, rather than outside?" he asked. "You look very sad. And my grandson looks very sad."

"Suffice to say Cooper doesn't like liars."

Laughing Bear nodded. "When he was in college a woman lied to him and almost took his heart in the process. He has had trouble trusting since then. But he will trust you again because his heart will guide him. Sometimes people keep secrets because they have no choice. You will reveal your secrets when you feel ready.'' He patted the back of her hand.

''My secrets won't harm anyone,'' she confessed, unconsciously admitting there was more than one mystery connected to her. ''Deep down, I'm a coward in the worst way, so I haven't been able to find the best time to explain everything.''

''Not a coward. Just waiting.'' Laughing Bear studied her. ''You do not look as sad now.''

''I don't feel as sad as I did,'' she told him, leaning over to hug him. ''Should I thank you or your Spirits?''

''Since I am the one who advised you, you can thank me,'' he said with a smile given more freely than his grandson's. He slowly rose to his feet.

She got up and hugged him again. ''Then thank you from the bottom of my heart.''

He smiled again and patted her shoulder. ''You are good for my grandson.'' He started to walk away, then stopped and turned around. ''What was your address where you lived before you came here?''

''My address?'' She hadn't expected his question.

He nodded. ''Yes. The street name.''

''River Road,'' she replied, still mystified. This time she told the truth.

Laughing Bear's leathery face broke into a broad grin that bordered on smug. He nodded as if he'd expected her answer. He turned back around and continued on his way.

Lighter in heart, Caroline left the library. She stopped at the grocery store for the only other thing that would soothe her, then made her way back to the boardinghouse.

''Well, I must say you look better than you did when you left this morning,'' Anna greeted her when she entered the kitchen.

"I feel better, too." Caroline set the grocery bag down on the table and unpacked it. She retrieved a bowl from a cabinet and a spoon from the flatware drawer. It was time to concoct her form of feel-good medicine.

Anna leaned against the counter and watched Caroline go to work. "Is there a method to this madness?"

She nodded. "Whenever I need to figure something out, I make my favorite treat." It consisted of a large scoop of French vanilla ice cream, another of chocolate ice cream, topped with marshmallow cream, peanut M&Ms, broken up chocolate sandwich cookies, a sprinkle of coconut and some cinnamon candies for spice. "Would you like one? I'll make it for you."

Anna held up her hand. "I think I can do one of my own. On a much smaller basis," she murmured, pulling a bowl out of the cabinet.

Caroline sat at the table but waited until Anna joined her before she dug in.

Anna took a small bite and rolled the various tastes around inside her mouth. "I don't think I've ever had anything quite like this. It's good. Is this what you always eat when you're depressed?" she asked. "I won't even ask about the calorie count. It would only depress me. It's bad enough we're eating this because you're feeling down."

Caroline looked smug as she made sure she had a little bit of everything on her spoon. "Are you kidding? When I want to feed my depressed inner child, I go for pizza. This is what I eat when I'm happy."

Chapter Eleven

By this time, she entered his dreams as effortlessly as he entered a room.

The mist still swirled around her like a possessive lover, but this time she merely stood there and looked at him. She didn't offer him her hand. But other things hadn't changed. He still couldn't see her face clearly, but he could feel her disappointment in him as if she openly wept.

She stood there for what seemed like the longest time. Without a word or gesture, she silently turned around and disappeared back into the enveloping fog. Her departure made him feel empty, as if he was the only person left on earth.

This time, she retreated into the mist before he rejected her.

Cooper woke up cursing the woman in his dream. He started to turn over and reach for Caroline. Then he remembered. She wasn't there.

Since the day he'd discovered her lie, he had deliberately kept his distance.

What he hadn't done was contact the San Mateo police and run a check on her.

He just needed time to think things through. Time to

sort out his feelings for her. Time to react like a man, not a cop.

He rationalized what Caroline had done: she'd had good reasons for withholding the truth.

But she'd still lied.

All these suspicions were Brady's fault.

When his friend had first approached him about Caroline, Cooper should have just told him to buzz off. To do his own detecting. That Cooper wanted no part of it. The trouble was, he was already attracted to Caroline and had used Brady's request as a reason to get close to her.

"You going to Jenna and Seth's for the party?" Steve asked, stopping by Cooper's desk. He perched on the edge.

"I told them I'd be there," he replied. He knew he didn't sound the least bit enthusiastic about the prospect.

Steve's features sharpened. "You haven't been over at the diner as much lately. Anything wrong between you and Caroline? I noticed she doesn't seem her usual cheerful self."

"Nothing that concerns you," Cooper said, tight-lipped.

"Amazing how you don't say a thing, but I can still get my question answered. No wonder Marge's has practically been overrun with single male customers during Caroline's shift," he commented, watching Cooper closely for a reaction. "She might not be wearing a sign that says she's available, but there's a lot of guys sitting over there who think they've got a chance with her."

Cooper refused to rise to the bait Steve had thrown out. It was bad enough that he'd reacted to Steve's less than subtle probing about him and Caroline. Cooper wouldn't be surprised if Steve was one of those guys sniffing around her. And if he was, Cooper would just have to break him into pieces.

What could he say? That he'd put some distance between them, meaning he'd basically shot himself in the foot?

They were supposed to attend the party together tomorrow. After the way he'd acted lately, he doubted she'd be willing to walk to the corner with him.

He didn't let one hint of his thoughts appear on his face. Steve, seeing he wasn't going to get anywhere, shrugged and moved away.

Everyone else pretty much left Cooper alone, because they didn't want their heads bit off. Even his grandfather had left him alone after telling him he would have to battle his demons himself.

Cooper hated it when people seemed to know his thoughts better than he did.

He picked up the phone, then replaced it. There were way too many ears in the vicinity. He'd wait until he got home. He wasn't going to stop by the diner, either. He knew there was already too much speculation about him and Caroline without adding even more fuel to the fire.

It wasn't until he was getting ready to leave the substation that Hedda approached him. ''A message,'' she murmured, passing him the pink slip.

''I'm off duty,'' he protested.

She shook her head, keeping her voice low so no one would overhear her. ''This one's personal. I don't think you want anyone else to know about it.''

The minute he saw the initials C.B. in the space for the caller's name, he sensed the contents of the message.

Caroline would be attending the party with Anna and Johnny.

This was one of those times when Cooper hated how

he kept such a tight hold on his emotions. If he was smart, he wouldn't bother going to the party tomorrow. But he'd already told Seth he'd be there.

He would have gone, anyway. After learning that Caroline would be there.

"Thanks, Hedda," he said quietly, carefully folding the note into a small square and putting it in his shirt pocket.

She patted his shoulder and returned to her desk.

Right about now, Cooper wasn't sure who was making him more crazy—Caroline or the woman in his dreams.

COOPER TRIED NOT TO LOOK too obvious as he scanned the people crowding the backyard. The largest knot of people was in the vicinity of the double stroller that held the babies of honor. So far, he'd managed to stay away from that group.

"You could pretend to enjoy yourself."

He turned his head and faced Seth Spencer.

"I am enjoying myself." He held up his glass of Coke. "There's nothing more interesting than watching a bunch of women act as if Susan and Dominick were the first babies born this century. The hormones are running high over there. A pretty dangerous place to be."

"Especially with Caroline Benning there."

Cooper's gaze sharpened as he swung back around. Sure enough, Caroline was standing by Jenna, picking up one of the babies.

He felt as if he'd taken a heavy-duty punch to the stomach.

Caroline looked so right with the baby cradled in her arms. The expression on her face took his breath away. The expression of awe and tenderness lent a glow he'd never seen before.

"Babies tend to do something to a woman," Seth said quietly. "Makes them even more beautiful, don't they?"

"What are you doing? Taking up where your brother left off?" Cooper asked, keeping his gaze centered on Caroline.

"He told me he'd talked to you about her." He didn't pretend ignorance. "About what Dad saw in the house during the wedding reception. I haven't talked to Dad about it any further. Maybe he's even forgotten about it by now."

"Elias forget about anything?" he said skeptically. "I don't think so."

Seth regarded him closely. "You've fallen for her, haven't you?"

Cooper kept his gaze trained on Caroline. Her light-streaked hair was a contrast to Jenna's dark hair. He thought of an angel even though he already knew she had a devilish soul.

The dark rose tank top clung lovingly to her upper body. There was no doubt she wasn't wearing a bra. The short denim skirt flirted with her bare legs.

She laughed as she looked at Jenna, her smile brightening as she looked at the other women in the group. As she turned, her gaze fell on him.

He knew the second she saw him because her smile stilled. Anyone looking at her wouldn't notice anything different, but he did.

He knew every square inch of her body and exactly how she would respond. He could also tell, just by looking at her, that she still wasn't too happy with him.

He couldn't say she was angry with him. He couldn't see even a hint of anger in her dark green eyes as she boldly returned his gaze. No, if anything, she was disappointed in him and it hurt like hell.

She lied to you, warned a voice inside his head. *She lied to everyone here and is still lying to them.*

But that was before she knew me, he reasoned, *as if defending her. And she had a reason for it. A good one.*

Caroline was picture perfect as she stood there with one of the babies in her arms. She looked like a woman made for motherhood.

From the beginning she had settled easily into the town's rhythm.

She fitted in with everyone as if she'd been born and raised in Tyler. As if she truly belonged here.

Dammit, she belonged to him.

Cooper never believed in primitive feelings, but right about now he was ready to go over there, throw Caroline over his shoulder and carry her off.

He didn't care where she was from, or how much family she had.

"Be careful, Night Hawk," Seth murmured before he moved away. "Your primal side is showing."

Cooper used his willpower to tamp down those feelings as he moved in the other direction. Farther away from Caroline.

Before he gave in to those uncivilized urges.

CAROLINE DIDN'T MISS the flash of light in Cooper's dark eyes. Or what it meant. She'd seen it too many other times. Like when he was making love to her.

She felt as if she'd been thrust into a vacuum where only she and Cooper existed.

"You look as if you wouldn't mind having a few of these little darlings yourself." Martha Bauer's voice cut into her thoughts. Several members of the Quilting Circle smiled and agreed with her, their gazes alternating between Caroline and Cooper.

"When the time is right," Caroline murmured, handing Susan back to Jenna, who tenderly laid the baby back in her stroller.

"Be careful," Jenna whispered to her. "I think they're already planning just when we'll be christening your little darlings."

"If that's what they want, they're going to have to be the ones having them," she said under her breath.

When she swung back around she noticed Cooper wasn't standing where he'd been before.

A tiny hitch in the vicinity of her heart told her she'd hoped he'd still be there. Furtive glances in other directions told her he wasn't anywhere about.

Had he left already? Granted, she hadn't expected to see him at the party. Knowing his distaste for social functions, and considering what had happened between them, she thought he'd stay away.

He hadn't been in the diner for some time. There were days when she wasn't sure whether she was going to kill him or go off in a corner and lick her wounds. Not to mention she was getting pretty sick and tired of every single man in the county coming in and asking her out, as if she would be grateful they were paying her attention. As if she was desperate for male company. One who dared voice that very thought was lucky to end up with only stew in his lap.

Cooper's abrupt disappearance from her life gave her her answer as to how he'd react if she told him the truth about herself.

"How much do you want to bet there's only one reason for him to be here?" Jenna whispered, bumping Caroline with her hip.

"And the same reason he left me," she said sadly.

Caroline was determined to smile her way through the

afternoon. She helped Jenna and a few of the other ladies pass out slices of cake to the guests. She laughed and talked to everyone, but the smiles were forced

During the entire time, she was acutely aware of Cooper. Whom he was talking to. What he was doing—mostly looking at her.

The afternoon was very warm and for her, even warmer.

Needing to be alone, she finally escaped into the house, with the intention of splashing some cold water on her face. She'd barely stepped inside the bathroom, and was starting to close the door, when it was pushed open.

"What are you doing?" she furiously demanded, careful to keep her voice low. The last thing she wanted was to have someone come upon them. Talk about creating even more gossip!

"Talking to you," Cooper muttered, pushing her into the small room and closing the door after him. The click of the lock sounded loud.

"Get out of here!" she ordered, forced up against the counter. "At this moment, this is the ladies' room, not the men's room!"

Cooper didn't say a word as he looked down at her.

When she realized his intention, she jerked her head away, but he didn't stop. He cupped the back of her head with his hand and held it fast as he lowered his face.

"Not fair!" she wailed softly, just as his mouth covered hers.

He stole her very breath as he kissed her with the raging hunger of a starving man. He kissed her as if the world was due to end in seconds.

She felt as if she was on fire from the inside out. And Cooper was the match. She held on to him tightly as he lifted her onto the vanity and stood between her legs.

"Cooper!" she gasped, tearing her mouth away from his. She started to wiggle away from him. When she felt his erection snugly nestled against her hips, she stopped before things got too out of hand. "This is crazy! We can't do this here."

"I was a fool," he muttered, tunneling his fingers through her hair, cupping the back of her head to keep it still. His lips moved down the side of her neck and along her bare shoulder. "I shouldn't have judged you without listening to everything you had to say. I can't sleep without you beside me."

They froze when a soft knock on the door, then the rattle of the doorknob, seemed to echo throughout the room.

"Is anyone in there?" It was Tillie Phelps.

Caroline smothered her whimper by burying her face against Cooper's shirtfront. She almost screamed when she felt his hand cup her breast. She settled for raising her face enough to nip the tender skin under his jaw. His only reaction was to tighten his hold on her.

"Is there a problem in there?" Tillie called out again.

"No, ma'am," Caroline managed to say. "I'll be out in a minute." She pushed Cooper away and hopped off the counter. "Now what?" she hissed. "She's probably standing out there waiting for me to leave."

He shook his head. "Not Tillie. She'll head for the kitchen to see what she can swipe off the food platters."

Caroline turned around and studied herself in the mirror. Other than a hectic flush to her cheeks and a slightly swollen mouth, she looked as she had when she came in.

"You are totally crazy," she muttered, trying to sound angry, but not succeeding very well when her blood was singing.

"I never used to be until you came along," He moved up behind her and wrapped his arms around her.

"That's right, blame it on me." She tried to finger-comb her hair and dismally failed.

"Let's get out of here." He bumped his hips against her. "Go somewhere where I can properly apologize to you."

Caroline should have wanted to make him suffer. It would have served him right for making *her* suffer. But that wasn't her style.

"Jenna will never forgive me for just leaving." She gave the last protest she could think of, even if it was halfhearted.

"I don't think she'll be surprised."

Caroline moved away from him and unlocked the door. She cautiously opened it and peeked out. Seeing the hallway was empty, she unceremoniously pushed Cooper out, then slipped out herself.

"Where are you parked?" she asked. "I need to tell Anna or Johnny I won't be going home with them."

"I'll wait for you out front."

Caroline stared at him for a long moment. "I missed you," she said softly before she turned and hurried down the hallway.

Caroline's softly spoken admission echoed in Cooper's mind as he went in the opposite direction.

"I missed you, too," he whispered.

He stopped long enough to say goodbye to Seth, who smiled knowingly. "Did you throw yourself on her mercy?" he asked.

"I don't grovel." Cooper didn't bother to pretend he didn't know what the other man meant. "But I know when to admit I was wrong."

"Must have been a doozy of a battle."

Cooper wasn't about to divulge what had caused the rift between them.

"Give it up, Spencer," he recommended. "The ladies in this town do a hell of a lot better job of ferreting out gossip than you ever could."

Cooper headed for his truck before he could be stopped again. When he reached it, he found Caroline already sitting in the passenger seat.

As he climbed in behind the wheel, she automatically slid over to sit beside him.

"After what happened, I wouldn't have blamed you if you'd told me to get lost," he growled, switching on the ignition.

She turned to look at him. "If I had, would you have gone quietly?"

He scowled at her. "Hell no!"

Caroline's smile was soft and knowing. "Then you know why."

Chapter Twelve

Caroline didn't want to sleep. If she succumbed to slumber, she would miss this time with Cooper. What she had here was better than any dream she refused to wake up from.

His apparent need to push the speed limit as he'd driven to his cabin in record time told her he'd suffered just as much as she had. She figured it was only because he knew where his fellow officers would be hiding out in anticipation of speeders, because it wasn't in Cooper's makeup to do anything to draw attention to himself.

Cooper was different than anyone she'd ever dated. And not just because of his cultural background. He was definitely more serious. But now she realized his smiles were rare because they were special. The few times she'd been blessed with a smile that seemed to come straight from his soul were the times she treasured most, because she knew they were meant solely for her.

She turned onto her side and propped herself up on one elbow so she could have a better look at him. He lay on his stomach, both arms shoved under his pillow. His hair covered part of his face, and his lips were parted as he emitted soft, snuffling sounds. She couldn't stop smiling.

What would he think if he knew he snored? Even if she considered it a cute snore.

Caroline couldn't remember ever feeling happier. From the time they arrived at the cabin to Cooper carrying her inside and to his bed, they'd been voracious. In a voice raw with need he'd told her what he would do to her right before he accomplished the deed. When they finally lay back, they were exhausted. But she preferred watching him sleep than sleeping herself.

Later she slipped out of bed. Because the night air was chilly, she took a quick peek in Cooper's closet and appropriated one of his plaid flannel shirts as a cover-up. She was rolling up the sleeves when a faint sound from outside caught her attention. Not thinking if it could be dangerous, she crept quietly through the kitchen and out the door.

She almost shrieked in fright when she found a dark figure sitting in one of the chairs on the porch.

"You should be asleep," Laughing Bear said, as if it was nothing unusual for her to walk outside of his grandson's cabin in the middle of the night.

Caroline pressed her hands against her chest, where her heart was thudding. "I thought some monster had come out of the woods," she confessed, dropping into the chair beside him.

He shook his head. "Not around here. We have no monsters in our legends." He looked up. "I can see the stars better down here. The Spirits like it better down here, too."

All of a sudden, Caroline realized the older man could easily figure out what had transpired to bring her there. She wished she'd stayed inside instead of coming out to investigate. What must he think of her?

"The Spirits like you," Laughing Bear said, still look-

ing toward the heavens. "You have a good heart, Caroline. It is more important what a person has on the inside
than on the outside. But you must stop keeping secrets."
This time he turned his head, looking at her as if he could
see through her ruse. "They will only keep you sad."

"Even if it's a secret you're afraid might hurt others?"
she asked, curling her legs under her body and draping
the long tails of the shirt over her knees.

"People are stronger than they think. From the time
they enter this world until the day they leave the earth,
they have trials that will help them, as long as they wish
it. My grandson has grown strong over the years, and even
one as young as you has learned to grow stronger. You
were meant to come here."

"I haven't admitted to myself that I'm in love with
him." It seemed natural that she confess her feelings for
Cooper to his grandfather first.

"When your heart knows, you do not need to say it to
anyone. I knew you were the one meant for Cooper the
first time I saw you," he said mildly. "Cooper knows it
even if he has not said the words."

"He hates secrets," she reminded him.

"Then you need to settle all your secrets to help calm
your spirit."

Caroline nodded. "You're right. It's time. I do need to
do it. I haven't been able to learn all I'd hoped to, so
maybe someone else will have the answers I'm looking
for," she explained, not even wondering how he seemed
to know so much about her. It was more a relief that
someone else understood the torment she'd been going
through.

Laughing Bear nodded.

"You trying to steal my woman?" A heavy-eyed Cooper slouched in the doorway. The jeans he'd donned were

zipped but not snapped. With little effort, he picked Caroline up in his arms and dropped back into the chair with her nestled onto his lap. He wrapped his arms around her, keeping her close to his chest. "I guess you and your Spirits are down here again to watch the stars."

Laughing Bear smiled. "I do not think she would allow herself to be stolen."

"I pretty much stole her from Jenna and Seth's place," he admitted.

"If you don't mind, the woman in question would like to speak for herself," Caroline huffily insisted from her warm cocoon within Cooper's arms. She glared at him. "And admitting you were acting like a Neanderthal is not exactly something to be proud of."

He cupped the back of her head, bringing her cheek against his chest, resting his chin on top of her head.

"She gets cranky when she doesn't get any sleep," he told his grandfather.

Caroline mumbled a few uncomplimentary comments about men and closed her eyes. Within seconds, she was sound asleep.

The two men sat in companionable silence, not caring to mar the moment with speech.

"Your past troubles are resolved." Laughing Bear made it a statement instead of a question. "Some people need to settle their problems in their minds and hearts before they can be shared. When that time comes they need to know everything is all right."

Cooper tightened his hold around Caroline, as if his grandfather's words held some type of threat destined to take her away from him. He'd judged her once before and he wasn't going to risk losing her again because he was pigheaded.

"Just as long as anything they're hiding doesn't break

the law," he said, needlessly reminding his grandfather
of his career choice and his own personal set of values.

"You need to remember, Grandson, that everything is
not black-and-white. You have to look beyond. Just as
you did with Caroline from the first time you noticed her.
She makes you smile, she brings laughter to your heart.
That is what matters."

"I guess that means if she follows me home again I
can keep her?" Cooper asked on a lighter note. He felt
as if his grandfather knew something he didn't. He also
knew that if Laughing Bear felt he shouldn't know about
it, the elderly man wouldn't say a word. For now, Cooper
gloried in the sweet feel of Caroline's sleeping form in
his arms.

The older man chuckled. "I told you she is all yours.
She will not be leaving Tyler, because everything she
wants is here." He cast his grandson a warning look.
"Don't blow it."

Cooper was surprised by his grandfather's use of modern slang, since Laughing Bear usually grumbled that
none of it made any sense to his ears.

"Looks like I better keep a closer eye on you or you'll
try to steal her, after all."

"IT'S GOOD TO SEE YOU smiling again," Anna told Caroline.

Caroline had stopped in the kitchen long enough for a
cup of coffee before heading for the diner. Since she'd be
working late, she knew she'd need all the caffeine she
could get.

"Summer has always been my favorite time of year."
She blew on the steaming surface to cool the liquid before
daring to take a sip.

"I'd say it has more to do with the man you're keeping

company with. I'm glad the two of you cleared things up." Anna patted her shoulder.

Caroline fairly radiated good cheer. "So am I."

"Are you still trying to get him to smile?" Anna asked.

She concentrated on her coffee, but a sly cat-who-ate-the-canary smile appeared on her lips. "Oh, he smiles," Caroline murmured. "When it counts." She flashed Anna a saucy wink as she left the house.

She was still smiling later that evening as she was busy refilling coffee cups and carrying orders to the tables.

"You're like a ray of sunshine, darlin'," Henry told her. "Somethin' good for these old, tired eyes to look at."

"If you think that lovely compliment will allow you to look down my blouse, you've got another think coming, mister." She pinched his cheek.

"Now, I wouldn't do that," he protested, looking properly wounded.

"Yes, you would, Henry," she whispered as she swept by him, "but that's part of your charm."

The elderly man immediately perked up. "It won't stop me from trying," he warned.

"Of course you won't. That's what I love about you," she told him with a smile.

Caroline delivered meals and refilled cups. Even at suppertime, the decaf coffeepot more or less remained on the burner. She'd learned early on that no matter how late the hour, most of the diners preferred their caffeine buzz.

She was proud of herself for not faltering when she spied Brady Spencer sitting in one of her booths.

"Hey there, Dr. Spencer," she greeted him, holding up the pot. He nodded and she picked up the cup on the table and filled it. "What can I get you?"

"I'm really in the mood for breakfast instead of dinner.

Think Marge could rustle up a ham-and-cheese omelette with hash browns and rye toast?'' he asked with a warm smile.

''You know she will.'' She jotted it down on her pad. ''We don't see you in here as much since you got married.''

''I was called out for an emergency surgery,'' he replied. ''Figured the least I could do is eat before getting home and saving Eden the fuss I know she'd make.''

''Seems even after all those long hours as an intern and resident you still don't have regular work hours,'' she commented.

''Not when a hot appendix is ready to burst,'' Brady agreed.

''I'll put a rush on your food,'' she promised as she moved away.

Caroline felt a rush of power go through her as she dropped off Brady's order. Before, she'd always tried to act the part of the invisible waitress whenever he or any member of his family had been in here. Tonight, she decided, it was time to start moving past that.

Brady looked up as she served him his food. ''Don't you ever sit down for more than a second?'' he asked.

''Sometimes.''

''How about now?'' He gestured toward the seat across from him.

She looked around. ''I don't see why not.'' She sat down. ''But don't stop eating on my account.''

''The way I feel right now, that won't be a problem. I'm hungry enough to eat the plate.'' He dug into his omelette.

''I hate to think what your mother thought of you eating plates,'' she quipped.

Brady's expression stilled. ''She wasn't around long

enough to worry about my eating habits," he said in a harsh voice.

Caroline didn't need to be hit over the head to realize Brady didn't want to talk about their mother. Not that it wasn't going to stop her. She'd just go about it in a different way.

"My father used to say he thought all girls nibbled their food daintily. He could never understand how I'd devour an extra large pizza with everything on it," she told him, hoping her confession would bring about one of his own. "As long as it didn't have anchovies on it."

He chuckled. "Obviously, you're not a cheap date when going out to dinner. My dad used to say that we boys could clean out the refrigerator in an hour."

"Your father is very scary." She suddenly gasped as she realized what she'd just said.

Brady almost choked on his coffee. "I wouldn't worry. I'm sure there's a lot of people who think the same thing. He comes across as scary, but he's actually a nice guy."

Caroline looked off into the distance. "I wish I'd known my mother," she mused. "Had someone to talk to me about all the girl stuff instead of feeling bad for my dad as he stumbled through the explanations. Moms are very important."

He didn't say a word for a moment, then said bluntly, "Our mother left us when we were kids. It didn't take us long to realize we could do very fine on our own."

"I'm sorry," she said softly, aware he had no idea of all the things she was sorry about. "But sometimes there are reasons people leave."

"Her reason is pretty well known and not all that pleasant." He took a deep breath. "Look, do you mind if we talk about something else?"

She could have subtly pushed, but she knew she

wouldn't get anywhere. Still, it was a beginning. Now she knew her half brothers hated their mother. And she couldn't really blame them. Violet had had no choice in the matter when she left Caroline, but she had when she'd left her sons.

Caroline looked up and watched Cooper walk into the diner. Her smile automatically kicked up a few thousand watts. He might not have smiled back, but the light in his eyes told her all she needed to know.

However had she survived before she met him? She knew one thing: she wasn't about to give up something so good.

"Caroline. Brady." He nodded warily at the other man.

"Hope you don't mind if your lady keeps me company," Brady greeted him.

"I don't mind as long as Eden doesn't," he said blandly.

Caroline rose to her feet. "Have a seat. I get off in a half hour."

"I thought that was my job," he murmured for her ears only as she moved away.

She shot him a warning look, but the heat in it had nothing to do with anger.

"Looks like you and the lady have become a hot item," Brady remarked as Cooper sat down.

"What the hell are you doing?" he demanded in a low voice.

Brady looked down at his plate. "Having breakfast."

Cooper leaned across the table. His face was dark with anger. "Leave her alone," he ordered.

Brady cocked an eyebrow. He leaned back in the chair, not intimidated by his friend's fury. "You really have fallen for her."

"I mean it, Brady, leave her alone." He got up and

walked over to the counter. He accepted a cup of coffee from Marge.

Brady stopped by Cooper as he left the diner. "I think I was wrong about her, Cooper. She seems pretty special. Don't screw it up," he advised under his breath.

Cooper's reply was less than polite.

Caroline turned up the volume on the radio when a soft dreamy song came on. She turned around and headed straight for Cooper.

"Dance with me, big boy," she invited, grabbing his hand and pulling on it.

He reared back. "No way," he said, digging in his heels.

"Come on. We're all alone now." She gestured around the diner. "And Marge is in the back." Caroline grabbed his other hand and pulled even harder. "It'll be good for you." She swayed her hips to the music in an inviting motion.

Realizing Caroline wasn't going to let him off easily, he slid off the stool and allowed her to lead him toward the open section of the diner.

Once there, he set his hands on her hips while she looped her arms around his neck. She tipped her head back so she could look up at him.

"This isn't so bad, is it?" she murmured.

"You think I'm going to argue when I have you in my arms?" They moved languidly to the sultry rhythm.

He felt the warmth of her nose buried in the hollow of his throat. Just that tiny touch, the sensation of her warm breath on his skin, aroused him. Their movements had him thinking how well they danced together in a more elemental way. He wanted her so badly he ached inside.

"Sometime we should try dancing outside," she whispered for his ears only, "in the moonlight." He tightened his grip on her hips as he felt his body harden in response to the sensual invitation in her voice.

"Sweetheart, you have a hell of a sense of timing," he muttered between gritted teeth.

She smiled. "Then I guess we'll have to dance more, won't we?"

Unfortunately, the song ended. And the applause started.

It wasn't until then that Cooper realized they had an audience, standing in front of the diner's windows. He swore under his breath.

"Now, now," she chided. "Bow to the nice people." She kept hold of his hand and managed a ladylike curtsy to their viewers.

"That was really pretty, you two," Marge called out to them as they left.

"Nice dancing in there, Cooper," one man called out. "We going to see you at any of the hotspots next?"

"Only if I'm in there to haul your sorry butt home," he retorted amid laughter.

"Expect your dance card to be full at the next dance, Cooper Night Hawk," one of the woman said with a laugh.

"Sorry, but his dance card is already full," Caroline replied, wrapping her arm through his in a possessive manner.

"I must be crazy to let you talk me into some of these things." He shook his head as he helped her into his truck.

"You had fun. Admit it." She twisted around to face him as he slid behind the steering wheel.

"I had fun," Cooper said reluctantly. "You know, I used to have a nice quiet life."

"Boring!" she sang out, leaning over to hug him.

"That's one thing you are definitely not." He switched on the engine. "Secure your seat belt."

"You really need to get used to hugs," Caroline told him, not offended by his gruff tone. She knew he wasn't the grump he liked to think he was. She just wished he would show his lighter side more in public, so others could see it, too.

"My family wasn't into hugs," he explained. "We didn't need them to feel close. We always knew we were loved."

"But hugs are nice." She snuggled as close to him as her seat belt would allow. "And you know I love to give hugs." She laid her head on his shoulder.

Cooper knew he should admit that, yes, hugs were nice. Especially Caroline's hugs. He'd learned from the beginning that she was a touchy-feely type of person. She'd touch his arm or his shoulder, and it wasn't long before she was reaching out to him with a hug or kiss on the cheek. He knew she didn't do this to just anyone, but to those she cared about. He'd seen her give Henry or Barney a hug that had the elderly men blushing from her attention. Cooper wasn't about to admit he was warmed from the inside out to be the recipient of her displays of affection. Caroline was a powerful presence in his life. So far, he hadn't told her how much. He wasn't sure he wanted her to know just how much she meant to him.

That she held his heart, and his soul, in her hand.

An image of the woman in his dreams wavered in front of him. If he hadn't had a secure hold on the steering wheel, he might have driven right off the road.

This time she looked a hell of a lot like Caroline.

Then he nearly did lose control of the wheel when he felt her warm breath in his ear.

"Dammit, Caroline," he growled.

"Let's go parking," she murmured.

"Parking?"

She nodded. "You know all the good spots. Let's take a trip down memory lane. Relive your wilder days. Come on, Night Hawk, let's go somewhere quiet and indulge in a hot and heavy make out session," she murmured. "If you play your cards right, you might even make it past first base."

"Damn, you're trying to make me feel sixteen again," he muttered, already feeling his body harden.

Caroline couldn't stop smiling. She knew it was due to being with Cooper. Those days of being apart had ripped into her like a wound. She didn't want to go through that kind of pain again. She knew the time was coming when she would tell him everything.

She was beginning to think the quilt wasn't meant to bring her to Tyler to find her half brothers, but to find Cooper.

She wished she could turn toward him and trace his features with her fingertips, but knew it wasn't a good idea while he was driving. She'd have to wait. She never tired of looking at him. In one of her fantasies she could see him as a great chief. He had the commanding presence of a man meant to lead people. She'd heard talk that no one would be surprised if one day he would be sheriff.

Cooper turned off the main road onto a bumpy gravel lane. Not too far down, he made another turn, then parked the truck on a rise overlooking the lake. He switched off the engine, found a radio station playing soft music, and turned in the seat, leaning back against the truck door.

"How's this?"

She looked around with interest. "Very romantic. Night sounds, moonlight on the lake, you, me." Her voice softened. "Everything we need."

He reached across and unbuckled her seat belt, so he could pull her toward him. She willingly went into his arms. She straddled his lap and looped her arms around his neck.

"We could have gone back to my place and done this there," he said.

She shook her head. "It wouldn't have been the same. I never went parking when I was a teenager," she confessed. "I wanted to find out what it was like."

"Then think about acting a little coy," he told her, tunneling his hand under her cotton top until his splayed hand covered her back.

"Oh no, I'm the town bad girl." She feathered light kisses across his cheekbones. "And I'm out here with the town bad boy." She angled her head and nibbled on his earlobe.

Cooper cupped the back of her head and brought her face up to his. He slanted his mouth across hers, kissing her with a hunger he'd kept in all day. She responded in kind, with sighs and soft moans that only spurred him on. He easily unhooked her bra and moved his hand around to cup the soft weight of her breast.

"First base," she murmured against his throat as her teeth grazed the roughened skin.

She busied herself pulling his shirt out of the waistband of his jeans so she could run her hands across the velvety smoothness of his chest.

"Ever hear the story about the couple making out in the car and a killer with a hook for a hand?" Cooper rasped.

"Mm, she hears a noise, he assures her there's nothing out there and later on, they find the hook secured onto the door handle," she murmured, working on the fastening to his jeans. "Second base."

Cooper gasped and jerked upward under her bold caress. "At the rate you're going, you'll be hitting for a home run in no time," he growled.

"Wow, major league so soon?" Caroline asked, peppering his face with kisses. Her breathing grew unsteady with arousal.

As did Cooper's.

"Let's go back to my place where we can do this right," he suggested in a raw voice. "Damn!" he swore when his leg hit the gear shift.

Caroline leaned back, then almost lost her balance. She cried out when her elbow hit the edge of the steering wheel.

"You win," she said, rubbing her injured elbow as she climbed off him.

Cooper wasted no time switching on the engine and turning the truck around. They had barely gone a mile on the main road when Cooper noticed flashing lights in the rearview mirror.

Caroline noticed it next. "Why isn't he driving around you?" she asked. "Isn't there an emergency somewhere?"

"No emergency. He wants me to pull over," Cooper groused, doing just that. He pushed the window button so that it rolled downward.

"Hey there, Cooper." Orson leaned his arms on the window. "Caroline." He smiled at her.

Cooper flashed him a look that threatened dire consequences for the other man. "You have a problem?"

The deputy shook his head. "Just wondered if you two had noticed any kids out and about. You know how they get on these long nights."

"It's been awhile." He stared the man down. "And I'm also off duty."

"Figured I'd ask," Orson said amiably. His gaze drifted downward, paused, then snapped back up. "Drive carefully now." He tipped his hat to Caroline and walked back to his vehicle.

"He's going to be real sorry," Cooper muttered, waiting until the other vehicle passed them. Orson gave them a smile and a wave as he drove on.

"He's also going to have a story, isn't he?" Caroline looked at her T-shirt, which was barely tucked in. She looked at Cooper's. His hair was tousled and if she wasn't mistaken... "Cooper?" She jerked her head downward.

Cooper looked down and noticed the open zipper. He dropped his head against the back of the seat.

"This is the kind of story they never let you forget, isn't it?" she said, wondering how he was going to handle what had to be embarrassing for him.

His lips twitched and he started laughing uproariously. "Oh yeah, it's one they tell at your retirement dinner. You know what's even better about this whole thing?" He pulled her toward him for a hard kiss that soon had them breathing heavily.

"What?" She was wide-eyed at his amusement. Cooper was such a private man that the idea he found the situation funny was a surprise for her.

"They'll all be wishing it had been them with you."

Chapter Thirteen

Don't Just Buckle Up for Safety When You're Behind the Wheel. Remember to Zip Up, Too!

Cooper stared at the brightly colored sign displayed prominently on the board in the hall. As if that wasn't bad enough, underneath the sign was an ad for dance lessons.

"I had no idea there was so much jealousy going on around here," he announced, balling the signs up and lobbing them into the wastebasket. "You know, you might find it easier if you tried to have a social life. Of course, that would mean the task of finding women who would be willing to take on such pitiful specimens." He shook his head in mock sympathy as loud boos were directed at him.

"I don't know if any of us could keep up with you," Steve told him, perching on a corner of the desk. "It's almost become a spectator sport waiting to see what will happen next."

"Just don't turn into Peeping Toms," Cooper advised.

Steve shook his head. "I never thought I'd see it happen. You falling so hard for a woman."

"Neither did I," he acknowledged candidly, leaning

back in his chair. "But it's still a wait-and-see proposition."

"If I were you, I wouldn't wait too long," Steve said.

Cooper thought of how it felt to have Caroline in his arms. How she tasted.

He wanted to announce to the world that Caroline was his. But he still held back. He didn't want to think that after all this time she'd leave, but he still wasn't sure it wouldn't happen.

"Look what we caught!" Orson Clayton shouted, coming into the station. He held the end of a rope high in his hand. On the other end was an angry brown-and-white goat, which was loudly bleating his displeasure. Stuck to one horn was a piece of cobalt-blue lingerie.

"Hey, Orson, it sounds like your perp's demanding to see a lawyer," someone shouted. "You read him his rights, didn't you?"

Karen came out of her office to find out what was going on. She laughed as she saw the colorful fabric dangling from the horn. She plucked the silk off and held it up.

"Why, Margaret Ingalls, death sure didn't do you any favors, did it?"

CAROLINE CURLED UP into the fetal position under the covers, but couldn't find any relief.

"Are you feeling any better, dear?" Anna asked, tiptoeing into the room. She set the tray she carried on the bedside table. She reached for the insulated carafe and poured water into a glass. "I picked up your prescription. The doctor said he wanted you to begin taking your medication right away. I also brought you some water. He said you need your fluids."

"I haven't felt like this in a long time." Caroline's words ended in a soft whimper.

Anna carefully sat on the side of the bed and handed over the glass and two capsules. Caroline held her head as she swallowed the pills.

"This flu has been nasty for everyone. Would you like anything else?" the older woman asked, brushing a stray lock of hair away from her patient's forehead.

Caroline was usually so healthy that she hadn't feared the virus that seemed to be traveling like wildfire through town. Alice had come back to work the previous day after her bout with the flu. Last night, Caroline had painfully learned that the commode was her best friend and her stomach could be her worst enemy. When Anna found her huddled in bed, she'd wasted no time in calling the doctor and insisting he come out to see Caroline. As predicted, she was diagnosed with the flu. He left, assuring Anna he'd have the pharmacy send something to settle Caroline's stomach and relieve her aches. The moment the medication arrived via one of the high school boys who handled deliveries, Anna had hurried upstairs to Caroline.

"Just a new stomach," Caroline whispered. "You are so sweet to do this for me. You don't have to, you know. I'd hate to think you'd catch this from me."

"Oh honey, there is no way I'd allow you to lie up here alone when you're feeling so bad." She placed the back of her hand against Caroline's forehead. "You still have a fever."

Caroline returned to her fetal position under the covers. "I hardly ever get sick. I've probably had the flu three times in my whole life. And never this bad."

"Then I guess it was just your turn." The older woman straightened her covers for her. "Try and get some sleep. That's the best thing for you."

She cocked her head when she heard the doorbell. "I

wonder who that can be," she mused, leaving the room. "You just call out if you need anything," she told her.

Caroline knew what she needed, and it had nothing to do with medication or juice. She crawled out of bed and slowly planted her feet on the floor. Stars danced before her eyes as she wobbled back and forth. She slowly made her way to the closet and carefully pulled the quilt down. She collapsed back onto the bed and pushed the covers back. She draped the quilt over her, then pulled the sheet up over it. She closed her eyes and while she couldn't sleep, she still felt a bit more secure.

WHEN ANNA OPENED the front door, she wasn't entirely surprised by the identity of her visitor.

"Hello, Cooper," she greeted him.

"Marge said Caroline's been real sick." Without waiting for an invitation, he stepped inside—an indication of his concern, since Anna always knew his manners to be impeccable. "Has she seen a doctor? Is she all right?"

She couldn't miss the slightly ashy cast to his skin. She never thought she'd see the day when Cooper Night Hawk would be scared of anything.

Lordy, the man was in love with Caroline!

"Cooper, she's fine," she assured him. "She's caught that flu that's been going around."

Cooper looked as if he wasn't sure whether to remain worried or be relieved. "She's never sick," he said numbly.

"She said that, too. I told her, sad to say, it was her turn."

He tipped his head back, allowing the tension to roll from his body. "Could I see her?"

"You're not afraid of catching it?" Anna asked.

"Since this bug started, my grandfather's been down

to my place every morning pouring some god-awful concoction down my throat. He swears it will keep it away. This can be the test." Stark need crossed his brow. "I'd really like to see her, Anna."

"As long as you understand that she's been up all night with a sick stomach and still feels miserable," she warned him.

Cooper didn't waste any time heading for the stairs.

"Second room on the left," she told him.

Cooper made it up the stairs in record time. He approached the open doorway and glanced in. Caroline lay with her back to the door.

"Caro," he said softly, not wanting to disturb her if she was asleep.

She stirred and looked over her shoulder. "Cooper?" Her voice held disbelief.

He hesitantly entered the room. He had been in her room only once before—in pitch darkness. He wasn't surprised that her private domain looked very much like her.

She started to sit up but he waved her back down. "You decided to catch the flu, huh?" he said, coming over to the bed.

"I look like a mess," she said softly, starting to put her hand to her hair, then limply dropping it back down.

This was a time when a lie was necessary. He wasn't about to tell her that he only had to look at her to know she was very ill. Her hair hung in lifeless strings around her face, her skin was a pasty color and her eyes lacked their normal sparkle.

"No, you don't."

She managed a feeble smile. "Liar. Have a seat," she invited.

He looked around.

Caroline patted the side of the bed. "If you feel brave enough. I haven't thrown up for a whole hour."

He winced. "Poor baby," he said, carefully sitting on the edge of the bed by her hip. He rested the back of his hand against her cheek.

"Anna already checked me for a temperature and it's done on the forehead," she told him.

"I just wanted to touch you," he admitted.

A hand appeared outside the covers and covered his. She laced her fingers through his. "I'm glad you came by."

"I probably should have brought flowers." He chastised himself for not thinking of it sooner.

She smiled. "I'd rather have you."

Cooper studied the lace edging Caroline's nightgown's neckline. The tiny blue rosebud print was a new sight for him. He was more used to her stealing one of his shirts as a nightgown when she spent most of the night with him. He wished he could wake up with her in his arms, but she always insisted on coming back to the Kelseys. She told him it was to protect his reputation, but he sensed it was more because she respected Anna and Johnny and felt it was best to wake up in her own bed. He admired her even more for her sensitivity toward others.

He had a good idea that more than half the town had figured out Caroline and he were sleeping together, but it was never mentioned. He felt as if everyone was giving their approval. Suddenly the prospect of a permanent match wasn't scaring him as much as it once would have.

He recognized the blouse that lay draped over the back of a chair as one he'd stripped off her a week ago. The earrings and necklace on top of the dresser once lay on his chest of drawers. The scent of her perfume lingered in the air, just as it did in his bathroom after she showered.

Somehow it eased his mind, so that he didn't feel as if
he'd stumbled onto an unfamiliar place.

"Don't tell me you've never been in a woman's room
before," she murmured.

"I'm taking the Fifth on that one," he said dryly.

"You look very uncomfortable." She reached up and
stroked his face with her fingertips. "It's not as if you
haven't seen me in bed before."

"It's always been my bed, and you weren't sick at the
time." He grasped her fingers and turned her palm so he
could kiss it.

"I guess I am a scary sight," she said.

He shook his head. "I'm just glad to know it wasn't
anything really serious. I hate to see you feeling so bad."

"I feel better now that I've seen you," she said sleepily. She smothered a yawn. "I'm sorry. Anna gave me a
couple of the capsules the doctor prescribed, and I guess
they kicked in."

"I have to get back to work, anyway. And you need
your sleep." He adjusted her covers over her shoulder as
she slid downward. He leaned over and kissed her gently
on the cheek.

"I expect a lot more of those when I feel better," she
murmured.

"It's a date," he whispered.

As Cooper got up, he noticed a series of bright colors
just under the sheet. He carefully lifted the edge so he
could get a better look at what was underneath. A quilt.
He wondered where it came from as he took a closer look.
He froze when he noticed embroidery on one corner.

The names he read hit him right between the eyes. He
swung around to look at Caroline. Her eyes were closed
and her breathing deep and even as she slept.

He didn't have to be a cop to put two and two together.

Her sudden appearance in town, the lies. Why she was so interested in the Spencer family. This quilt, which must have left Tyler with Violet Spencer, was the final piece of evidence.

She was Violet Spencer's child.

Apparently she'd lied about much more than her hometown. How could she?

Dammit, he didn't want Brady to be right. He didn't want to think the worst of her. But how could he look at this evidence and not conclude the worst?

He carefully covered up the quilt with the sheet again. He knew what he had to do.

He was quiet as he escaped the room before he gave in to his baser instincts and woke her up so he could demand an explanation.

"Does she need anything?" Anna asked as he descended the stairs.

"She's asleep," he said abruptly, not breaking his stride.

"Cooper, is everything all right?"

"Fine," he said in clipped tones as he strode to the door.

Anna stood in the open doorway and watched him walk to his vehicle. The very set of his shoulders told her something wasn't right.

She went back upstairs and tiptoed into Caroline's room. She gazed at Caroline's sleeping face with the expression of a worried mother.

"What happened?" she whispered, knowing she wouldn't be receiving answers anytime soon.

COOPER TOOK SEVERAL DEEP calming breaths. They didn't help. He radioed in to the station that he needed to take some personal time.

"Is Caroline all right?" Hedda asked.

"She's fine," he said. "There're just some things I need to do."

"I'll tell Karen." She signed off.

Cooper pulled out his cell phone and in short order made four phone calls. His message was delivered in a terse voice. The recipients assured him they would not be late for the meeting.

He didn't bother stopping by his cabin to change out of his uniform. He needed the official clothing to help him with what he was about to do.

Elias's house wasn't far from the Kelsey Boarding House, so Cooper was the first to arrive. Elias looked faintly puzzled as he let Cooper in, then directed him back to his office.

"I hope you don't mind if we wait until Seth, Brady and Quinn arrive," Cooper said, declining the offer of a chair or a drink.

"Of course." Elias leaned against the edge of his desk. "You have to understand that I'm naturally curious about this meeting you asked for."

Cooper stood at the window and looked outside. The serene view was lost on him as mental pictures of Caroline kept flashing through his mind.

Quinn was the first to arrive, then Seth, both men in a suit and tie, while Brady, the last to arrive, was wearing a rumpled shirt and chinos.

"A long night," he muttered, spearing Cooper with a sharp gaze. "You found something."

Elias turned to his son. "Is this about Violet's child?"

Cooper kept his eyes trained on Brady. "Caroline Benning is actually Caroline Bennedict, daughter of Ray and Violet Bennedict," he announced. "She has a quilt that was obviously made by the Circle. The names Elias, Violet, Seth, Brady and Quinn Spencer are embroidered in one corner.''

Elias froze. "My God, the waitress is Violet's daughter?"

Cooper picked up a notepad on Elias's desk and began writing.

"Violet Bennedict died in childbirth. Ray took Caroline and moved to California. This is Caroline's birth date. Ray Bennedict died a couple of months before she arrived here." He handed Elias the notepad and returned to his spot in front of the window. "She was clever enough to keep it all simple so she wouldn't trip herself up. She used a last name similar enough to her own so that she could easily answer to it. She spoke openly about her father's death."

He didn't bother explaining about how she'd purposely lied to him about San Mateo, trying to throw him off the trail of the truth.

"If it hadn't been for Elias noticing her studying your family photos so intently, no suspicion would have been raised."

An astonished Elias read what Cooper had written on the notepad, then listened to his curt recitation. "This isn't possible," he muttered. "Why didn't she tell me?" He reached behind him for the security of his desk as he leaned against it. His skin had turned a pasty gray color.

"We've known for a while that we had a half sister somewhere," Quinn said, "but are you trying to say that Caroline is she?" Quinn didn't wait for a reply. "Does she have proof? Anything other than the quilt?"

"It appears she hasn't come right out and claimed anything," Cooper replied. "Brady wanted me to find out and this is what I've learned. I've seen the quilt and there's no doubt the Tyler Quilting Circle made it."

"Dad?" Brady immediately went to his side and picked up his wrist with the intention of taking his pulse. With a sound of irritation, Elias shook him off. "You just had a shock," Brady said insistently.

"Hell, yes, I had a shock," he snapped, glaring at his son. "I just found out there's a very good chance I had a daughter twenty-two years ago."

"*What?*" All four men stared at him in stunned amazement.

Elias's hand was trembling as he lifted it to his forehead. "Her birth date says it all. Violet *was* pregnant when she left me. She never told me." He groped his way around the desk until he could drop into the chair.

"Dad, that doesn't mean she's your and Violet's daughter," Quinn insisted, automatically falling into the guise of attorney protecting the family interests. "I hate to say it, but it was common knowledge that Violet was having an affair with Bennedict before she left us. Besides, how do we know Caroline hadn't researched the family with the intention of getting money out of you?"

"She's been curious about us from the beginning," Seth inserted, taking his brother's side. "Who knows what Bennedict told her all these years?"

Brady remained quiet during the exchange. He concentrated on his father, along with keeping one eye on Cooper.

"What do you think about this, Cooper?" he asked quietly. "Is she a con artist?"

He turned to face them. "Has Caroline approached any of you and asked for money?" He speared each of them with his gaze, waiting until a shake of the head confirmed what he already knew. "Has she done anything to make you think she's a member of the Spencer family? That she wants anything from any of you?'' He again waited and received negative replies from each of them.

"What did she say to you when you confronted her about the quilt?'' Seth asked.

Cooper refused to look at him. "I didn't confront her.'' His quiet reply echoed in the equally silent room. "She's down with the flu. She's pretty miserable right now.''

"Probably just as well nothing was said,'' Quinn said. "No reason to scare her off before we find out what her game is.''

Seth cocked his head to one side, studying Cooper's set features. "Cooper, you said you saw the quilt today. When I stopped in the diner this morning, Marge mentioned that Caroline was home sick. Do I assume you stopped by the boardinghouse to see Caroline and in the process saw the quilt? She didn't notice you examining it?''

"She was asleep. Are you happy now?'' Cooper swung around. "Brady, you asked me to find out about Caroline. I did just what you asked. And now I feel lower than a snake.'' He shook his head as if to clear it. "No more,'' he muttered, as he stalked out of the room. The sound of the front door slamming sounded like a gunshot reverberating throughout the large house.

Brady was the first to break the charged silence between father and sons. "Well, that went well.''

"I should have seen the similarities to Violet,'' Elias muttered, still lost in thoughts from years ago. "It was there in the shape of her eyes, the way she lifted her chin. Her smile.'' He looked up at his sons, who now loomed over him with varying degrees of alarm registering on their faces.

"Dad, you don't seriously think she's your daughter,'' Quinn argued. "Besides, who says the birth date listed on her driver's license is correct? It's all too easy to obtain fake identification papers if you have the money for them."

"Do you think she's a Spencer because of the quilt? We've no proof it was made by the Circle," Seth asked.

"I remember the quilt very well," Elias said quietly. "The ladies gave it to us not long after we arrived in town. It was a welcome gift. Violet took it with her when she left. I never understood why." His voice broke on the last.

"Dad, Violet had an affair with Ray Bennedict," Seth said gently, not wanting to distress his father any more than he might have to. "It's conceivable that Caroline is his child."

His father shook his head and held up his hand to silence further protests. "This needs to be sorted out immediately."

"I agree," Quinn said. "I'd like to have her investigated."

"Cooper already investigated her," Brady interjected. "He found out what we wanted to know. I don't think he's too happy with himself, either."

"There's been a lot of talk about the two of them," Quinn said. "Maybe he feels a need to protect her."

Seth laughed. "Come on, Quinn. Think who you're talking about. Would Cooper ever protect anyone? Hell, he gave his own grandfather a speeding ticket last fall. Just because she's in his bed doesn't mean he'd defy the law for her."

"I wouldn't use those exact words around him. You might end up with a broken nose." Brady walked over to the bar and poured healthy measures of whiskey into four glasses. He passed them out and kept one for himself. He raised his glass in a toast. "Gentlemen, for better or worse, there's a new member in the family. Funny, once upon a time I thought it would be neat to have a sister. I just didn't realize it would take this long to get one.''

Instead of joy written on their faces, each man displayed a sense of solemnity as he raised the glass to his lips.

WHEN CAROLINE AWOKE she realized her fever had broken, the body aches and headache were gone. She crawled out of bed, took a shower and dressed. She picked up the tray Anna had left on the bedside table and carried it downstairs.

"Don't you look better," Anna greeted her when she entered the kitchen.

"I feel better, too. Maybe it's behind me. Thanks for the tea and the TLC. They seem to have done the trick." She set the tray down on the counter. "Cooper must think I'm horrible. I fell asleep on him."

"You'll find out that men don't scare that easily." Anna wiped her hands on a dish towel. "Caroline," she hesitantly began, "about your quilt..." She didn't miss the sudden stillness in Caroline's stance.

"Yes?" she asked warily.

Anna gestured for Caroline to take a seat. She turned on the gas under the teakettle and bustled around, getting clean cups. She soon set two cups of tea on the table.

"Your quilt was made by the Tyler Quilting Circle," Anna explained. "It was given to Elias and Violet Spencer not long after they moved here. Six months later, Violet Spencer left Tyler—with another man."

Caroline's hand trembled as she picked up her cup of tea and sipped the hot liquid. "Ray Bennedict," she whispered.

"Yes, dear." She covered Caroline's free hand with her

own, dismayed to find the skin cold to the touch. "No one knows the entire story. I don't think even you do."

Caroline shook her head. She opened her mouth to speak, then stopped. She swallowed a couple times.

"I found the quilt the day I packed up my father's personal belongings," she whispered, staring into her cup as if the contents would give her the answers she needed. "I knew I was born in New York and raised in California. He said very little about my mother. I assumed it was because it was difficult for him to talk about her." When she raised her head, her eyes brimmed with tears. "It was only pure luck I found out about Tyler." She wiped her face with the back of her hand. "As soon as I could make the arrangements, I came out here to see what I could find out about my other family. Maybe learn more about my mother."

Anna smiled and reached into her apron pocket, pulling out a handkerchief. She pressed it into her hand.

"Considering Elias's anger after Violet left him, I think you'll have to understand that you might not learn very much from him," she said. "I'm afraid I didn't know Violet very well. She didn't live in town very long."

Caroline blinked rapidly to stem the flow of tears. "So all I really have of her is the quilt," she whispered, her voice starting to sound a little raw from her crying. "There were only a few pictures from when she was pregnant with me. No letters, nothing."

Anna took her hands in hers, rubbing them briskly, since they still felt chilled to the touch. "You have to remember that your mother didn't expect to leave you so quickly. As a mother, I can tell you those nine months are spent imagining your baby going through all the stages. From a toddler managing her first steps to her first day in kindergarten to going to her first dance." She patted the back of her hand. "I'm sure she would have been there for you if she could have been."

Caroline nodded jerkily and asked the question that haunted her. "Do you think Cooper saw the names on the quilt?"

"I believe he did." Anna wasn't going to lie to her. "He didn't say anything, but he appeared upset when he left here."

"Cooper doesn't let anyone see what he feels," she murmured. "I wasn't deliberately lying to anyone. I didn't think I should just come into town and announce that I'm the Spencer brothers' half sister. I'm not known here. They are. I thought if I spent some time here and got to know everyone and they got to know me... I didn't expect—" Her voice broke off.

"That you'd fall in love with Cooper Night Hawk." Just as she'd done with her own children, Anna wanted to gather the younger woman in her arms and assure her everything would be all right. But she'd seen Cooper's face when he left the house. To say he wasn't happy was an understatement. She could only hope that he would listen to Caroline and understand why she'd done what she had.

Caroline nodded, looking utterly miserable for someone in love. "He caught me in a lie about who I really am and he was upset with me," she explained. "Honestly, I don't want anything from the Spencers. I just want to know my half brothers."

Anna nodded. Now she knew what had caused the rift between the couple.

She got up from the table and did what she did best. She opened the cookie jar and filled a plate with oatmeal chocolate chip cookies she'd made in anticipation of her grandson's visit later that day. She set the plate down in front of Caroline.

"I think you need to talk to Elias," she said finally. "And Cooper."

"Will they hate me?"

"I don't think that will happen," she assured her. "Elias is a reasonable man. And Cooper will probably be more hurt than angry. You see, men don't like it when we women keep important things from them. Even if we feel it's in their best interests."

"It wasn't because I didn't trust him," she insisted, sniffing loudly. "At first I didn't know Cooper well enough to confide in him. Later on, well, everything had gone on for so long and I knew he was friends with them and..."

Anna tapped her fingers against Caroline's hand to stop her recitation.

"Dry your eyes and blow your nose," she ordered, not unkindly. She shook her head in amazement after Caroline had followed her directions.

Instead of eyes reddened from her tears, they were a deep shimmering green. Her nose betrayed only a faint pink on the tip, her cheeks the same color.

"I cry and my face swells up and my eyes turn a horrible red color," Anna commented. "You sit there and cry buckets and all you do is look even more beautiful. Perhaps it's just as well. You have to look your best for your man."

"Anna." Caroline looked up, her expression less tense than before. "Would your mother have known anything about my mother?"

"We can ask."

AS ALWAYS, SHE STOOD on the edge of the mist-filled forest. She looked toward him, with one hand reaching out to him.

It would have been easy to take her hand. Very natural to take her hand and see where she would lead him.

Her smile was different from the other times. This time it warmed him. Left him with a feeling that everything was going to be all right.

But he knew it wasn't going to happen unless he did something about it.

She held out her hand again, beckoned to him.

No, he couldn't take it yet. It wasn't time. This time, she seemed to understand his hesitation, because she didn't look sad when he stayed back.

She said nothing, but he could feel a voice inside his head promising him everything would be all right as long as he believed in Caroline.

This time when he woke up, the frantic fear was not there.

Through an evening of soul searching, he'd finally come to terms with Caroline having lied about her name, lied to him. It took his hard head a while to realize that what was going on inside him was his problem, not hers. He was wrong to blame Caroline for what he was going through.

After what had happened at the Spencers, he knew there was a chance, albeit a slim one, that that Caroline could be Elias Spencer's youngest child. If that was the case, then he also had to assume that she had no idea of that fact.

If she was, he would have thought she would have approached Elias the moment she arrived in town. He already knew she never did anything without a good reason.

Such as giving him her virginity. An act that still left him feeling humbled at her complete trust in him.

He sat back up and plumped his pillows behind him.

Had he ever known anyone like Caroline? Had anyone ever affected him as deeply as she had?

What would happen when Elias decided to confront her? Cooper could see it all now. Quinn would be playing the part of the analytical attorney because he thought perhaps she was there for a share of the Spencer money. Seth would do his part, too. Which meant Brady wouldn't want to be outdone.

Caroline against four men who would each have an agenda of his own. Four men who were known to never back down from any confrontation.

"Who's going to protect them from her?"

Chapter Fourteen

Caroline's hand was trembling when she replaced the telephone receiver. It had been days before she started to feel healthy again, but her trembling had nothing to do with her recent illness.

Anna stood nearby trying not to look interested, but considering the caller was Elias Spencer and she'd been the one to answer the phone, she was very interested.

"Mr. Spencer just asked me if I would come over," Caroline said once she recovered her voice. Her first thought was to call Cooper. He'd phoned several times and talked to Anna to see how Caroline was feeling, but she hadn't talked to him since that first day. He hadn't asked to speak to her, and she hadn't the courage to take the initiative. Her first thought was that she truly had lost him.

"Mr. Spencer asked if I could be there at eleven." Caroline's chest felt so constricted, she started to wheeze. "Anna, I can't breathe!"

"Cup your hands and breathe into them," she ordered briskly. "Why is this upsetting you so much? Oh dear, you're truly not over this virus, are you? Let me call him back and tell you're still unwell." She reached for the phone.

"No!" Caroline surprised herself with her vehemence. "It's just nerves. After all, I've barely spoken to the man."

She couldn't imagine why Elias wanted to see her. While she'd wanted to talk to him, the cowardly part of her still hadn't expected to do it so soon. She wasn't ready to tell him everything! She straightened her shoulders and started up the stairs. She'd thought when the moment came it would be one of her choosing. It appeared that was out of her hands.

Anna watched her go up. "Are you sure you're all right?" she called after her.

"I'll be fine," she answered, then muttered, "right after I throw up."

"WE NEED TO TALK TO HER."

Elias looked at his sons, pausing at each face. They looked as haggard as he felt. Along with a healthy dose of suspicion. Easy to understand why. Caroline had lied to everyone about her background. It wasn't easy to trust anyone's motive when they started out with a lie. He'd paced the floor all night, reliving those last few days with Violet. Wondering why she hadn't told him she was pregnant. She had to have known. Just as she had to have known whose baby it was.

He'd wondered if that was why she'd left so abruptly. Had she hated him that much?

After Cooper's revelation, he found himself asking a lot of questions, with no way of finding out the answers. He'd spent the past few days talking to a reliable private investigator, who'd found out everything he needed to know.

Such as the information that Caroline *was* his daughter. Which had him desiring to learn everything he could about Caroline Bennedict. What he learned confirmed that she was his daughter even if her birth certificate listed Raymond Bennedict as her father. There was no doubt on that score, since Raymond Bennedict had been sterile.

"This could be tricky," Seth said, sitting in one of the chairs.

"In more ways than one," Quinn agreed. "We still need to cover all the legal ramifications."

Brady had a plan. "I suggest we ask her over and take it from there."

Elias smiled. "Good, because she'll be here in about—" he consulted his watch "—five minutes."

"There's a lot to discuss first," Quinn protested, jumping to his feet.

Elias lifted his head when he heard the doorbell chime. "Which we'll do as soon as she comes in." He left the room.

The three brothers looked at each other, but by unspoken agreement said nothing.

When Elias reentered the room, Caroline walked in front of him.

She looked more decorous than usual in a blue print sundress that floated around her calves. She carried her large canvas tote bag. Her features were composed, as if her coming here was an everyday occurrence.

"Would you care for something to drink? Iced tea, water, soft drink?" Elias asked in his formal voice.

"Iced tea, thank you." She took the chair he gestured to and set the bag down next to it.

Elias called out to Eva, his housekeeper, asking for iced tea to be brought in.

Caroline sat in the chair with her ankles neatly crossed, hands clasped in her lap. Her smile was polite as she easily returned the stares the three younger men were giving her. If she felt the least bit intimidated she didn't show it.

Elias waited until Caroline's iced tea was served to her and the housekeeper left them alone.

"I suppose you're wondering why I asked you here today," he began.

"Yes, but I guess I knew this day would happen sooner or later," she murmured. She took a sip of tea, then set the glass back down. She picked up the tote bag and pulled out a multicolored length of fabric.

Elias sucked in a breath as he stared at the quilt he hadn't seen in more than twenty-two years.

"May I?" he asked in a quiet voice, holding out his hand.

She inclined her head and held out the quilt.

Elias picked it up with quiet reverence and unfolded it until he found the corner with the names. He reached blindly for his chair and dropped down into it. The heavy fabric spilled down around him.

"This was very special to her," he said in a low voice. He looked up at his sons, then at Caroline. "Caroline, you aren't Ray Bennedict's daughter, you are mine."

The glass she held in her hand again wobbled dangerously. Quinn, the closest to her, swiftly reached out and took it from her before it fell.

"What are you talking about?" she said numbly, her face white with shock. "No, my father is Ray Bennedict. I realize I am their half sister—" she gestured toward the Spencer brothers "—but no, I'm sorry, I am not your daughter. I'm only here because of the quilt. I looked through papers and found a mention of Tyler and thought I would come here to meet my half brothers," she said in a rush. "I don't want anything. I don't need anything.

I just wanted to know the rest of my family. My *half brothers.*'' She emphasized the words.

"Then why did you give a false name when you came here? Why didn't you say anything?" Seth accused.

"I've seen enough movies to know people don't like a supposedly long lost relative showing up on their doorstep. I thought if I stayed here for a while, got to know you, and in the process, you got to know me, it would make it easier. But all I did was complicate things more.'' Caroline blinked rapidly to keep back the threatening tears. "My father never lied to me," she whispered.

Elias shook his head. "I am sorry you have to hear it this way, Caroline, but I have the proof. Ray Bennedict was sterile. I realize we'll never have all the answers we'd like, but I'd like to think we could make a start from here.''

Caroline looked at the other three men, who didn't look as welcoming as Elias did. "If you want me to sign legal documents that I won't interfere with the family money, I'm more than willing to do so as long as you don't try to interfere with any of the holdings my father left me." She sent Elias a challenging look. "For twenty-two years I've known Ray Bennedict as my father. I don't intend to give that up just because it's turned out not to be true.'' She looked around the room. How could she explain to him that his telling her she was a Spencer didn't make her one? Which made something else come to mind. "How did you find out all of this?" she asked.

"I hired a private investigator," Elias replied. "I needed to know what happened after Violet left here.''

Caroline shook her head. "No, not just that. I want to know how you learned I was Violet's daughter?''

Doorbell chimes sounded, then a commotion at the door alerted them to an unexpected visitor.

"I'm not receiving anyone," Elias called out, not caring if he was heard.

"Me, you'll receive," Cooper said as he strode into the room. He looked first at Caroline, then the others. "I called the boardinghouse and Anna said you were here," he told Caroline. "Is everything all right?"

His appearance alone was enough to answer her question.

"You were the one to tell them, weren't you?" Her eyes flashed a fire that spelled DANGER in capital letters. "Somehow you found out and you told them."

He nodded.

"Without saying anything to me first."

He nodded again.

"You cared more for them than me," she said in a cool voice that was rapidly growing colder.

"Not one of my better moments," he confessed. "But I felt they needed to know, and you were too sick to discuss it then. I saw the quilt under your sheet," he explained.

"Not one of your better moments," she repeated. "How true that is."

"Cooper," Brady interrupted, "if you're here thinking Caroline needs some protection against us—"

"Far from it. It's more like you needing protection from her," Cooper replied, still keeping his eyes on her. "When she's on a roll, nothing can stop her."

"Mr. Spencer just told me that he's my father," she announced baldly. "Did you know that, too?"

Cooper crossed the room and crouched down in front of her. He took her hand in his. She started to pull it away, but he tightened his grip. "So all of this is as much a surprise for you as it is for them."

Caroline stared at him for several moments. He had no

time to react before her hand lashed out and struck him. "I may have handled this wrong from the beginning, but it wouldn't have hurt you to talk to me first." She got up and stepped around him. She stopped in front of Elias. "The quilt is yours," she said quietly. "And I would like a chance to get to know you and the others." Her gaze took in the three brothers. "I have some things to make right in this town and I would like the opportunity to do it myself. The only thing that concerns me is my name. I'll leave everything else up to you. What you wish to tell anyone I'll also leave up to you." With that, she left the room.

Cooper stood up. There was an imprint of her hand on his cheek.

"She has the beginning of a good left hook there," Brady commented, inspecting his face.

"I'd guess that the lady is more than a little upset with Cooper," Seth volunteered.

Cooper scowled, then winced. "What was your first clue?"

"She's a Spencer all right," Quinn declared. "She didn't even hesitate when she slugged you."

"And to think I came here figuring you were the ones who needed protection," Cooper muttered.

"Have you told her you're in love with her?" Elias asked.

"That's no guarantee she'll want to stay here. Her life is in California." Cooper gave an evasive answer.

"Man, it hit you hard, didn't it?" Brady asked. "And all because I asked you to check her out."

Cooper's glare was turning deadly. "Remind me later to thank you."

"She'll stay," Elias said confidently.

Cooper had had enough. "She was right. I should have talked to her first before coming to you."

"I don't envy you. You're going to have to grovel big time to get back in her good graces," Brady said.

Cooper's reply was less than polite.

Elias winced when the front door slammed shut after Cooper. He looked at his sons.

"I'd say we know who will be receiving the next quilt."

"HE SENT FLOWERS," Anna announced, carrying a vase filled with yellow roses.

Caroline started to brighten when she saw the beautiful arrangement, then forced herself to hold back. "If I told you to throw them out, you wouldn't, would you?"

Anna gazed at the flowers with pure adoration. "Not a chance." She held out the card.

Caroline took it reluctantly and opened it. "'I was a fool and willing to admit it,'" she read out loud.

"You'll have to put him out of his misery soon," Anna said. "It's been three days."

"Three days isn't long enough to make him suffer," she replied.

She'd spent most of the past three days with Elias. She learned about her mother and he learned about her years in California. Why Violet never left any information about her former life they would never know, and it saddened them both. Elias mourned the years he'd missed with Caroline and constantly invited her to come live with him. She insisted she needed her independence and that this was best while they found their footing. They were able to start a decent foundation to build upon.

During those days, Caroline also made some plans of her own.

She hadn't fallen out of love with Cooper. No chance of that happening. But romance and relationships were still new to her.

It was Elias who advised her, during one of their visits.

"You need to talk to him. Tell him you were in the wrong."

Caroline looked up at the man she was just getting to know. "Just like a man. Blame it on the woman."

Elias wasn't deterred by her light accusation. "Who came here lying about herself?"

She flushed. "All right, so it isn't all his fault," she muttered.

"All?" he said dryly.

"Don't push your luck or his." She flopped back in her chair. They were seated on the patio enjoying a quiet afternoon. "I just need to think."

"I would hazard a guess that Cooper has some thinking of his own to do." Elias looked at her.

"He's had enough time," she decided suddenly.

"Then do something about it," he challenged.

She arched an eyebrow. "Don't think I won't."

Elias burst out laughing. "Maybe it's Cooper I should feel sorry for. Except it's obvious the two of you are meant for each other."

By the next day, Caroline had planned everything down to the smallest detail.

Cooper didn't have a chance.

"WHY DID I GET STUCK with this lousy duty?" Cooper grumbled into the microphone as he stared down an empty road.

"Get with the program, Night Hawk. You're acting like we did this deliberately. You've got speeder duty because you drew the short straw," Steve replied.

"Like speeder duty is necessary right here. Tell me the last time someone caught a speeder on this particular road?" he argued. "The only good thing about it is at least I'm close enough to go home, since we both know nothing will happen around here."

Steve ignored his less than subtle threat. "Just keep a lookout for speeders. And be glad we didn't send you any farther away. You haven't exactly been the easiest person to work with lately."

Cooper was about to suggest that Steve leave that subject alone or lose his head when he heard the sound of a racing engine. He looked up, and a flash of red sped past him before he could blink.

"What was that?" Steve asked.

"What do you think? That speeder you told me to be on the lookout for." Cooper switched on the siren and pulled out. He cursed under his breath as he floored the accelerator in order to catch up. He didn't need radar to know the driver was going a good thirty miles over the speed limit. He spent the next few miles cursing, until he noticed the sports car start to slow down and pull over to the side.

Since no one else in town owned a red Miata convertible, he knew who he would find in the driver's seat.

Caroline not only sat behind the wheel, she was dressed in a pair of shorts so short he wondered why she'd bothered putting them on. If that wasn't bad enough, she had paired it with a halter top that barely covered the essentials. She looked up, tipping her sunglasses down her nose.

"Is there a problem, Deputy Night Hawk?" she asked in a throaty voice that sent frissons of sensation down his spine.

He had to work his jaw a couple of times before he

could speak. "Could I see your license, registration and proof of insurance, please? You were going seventy-five in a forty-five mile an hour zone."

She opened her purse and pulled out her wallet. She pulled out her license and handed that to him. He couldn't keep his eyes off her as she leaned over to rummage through the glove compartment for paperwork. The length of bare leg that teased him was almost his undoing. Even outside in the open air, he could smell her perfume.

"I've never seen your official side before, Deputy," she murmured, handing him the appropriate papers. "Interesting."

Cooper stared at the documents he held in his hand. He had to read them twice before they started to make sense. He looked over at her.

She offered him a demure smile. "Is there still a problem, Deputy Night Hawk?"

"This temporary license is for the state of Wisconsin."

Her eyes were guileless as she gazed up at him. "Yes, it is. Considering I live in Wisconsin, I thought it would be a good idea to apply for one."

He didn't stop to think. He tossed the papers into the passenger seat and leaned over, bracing his hands on the side of the car.

"You've put me through hell thinking you would pick up and leave once you got to know your father and brothers," he stated between clenched teeth. "I thought for sure you'd head back to California."

"Maybe you should have asked me if that was what I wanted."

Cooper combed his hands through his hair, feeling frustration roll through his blood. He barely registered his name being called over the radio. He cocked his head to one side and murmured into the microphone clipped to his shoulder, "What?" He didn't care if he wasn't following policy.

"Catch your speeder?" Steve asked.

Cooper looked at Caroline. "This was a setup."

"I guess that means you did." Steve chuckled. "Don't worry, I already signed you out."

Cooper turned back to Caroline.

"You couldn't have just told me you were staying for good?" he said hoarsely. "I thought you hated me for telling the Spencers."

"You never returned my calls. Then I was afraid you wouldn't care if I stayed in Tyler." She appeared to be holding her breath. "And no, I don't hate you. You did what you felt you had to do. I was the one in the wrong. Not you. I should have confided in you a long time ago. You probably could have helped me handle it the right way. By the time I realized I should have, I was afraid it was too late. I was afraid telling you would have you hating me for lying to you in the beginning," she confessed. "And then all of this happened and I felt as if everything was falling apart. And again, I was afraid you'd hate me. I wanted to talk to you so bad."

"I had some things to think over, too," he admitted. "I was going to call you tonight."

Her face lit up. "I came to realize that for all that time, you believed in me. I'm so sorry I didn't believe in you as well," she whispered.

He didn't waste any time before opening her door and pulling her out of the car. His kiss convinced her more than any amount of words could have.

"I think I should tell you that I only intend to change my name once," she warned him, when he allowed her up for air.

He grinned. "Is this a marriage proposal?"

"You got it, buster." She met his gaze head-on. "Do you think I'm going to allow any other woman to see those smiles of yours, Cooper Night Hawk? No way! I worked hard for those smiles and I'm not sharing them with anyone. They're all mine."

"It's a small town. Not anything like what you're used to." He felt obligated to warn her even if he wasn't about to give her up.

"You're here, that's what counts." She pressed herself against him. "Hey, big boy, you've got the rest of the day off. Let's go someplace private and seal the deal."

Cooper picked her up and spun her around. His laughter startled the birds in the nearby trees into flight.

She stood there with her hand outstretched. This time, he stepped forward and held out his hand to touch hers. Her smile radiated summer warmth and she seemed to glide instead of walk into the mist. He followed her without a second thought.

The mist disappeared as quickly as it appeared. Now she stood in sunshine. There was no resemblance to Caroline now. She was Caroline.

"It wasn't so hard after all, was it?" she said to him.

This time, when he awoke, he was smiling.

"Your dream again?" Caroline asked sleepily.

"Yes." He held her close. "But it's all right."

She yawned as she curled up against him and stretched her arm across his chest.

"Everything is all right," he whispered.

It had been a long time since gossip had been this good.

As if it wasn't enough that Caroline Benning's real

name was Caroline Bennedict, now they found out she was to become Caroline Night Hawk.

A proud Elias Spencer walked her down the church aisle. Laughing Bear was Cooper's best man, while Anna proudly presided as Caroline's matron of honor. During the reception, Brady enjoyed telling people it was because of him they'd got together. Cooper told him if it made him feel better to tell that story, feel free, but he'd been planning to ask Caroline out long before Brady approached him. He just hadn't gotten around to it yet.

What everyone talked about the most was the smile that never left Cooper's lips from the time his bride floated down the aisle toward him, all through the ceremony and the reception.

"We knew it all along," the ladies of the Tyler Quilting Circle announced as they presented a quilt to the couple.

It wasn't long before the ladies knew they would be planning a new quilt, when Elias announced his engagement to Lydia. Caroline hugged her father, declaring she couldn't wait until his wedding.

Cooper couldn't take his eyes off Caroline in her satin and lace gown, which bared her shoulders and clung to her waist before it flared out to the ground. She'd taken off her veil just before the reception, after pictures had been taken.

"You've done it," he told her as they danced to the first song.

"Yes, and you're all mine," she said smugly.

"Not just that, you wild thing. You're my dream woman," he said, his voice warm with his love. "In more ways than one."

Caroline looked as if she was going to cry. Instead, she reached up and pulled his face down to hers for a kiss.

"And that's just the beginning of what you'll be getting," she vowed, with a dazzling smile.

Looking down at her, Cooper had no doubt of that.

RETURN TO TYLER
continues next month with
special stories focusing on the
town's past. Discover how the
NightHawk legend began in

NIGHTHAWK'S BRIDE

by Jillian Hart
from Harlequin Historicals.

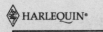